FAMILY TIES

A MARK PEMBERTON CASE

NICHOLAS RHEA

AGORA BOOKS

ABOUT THE AUTHOR

Nicholas Rhea was born in Glaisdale, a Yorkshire Moors Village, in 1936. The oldest of three sons born to an insurance agent and a teacher, he won a scholarship to Whitby Grammar School but left at 16 to become a police cadet. In 1956, he joined the North Yorkshire force in Whitby.

He began to write seriously in the late 1950s after years of casual interest, having his first short story published in the Police Review. Continuing to rise through the ranks at the region's Police Headquarters in Northallerton, he published his first novel, Carnaby and the Hijackers, in 1976.

Rhea is primarily known for his Constable series, inspired by his many years of police service. He retired in 1982 to concentrate on his writing, encouraged by an interest in his Constable books from Yorkshire Television. This was to become the highly popular Heartbeat series, which ran for 18 seasons and over 350 episodes.

Rhea had four children and eight grandchildren and lived with his wife in a quiet North Yorkshire village. He died in 2017.

Carnaby and the Assassins

Carnaby and the Conspirators

Carnaby and the Saboteurs

Carnaby and the Eliminators

Carnaby and the Demonstrators

Carnaby and the Infiltrators

Carnaby and the Kidnappers

Carnaby and the Counterfeiters

Carnaby and the Campaigners

FAMILY TIES

CHAPTER ONE

'I've got a most enjoyable task for you, Detective Superintendent.' The Chief Constable smiled at Mark Pemberton across his spacious desk. Pemberton, his thick blond hair cut to perfection and his expensive dark suit rivalling the fastidiousness of his boss, stood to attention as he awaited some indication of Moore's intentions. 'It's the ideal duty for you, I'd say. But first, tell me this, Mark. When did you last take a day off?'

'I get my weekly rest days like everyone else, sir,' was Pemberton's immediate response.

'I know you are allocated your days off, but you don't take them, do you? I see from the duty sheets,' and the Chief waved the relevant documents in the air, 'that you have not taken one day off work in the last six months. You work all the time, Mark, you never relax. You know what they say about all work and no play…'

'I enjoy being at work,' Mark told Moore. 'I enjoy the companionship, the interest, the atmosphere; I don't claim any overtime or compensatory time off for working on my rest days.'

'I'm aware of that, but everyone needs to take a break, you

know. I can't do with workaholics in my force. You set a bad example to your colleagues.'

'A bad example?' cried Mark, hurt at the accusation.

'Yes, a bad example. When a senior officer like yourself works all hours God sends, it makes the subordinates think they should emulate him. And they shouldn't be subjected to that kind of subtle blackmail! I'm all for loyalty among my staff and I do value a hard-working officer, but no days off in six months? That really is taking things too far.'

'I'm at a bit of a loose end in my leisure time, sir, since my wife...'

'I'm well aware that you haven't really come to terms with June's death; I know it takes time to adjust and I know you're lonely, but you must take time off. You do need to relax; I'm serious about this. Work isn't everything, Mark. Join a club, go to night classes, try rambling, landscape painting or something.'

'I've tried, sir, I've tried to join things, but the demands of the job mean I can't commit myself to anything in the long term. There's no way I can undertake a three-month series of night classes on, say, art appreciation. When I get called out to investigate a murder or some serious crime, things can't wait; I can't tell the victims to hang on until I've learned to understand Picasso or while I learn to make parsnip wine or teach myself Spanish!'

'Now you're being facetious, but there's no excuse.' Charles Moore was adamant. 'Other senior detectives manage to do it, they have a social life and enjoy their normal allocation of time off. Anyway, I've expressed my concern and, to be honest, you do look shattered. I am concerned about you, Mark, I really am. So, if you won't take time off, I'll have to make the arrangements for you. There, I've said my piece and in anticipation of your reaction, I have the perfect duty for you.'

'Sir?'

'It's a very cushy number, it's tantamount to a holiday in the countryside. Almost two weeks' full rest — and it will be considered a duty. I'm ordering you to undertake this task, so you can't back out. It's my way of compelling you to take things easy, at least for a few days.'

'I'm not sure how to react, sir.'

'You sit there, and you listen to me, that's how you react,' and Moore pointed to a chair in front of his desk.

'Very good, sir,' and Detective Superintendent Mark Pemberton obediently sat on the polished chair before his Chief Constable. The handsome Chief flashed the dazzling smile for which he was renowned, pressed the intercom button on his desk and said to his secretary, 'Two coffees, please, Anne, black without sugar.'

Moore said nothing further until the coffee arrived; it came within a minute and Anne said, 'Will that be all, sir?'

'For the moment, thanks,' Moore nodded, and she left.

Mark sipped from the hot, strong coffee and waited, knowing better than to take the initiative. Moore would begin when he was ready, and, for the moment, he was scanning through a thick file marked 'Secret'.

Then he flashed his smile and asked, 'You've heard of Thirklewood Hall?'

'Former seat of the Earls of Thirklewood? Presently a girls' school, but soon to end its life as a school before being refurbished and restored as the home of the present Earl who lives nearby. In two years or so, it will be opened to the public as our newest stately home. The school is moving to larger premises on the coast, on the outskirts of Rainesbury. It was all in the local paper.'

'Exactly. So you are going to spend a few days at Thirklewood Hall with all expenses paid, food and accommodation included. It's all courtesy of the force. How's that suit you?'

'But it's still a girls' school, isn't it?' Mark began to frown, suspecting some devious plot by his Chief Constable.

'The pupils will evacuate the premises this week and the

furnishings will be removed by the weekend. It's end of term, the end of the school's life at Thirklewood Hall in fact. The building will be empty throughout the summer months; then in the autumn, probably September, the contractors will move in to begin the task of restoring the house to its former glory.'

'So the place will be deserted during the summer?' said Mark.

'Quite. There will be a couple of months or so before that work begins so, in the meantime, we're going to use the premises. Unfortunately, the accommodation is a bit spartan, there are long dormitories and communal loos, but there are some private rooms which were used by teachers and members of the other staff who lived in. You can make use of one of those.'

'Me? I'm to live in, sir?'

'Of course, this is a holiday, like I said. Well, sort of a holiday. Your food will be provided, there are recreational and sports facilities, a library, space for walks in the surrounding parkland. I'm sure there will soon be a bar and a television lounge. Just like a hotel in many ways.'

'So what's the catch, sir?' Mark smiled, sensing the teasing mood of his Chief.

'Whatever makes you think there's a catch, Mark?' laughed Moore.

'I've known you long enough to realise that you wouldn't send me to a place like that unless there was a catch!'

'Caleb Hodgson Hartley, he's the catch,' said the Chief Constable. 'He's the new Vice-President of the United States. He's not very well known yet, especially among the general public of this country.'

'I can't say the name means much to me,' admitted Pemberton.

'Well, he intends to change that, he wants the English to sit up and take notice of him, so he's coming here for the same reason that lots of Americans do — to look up his family roots and to visit the graves of his ancestors. He reckons he's got Yorkshire blood in his veins.'

'It will be a private visit, will it?' asked Mark.

'Very much so. That's why we're using this Hall and not a hotel. Thirklewood Hall is ideal, it's extremely private and it is more secure than any other similar place. No other premises overlook it, and it's large enough to accommodate Hartley and his bunch of Vice-Presidential minders.'

'So what's my job, sir, if he's accompanied by dozens of his own minders?'

'They, along with the Diplomatic Protection Group of Scotland Yard, are responsible for his safety at all times when he's outside the house. As the police force responsible for the area in which he will be residing, we are responsible at all times when he's inside the house. That's quite normal. In this case, you are responsible.'

'Me, sir, alone?'

'No, you'll need to select a complement of officers. Make your own choice, men and women. Take enough to guarantee his security at all times when he's residing in the Hall.'

'Some holiday, sir!'

'It's not as bad as it sounds. Your task is to supervise his internal security — quite a doddle of a job, really. You will liaise with the Diplomatic Protection Group of Scotland Yard and our own Special Branch; they are in touch with the White House and the US Embassy in London.'

'So if he's bringing all his own cavalry, the visit must be official? I thought it was private?' queried Pemberton.

'This part of his visit is private, Mark. He's got official commitments in the UK both before and after his stay at Thirklewood Hall, but when you're deputy to the most powerful man in the world, you have no private life and you need official protection at all times. When he's at Thirklewood Hall, there will be no public engagements, he'll not be attending government meetings or talking to the press and the public will not be told of his presence or whereabouts at that time. To that extent, it's a private visit.'

'Fair enough, but who are his Vice-Presidential minders?'

'The Vice-President's party will include a mixed bag of officers from the US Treasury, the Marines, the FBI, the CIA, and others on the White House staff, about seventy in total. That is in keeping both with his status and with an overall assessment of the risk to his life. He is not a top-grade risk otherwise he'd have had more minders and we'd upgrade our own staffing.'

'A mini-army, in other words!'

'By our standards, yes. You'll have fewer officers to work with, of course, but you will need to draw up some form of duty rota so that the interior of the house is protected twenty-four hours a day during his stay. And you must appoint a deputy for yourself because I insist you take some time off during this commitment. Now, study the file and let me know your requirements with the names of your selected officers, and I shall see that your requests are met — provided they're reasonable!'

'When do I start, sir?'

'Now,' said Moore, handing Mark the file.

CHAPTER TWO

The file was marked 'Operation Roots' and it included a verbose description of Thirklewood Hall. It was couched in architectural terms, some of which could only have been understood by experts. Reading it in his office, Mark guessed it had been taken directly from Nikolaus Pevsner's series, *The Buildings of England*, but his attention was drawn to the fact that the huge house had seven doors on the ground floor, many large and vulnerable ground-floor windows, several fire escapes leading from the upper storeys and lots of adjoining outbuildings, all of which would require close supervision.

Built in the seventeenth century, it had endured many alterations, extensions and modernisations, but in its present form the house could accommodate 120 students and 24 staff. There were four self-contained suites, one of which had been used by the headmistress both as living quarters and as her office. After some rapid but discreet improvements, this would be utilised by the Vice-President. Before the Hall's 1947 conversion into a school, that suite had been part of the private apartments of an earlier Lord Thirklewood. Even then, the house had been open to the public and throughout its long history, its larger rooms had been used for public functions such as dances, parties, exhibitions and wedding receptions.

During the war, the house had been commandeered and used for billeting troops, whereupon His Lordship had moved into a more compact and up-to-date house within the grounds. Reluctant to return to the draughty old house after the war, Lord Thirklewood had leased the beautiful premises to a girls' school. And now that short period of its long history was coming to an end. The lease had expired.

The file included additional details such as the Hall's sewage system, method of water supply, location of the drains and power points, and a plan of the interior. A map of the grounds was also provided. It showed the surfaced road which led from Thirklewood village to the big house and revealed a bridleway access at the rear of the parkland. There was also a footpath which followed the bed of a small stream close to the house. The footpath was open to the public, but at no point did it provide a view of Thirklewood Hall; nonetheless, a short diversion from that path at several points would gain a splendid aspect of the house. Mark noted several points which needed scrutiny from the security aspect although these factors, being external, were the responsibility of Scotland Yard and the Americans. They would have to consider possible sniper positions or points of ambush.

The file contained a brief biography of Caleb Hodgson Hartley. Born in 1933 at Utica in the State of New York, he was the eldest son of Caleb James Hartley and his wife Jennie, née Ellis.

His father had made money in property speculation, land dealing and building, while his mother had been a nurse; the young Caleb Hodgson Hartley had done well at school and had studied law at university, following which he had begun a career as an attorney. Republican politics had attracted him before he reached the age of thirty, and his skills at oratory plus his ability to understand the complexities of government finances quickly earned him a State governorship.

For all his qualities and the respect he had earned from other politicians, his appointment as Vice-President had come by default — it had been discovered that the man first appointed had falsified some income tax returns, so that man had been compelled to resign after a few months in office. Much to the surprise of the country, the electorate and even himself, Caleb Hodgson Hartley had found himself Vice-President of the United States of America. He was married to Linda, née Irving, and had three children, a son aged twenty-nine and two daughters aged twenty-seven and twenty-five. There were no grandchildren.

A confidential addendum said that some of his earlier pronouncements had not been favourable to the British; he had criticised the British government over its attitude to Northern Ireland, its action in the Falklands and its commitment to a military presence in the Middle East. On several occasions, he had shown overt political antagonism towards Britain and its government.

He had, however, also been outspoken about the Libyan leadership and had condemned the taking of the Beirut hostages in 1986. Over his years as a politician, he had earned a reputation for being very outspoken on many issues and his remarks, regarded by some as being either thoughtless or spur-of-the-moment, had antagonised fanatical followers of Islam who regarded America as the Great Satan. Thus Hartley was considered 'at risk' from several Middle East factions, especially Iran. One of his actions had been to devalue the life of the American hostages by saying that the US government could not be held to ransom if what was taken by others was of no value. This had caused an uproar back home and he had made matters worse by saying he would be prepared to make a deal with the hostage takers, but on very lowly terms. That speech had antagonised the American people — many felt he had no sympathy for the plight of the hostages — whilst Iran had regarded it as an insult to their country because Britain had always had a policy of 'no deals with terrorists', thus making their stakes much higher. One Iranian spokesman had interpreted Hartley's comments as a statement that Iran dealt only in rubbish and was not therefore worthy of serious attention. The shooting down of an Iranian airliner by the Americans in 1988 was seen by the ayatollahs as a direct follow-on of Hartley's range of insults to the Middle East, particularly as he had personally refused to condemn that action.

Now that he was in high office, however, with the inevitable strong and historic Anglo-American links, it seemed he wished to appease his English critics, especially those in a governmental or official position, by claiming English ancestry. At one point, he had said that by speaking his mind, he was following the traditional outspoken bluntness of his Yorkshire forefathers. The file added that he was seeking to confirm his Yorkshire links during the forthcoming visit.

The file went on to say that Hartley's claim to English roots had been prompted by the discovery of some family letters and also by the fact that his grandfather, Luke Caleb Hartley, had settled in Canada in 1916. Hartley said that Luke Caleb had emigrated from Yorkshire, England. Grandfather Hartley had subsequently moved from Canada to the United States, settling only some 120 miles from his original home which had been at Brockville on the Canadian side of the St Lawrence river. His new base was at Utica, one of several towns of this name in the United States; this Utica was 140 miles north-east of New York.

A Foreign Office note in the file stated that there was a large family of Hartleys whose origins were on the North York moors. The Vice-President believed these were his ancestors and it seemed he had undertaken some preparatory investigation into his own family history. For example, the file said there were several Hartley family graves in St Monica's churchyard at Wolversdale, a village deep within the North York moors.

It was an area once noted for wild wolves, the last wolf in England being supposedly caught here by a Hartley way back in

1693. An existing family of Hartleys lived at Pike Hill Farm, Wolversdale, their eldest member being a Mr George Caleb Hartley; he had been approached, in preparation for the impending visit, by a member of the Embassy staff, but had stressed that his family knew nothing of any relations in America or Canada. They had no knowledge of their eminent and newly discovered distant cousin. The file added that Vice-President Hartley was going to pay a visit to the Wolversdale Hartleys in the hope of establishing a family connection. An appointment had been made via the American Embassy. It was for Tuesday, 12th July, when the Vice-President would meet Mr George Caleb Hartley, who was a retired farmer. As a working farmer, Mr Hartley had occupied Pike Hill Farm; his son, Alan Caleb Hartley, now occupied the house and ran the farm while George lived in a bungalow built on the land.

Another scheduled visit was to Hull, on Wednesday, 13th July, where it was believed an ancestor had founded the highly successful store which was still known as Hartleys of Hull. Humberside police would be supervising that event.

The file added that George Hartley had assured the Embassy representative that he would welcome the Vice-President and would do his utmost to provide him with any possible evidence to support his quest — he said, for example, that he would check the names on the family graves in Wolversdale.

While reading the file, Mark found himself wondering why this American politician was going to so much trouble to establish his English ancestry after being so antagonistic towards some of Britain's recent overseas policies.

But the wiles of politicians are not for mere police officers to understand and he decided it was none of his business. Mark told himself that he must not get involved in the politics of this visit. He had one clear and simple duty: the protection of Vice-President Hartley while he was staying at Thirklewood Hall.

In considering his staffing requirements for twenty-four-hour cover within the house between now and the end of the visit, Mark calculated he would need fifteen personnel. This would allow for a deputy, days off for everyone and all other aspects of a full-time residential duty. It then dawned on him that the team he had regularly used in the Incident Room during murder investigations would be ideal. They worked well as a group, they knew one another, and they could be trusted implicitly. He decided to make a formal request to the Chief Constable for those officers, provided, of course, that no murder investigation occurred.

In the belief that there was no time like the present, he called in his secretary, Barbara Meadows, and dictated the necessary application for personnel. He told her that she would be required to fulfil her usual role as secretary to the Incident Room and that she'd have to live at Thirklewood Hall.

Then he signed the application and she promised to forward it immediately to the Chief Constable. Mark told her he was now going to inspect Thirklewood Hall and said that if the application was approved whilst he was away, she must immediately inform the officers concerned and instruct them to stand by for their forthcoming duty on Operation Roots — they'd probably be required from next Monday.

His first priority was to examine Thirklewood Hall; he must identify all the internal operational problems. He picked up the telephone and dialled the number of Thirklewood Estate, then asked for the estate manager, a Mr Robin Blanchard.

'Blanchard.' The voice had a distinct Home Counties accent.

'Detective Superintendent Pemberton speaking from Great Halverton police headquarters,' Mark announced himself. 'I understand you are my contact for the impending visit of the American Vice-President?'

'I am indeed, and I was expecting a call from you. You will wish to see the Hall?'

'Yes,' said Mark. 'I was wondering about tomorrow? Say ten thirty?'

'Friday? No problem.' The fellow sounded most accommodating. 'Come to the estate office, not the Hall; we're just inside the main gate on the right. I'll be there with the coffee warming for you and then we'll tour the house.'

'Thanks,' said Pemberton.

'I'd better warn you that the place will be in a bit of a mess, we'll still be clearing up after the departure of the school.'

'That won't bother me!' Mark assured him.

Pemberton was in his own office sharp at nine o'clock the following morning and found a summons from the Chief Constable who wanted to see him straight away. Mark responded, whereupon Moore asked why he had selected the Incident Room team for Operation Roots.

Mark explained his reasons and added, 'I'd like them to bring the file on the Muriel Brown murder, sir. They could re-examine that while they're sitting around in the Hall.'

'Muriel Brown? That was before my time, wasn't it?'

'It's an old case, sir; it happened eight or nine years ago. Muriel Brown was murdered in her own car, stabbed to death after being raped. The car, with the body inside, was abandoned on the moors but the killer was never traced. I thought my team could program that case into HOLMES; it happened before we had the benefit of HOLMES and so we might just turn up the murderer.'

'It sounds a good idea, but I want you to relax, you understand? I don't want you to go chasing after killers, not on this duty commitment.'

'I understand, but I do need to keep my team busy during what will be a very boring assignment, and this unsolved murder is ideal.'

'Well, so long as you let them get on with it at their own pace and don't start chasing them for results — yes, I agree, Mark. Consider your application approved. Take the full Incident Room equipment with you. You will appreciate, of course, that if there is a new murder investigation to undertake during Operation Roots, those officers and the computer equipment will have to be recalled.'

'Yes, sir, I realise that.'

'So if that happens, how will you protect your American gentleman? You'll have to recruit a new, inexperienced team at very short notice!'

'I have plenty of very capable officers in reserve, sir; that would cause no problems,' stated Mark with confidence.

'Fine, then I give you my support. So what are your plans for today?'

'I'm going to visit Thirklewood Hall, sir, to inspect it.'

'Good. Keep me informed.'

Mark arrived at Thirklewood Hall five minutes before his appointed time and was immediately shown into Blanchard's tidy office. Blanchard stood up with a hand extended in greeting and Mark shook it. Blanchard, a stocky sandy-haired man in a Lovat green suit and brogues, showed Mark to a richly upholstered leather chair. A secretary brought some coffee and Blanchard moved his chair from the desk to be seated closer to Mark.

He noticed that Blanchard's face was freckled and that his eyes were almost green; he would be in his late forties, Mark estimated, but looked absolutely right for this role — confident, well-dressed and in command of himself.

'The house is in a bit of a shambles, I'm afraid,' Blanchard began. 'The school's just gone, as you know, and there's still a lot of debris to clear away. It all looks very shabby indeed. I'm afraid they didn't spend much on modernisation or maintenance. The showers are still wartime vintage, there are no carpets on most floors, just brown canvas, although they have left the curtains behind and the Head's suite isn't too bad. A bit old-maidish, if you know what I mean, but clean. I'm afraid there's not a lot we can do to improve the place right now although I believe the Americans are bringing some home comforts with them — they have their own cooks and maids, they'll be stocking the kitchen and the bar and will be bringing a television set or two. They might even decorate some of the areas they'll be using, and they've said they can rustle up some carpeting and rugs. You and your officers will be making use of their facilities, you realise?'

Mark smiled. 'Thanks — our lot wouldn't dream of spending a penny on decorations. So do I warrant a room of my own?'

'You're to have the French teacher's room. It's quite pleasant and overlooks the lawns to the South.'

'And my officers?'

'I've allocated them the nicer rooms — first come, first served! Mr Moore said you'd be bringing a contingent of about a dozen?'

'Fifteen probably,' said Mark. 'I can let you have details when I return to my office.'

'No problem, but some might have to use dormitories. There is a section for women too, they can have their privacy in the west wing. I've tried to keep your officers separated from the US Embassy teams, I thought you'd welcome that.'

'And the great man himself? He's in the Head's old suite, I believe? I'll need to look at that, from a security aspect. You know I'm responsible for all internal security?'

'I do indeed, Mr Pemberton, and I'll do all I can to help. Now, while the Vice-President is in residence, large wooden notices will be positioned at the main gate and at the rear entrance to announce that the school has left these premises; there will be a contact address and the school's new telephone number. The notices will add that the Hall is undergoing extensive alterations. Those signs will say the house is closed until further notice — that should deter casual visitors. The school has written to all its suppliers and other contacts to announce its departure and its new location. We shall open to the public many months after you have left. Any comings and goings from the house before and during the Vice-President's stay should not attract undue attention among the villagers.'

'I imagine they are accustomed to strangers around the place?'

'Yes, when the school has been on holiday in the past, the Hall has often been filled with seminars, conferences and the like. The locals are accustomed to seeing people around, both locals and those from overseas.'

'Some members of my force have been here, I believe,' said Mark.

'Yes, it all helps to keep the building busy. When this was a school people came from far and wide and didn't seem to mind the primitive sleeping arrangements during a short stay.'

'It would be like camping,' grinned Mark. 'Fun for a day or two. Now, the timings for my arrival. The Vice-President is due to arrive at this house on 11th July, a Monday. I'll have to move in some time before then to prepare, probably a week earlier, say Monday, 4th July.'

'American Independence Day, eh? Most appropriate and not a problem at all. I hope it's a good omen for all concerned.'

'I'll have to bring an advance party of my officers,' Mark said.

'And we'll need to establish extra telephone lines, install our computers and word processors and so on. We will bring all our own equipment, desks, filing cabinets, photocopiers and so forth, all to be installed before Hartley arrives. The one thing we do need from you is space for our offices.'

'There is plenty of office space — disused classrooms are all over the Hall. Help yourselves. It's first come, first served, as I said earlier. There'll be an advance party from the Embassy too, so you'd better get the best of what's available! Just make yourselves at home. Well, if you've finished your coffee, I'll show you round.'

Mark was driven along the rising, winding drive through sycamores until the house came into view. It was a splendid mansion with a pedimented entrance above a dual flight of curving stone stairs. Said to have been designed by Sir John Vanbrugh, the mansion was on two storeys above a basement, and had wings to the East and west. In front of the entrance was a courtyard surrounded by high walls with iron gates across the entrance; this was an added and welcome security feature.

Soon he was being guided around the interior. Blanchard, with evident pride, showed him the entire house and tried to explain how it would be improved for its forthcoming public visitors while repeatedly apologising for its current untidy and battered state. Battered walls, battered doors, battered floors, battered dormitories and battered bathrooms all bore the signs of repeated use by boisterous girls aggravated by a lack of funds to repair or conceal the damage. In the far future, all would be fresh and gleaming… But that could not be done in time for the incoming police officers, apologised Blanchard.

Mark inspected his own room and the rooms allocated to his team, then asked to see the Vice-President's quarters and the seven external doors. The tour took about an hour, with Mark asking pointed questions about fire escapes, window locks, fragile doors, cellar entrances and a host of other obvious risks to security. He was also concerned about the likelihood of electronic listening devices being planted in the fabric, and of time bombs or incendiary devices being positioned. At first glance, many of the security defects could be remedied by the attention of a skilled workman or two, and Blanchard said this would be done — the US Embassy had offered to pay for any such improvements.

Mark asked, 'Have any improvements been done since the school evacuated the premises?'

'No, there's not been time, we've just done a little general tidying up. A few broken windows fixed, toilet seats repaired, that sort of thing.'

'Who did that?' asked Mark.

'Our own staff,' responded Blanchard.

'From the time my officers arrive,' Mark said, 'everyone who enters this building must be approved by us. And I mean everyone. We need to concern ourselves with matters like someone planting listening bugs or bombs. I shall instruct our security experts to sweep the entire complex for devices, electronic or explosive; they'll arrive on Monday.'

'I understand.'

'Once they've declared the Hall clear of danger, we will make the building secure. It will be a sterile area, Mr Blanchard, and once that is achieved, we can then admit authorised personnel to carry out maintenance work, install telephones and computer lines and so on. Everyone working here will be security-vetted and will be issued with a security pass, including you and me!'

'Fair enough — I understand. I once managed an estate which hosted the Queen on occasions, so I do know the routine. I'm always here to help.'

'Thanks, it's nice to have our actions understood!' said Mark.

Having made this initial inspection, Mark said, 'Well, Mr Blanchard, thanks for your co-operation. My next duty is to move in here. I'll arrive on Monday morning, around coffee time!'

'The pot will be on,' promised Blanchard.

CHAPTER THREE

B y mid-afternoon on Monday, 4th July, Thirklewood Hall was buzzing with activity. Most of Mark's officers had arrived, with Detective Inspector Paul Larkin as Mark's deputy. Aided by Detective Constable Duncan Young, he was busy installing HOLMES — the Home Office Large Major Enquiry System, a sophisticated computer which was used on all major investigations and murder enquiries. Further computer equipment would provide immediate access to a whole range of information from national and international intelligence sources, vital if complete security was to be achieved.

Electronic surveillance experts from the Regional Support Services had arrived; some were checking every inch of the house for hidden devices, while others installed security cameras over the seven entrances. Explosives experts, along with police dog Ben, were scanning the interior for bombs while outside, the advance party of Americans was doing likewise around the grounds, distant outbuildings and all external parts of the Hall. All the drains and manhole covers, for example, were being inspected and made secure.

Ten officers from Scotland Yard's Diplomatic Protection

Group and fifteen US personnel had arrived and were installing themselves and their equipment.

There were secretaries and domestic staff, computers and crockery. Several American cooks had arrived too, along with a pantechnicon containing food and office equipment. Mark was delighted to learn that he and his officers would be fed by the Americans — their food was always scrumptious!

Robin Blanchard hovered around the activity, bemused by the noise, the shouting, the hammering, the requests for more coffee and the general bustle of this preliminary work.

'This is even noisier than the school!' he shouted to Mark above the din. 'And I never thought I'd ever say that!'

Mark had commandeered one of the smaller classrooms as his office. On the ground floor, it overlooked the forecourt at the front entrance and got most of the sunshine. It was large enough to accommodate Barbara along with her desk and word processor as well as his own desk; next door was Detective Inspector Larkin and two detective sergeants, while the other team members had the joint use of a much larger room. This had been the school lecture theatre and was at the end of a corridor, just beyond Larkin's office. The men had nicknamed it the Potting Shed because of its links with Operation Roots. Already, a colour photograph of Vice-President Hartley had appeared on a wall of the Potting Shed and a blackboard contained the known details of his programme of visits; Mark was delighted that his officers were showing their usual commitment to the task.

The man in charge of the American operation was called John T Dunnock, a member of the White House staff, and he made himself known to Mark, promising every possible assistance. A large round man with a friendly face and rimless spectacles, he seemed extremely easy-going, but Mark knew this was deceptive. To have achieved that position, he would be tough, although pleasant. He introduced Mark to some of his key personnel, showed him the office he was using and explained some of his own requirements and procedures. One factor was that when Hartley went off to visit Hull and the moorland villages in search of his roots, several aides would accompany him.

'We'll keep you informed of our movements and timings at all times,' Dunnock assured Mark. 'Mr Hartley likes an early night, by the way, and so we would ask your officers to remember that when they are moving around the house. Otherwise, he won't make any unreasonable demands upon you.'

Mark explained his own security arrangements, and so the procedures for protecting Vice-President Caleb Hodgson Hartley swung easily and efficiently into action. On American Independence Day, Thirklewood Hall was preparing to welcome its most important guest.

* * *

By Tuesday evening, the procedures were slipping into a comfortable routine; names of all the staff, American, British and Thirklewood Estate workers, had been fed into Mark's computers.

Security clearance had been finalised and passes issued. Duty rotas had been compiled, relationships established with the American aides and DPG officers, eating arrangements determined and personal corners of the building discovered. As everyone bustled around him, Mark found himself with little to do. Paul Larkin was firmly in control and his team were already programming details of the Muriel Brown murder into HOLMES. He knew they would look forward to regenerating aspects of the murder, unsolved for the past eight years or so.

Mark's room was not particularly welcoming. There was a plain metal-framed bed with a lumpy mattress, a battered wardrobe and dressing-table, a tattered rug and an old photograph of a Victorian man on one wall. It did have an adjoining toilet and shower, and it did overlook the front of the house, but otherwise it was not the ideal place to spend one's off-duty moments. There was always the bar, of course, or some work on the Muriel Brown murder.

After breakfast the following morning, Wednesday 6th July, Mark completed his supervisory tour of the Hall, had a brief conference with the White House officials about internal security, and then found he had nothing to do. Detective Inspector Larkin was working hard and so, for Mark, it was just a case of waiting for Hartley; he wandered into the Potting Shed and saw that his officers were occupying themselves with the Brown murder. The Chief had been right. This was a holiday, there was nothing much to do.

He should be able to relax but couldn't.

'Take time out, sir,' suggested Detective Inspector Paul Larkin upon noticing Mark's restiveness. 'Have a day off, I can look after things here.'

Mark shrugged his shoulders. 'I've nowhere I particularly want to go,' he said quietly.

'Lorraine's off duty today, sir.' Paul smiled. During previous enquiries, he'd seen Pemberton's happiness in the company of this tall, bewitching policewoman. 'She was talking about going over to Wolversdale, to see where this American's roots are.'

'Was she? Why would she want to do that?'

'Curiosity, sir,' smiled Larkin. 'Something to do.'

Mark wandered around the ground floor of the house, chatting to more White House, Scotland Yard and Special Branch staff, checking security of the doors and windows for the umpteenth time, and then he spotted Detective Constable Lorraine Cashmore. She was studying a map on a wall, her lithe, slender figure casting a shadow in a shaft of sunlight. Six feet tall with small breasts and the slimmest of legs, she might have been a model but had joined the force where her intuitive skills and dedication to her work had quickly resulted in a transfer from uniform to CID. Mark approached her.

'Morning, Lorraine,' he said, moving to her side.

'Oh, hello, sir.' She smiled at him, her dark eyes soft and gentle. 'I was looking for Wolversdale. I thought I'd have a run over there.'

'Me too,' he lied easily. 'I know the village. I've got time off… so, well, care to join me? I'll buy you a lunch in the Big Bad Wolf.'

She was somewhat hesitant, realising that a junior officer should not become too friendly with a senior member of the staff, but she relented when Mark said, 'It is to do with our task, Lorraine — at least, that's what I'll tell anybody who asks!'

'All right,' she said.

'My car's in the car-park,' he added. 'I'll just tell DI Larkin where we're going.'

Larkin was genuinely pleased. He liked to see Pemberton with a woman — the poor fellow never took time off and seldom went out unless it was connected with his work. Now he was heading for the romantic heather-clad moors with a lovely woman at his side! Larkin sighed. He had a wife and family to think about… He pressed a button to test HOLMES for information about red cars observed near the scene of Muriel Brown's death.

Happy that the system was working, he bent to his task. He scanned the statements for further references to red cars. It would be gratifying to solve the Muriel Brown murder.

* * *

DURING THE FIFTY-MINUTE drive to Wolversdale, Lorraine told Mark she'd always wanted to research her own family history but had never had the time. She had no idea where to begin and had hit upon the idea of investigating Hartley's background, purely out of interest. She thought it might help her to decide how to research her own family tree.

Mark agreed it was a good idea and told her of the Chief Constable's instructions that he should take more time off. He added that he regarded this outing as time off; true, it was remotely linked to his duties, but a day exploring the moors with an attractive woman could hardly be classified as official duty. Mark took a short cut along a deserted moorland road which eventually dropped steeply into Wolversdale. The road was no wider than his car, and grass grew along its centre. After a series of sharp bends and cattle grids, the road widened into the dale. The broad dale, so typical of the North York moors, was home to a scattering of farms, a bubbling stream, a Methodist chapel and a patchwork of dry-stone walls. The road led down the dale towards the village and soon they could see the outline of St Monica's Catholic church at the bottom of the hill. It was large and Gothic, having been built 120 years ago to replace an earlier building which had become too small. That smaller building was now the Catholic school, while its huge neighbour had the capacity of a cathedral.

In spite of its size, it was a mere parish church in a small North Yorkshire moorland village, Wolversdale being known as the village missed by the Reformation.

Spread before the church was the graveyard. Mark parked beside the metal gate and entered with Lorraine close behind. As they walked along the gravel path between the tombstones, Mark noticed a large grey-haired man swinging a scythe. With his back to the newcomers, he was clearing away the long grass which flourished near each stone. He used the ancient tool with considerable skill.

Mark approached him.

'Good morning,' he began, and the man stood erect to face him.

For Mark, it was like staring at the photograph of Caleb Hodgson Hartley. The man's features were identical to those of the Vice-President — sturdy appearance, strong jaw, squarish features, heavy cheeks and thick neck with a head of iron grey hair, neatly trimmed. He would be in his middle or late sixties. This man was surely a Hartley.

'Now then,' greeted the man without a smile. 'Visitors, are you? Tourists?'

'Yes,' said Mark. 'I'm looking for the Hartley family graves.'

'Then you've found 'em.' The man spoke in a heavy North Yorkshire moorland accent. 'These here,' and he swept an arc with the scythe to indicate the general area.

'Oh, thanks,' smiled Mark.

'Why do you want to see 'em? You're not a Hartley, are you?'

'No.' Mark decided to adopt his official role. 'I'm Detective Superintendent Pemberton of the local force, and this is my assistant, Detective Constable Cashmore. Are you Mr George Hartley, by any chance?'

'I am,' said the man, straightening up. 'George Hartley from Pike Hill Farm, that's me. So, why all this interest in the Hartleys all of a sudden?'

'You know about Mr Caleb Hodgson Hartley, the Vice-President of the United States?' From details in the file, Mark recognised that this man was the eldest of the local Hartleys.

'Aye, I do,' and Hartley volunteered nothing further.

'He's coming here to look up his family roots,' Mark continued. 'He'll want to see these graves.'

'I can't understand why he thinks we've got links with his family,' grunted the big man. 'I know nowt about any American cousins, let alone a big-wig like yon chap.'

'He looks just like you,' said Mark. 'Same facial features. And he's called Caleb like you. Your middle name, I believe? A family name?'

'How come you know that?' The man looked shocked.

'My job is to arrange his security while he's here.' Mark explained his role, adding (with tongue in cheek) that the securing of some background information was part of that duty. 'We know he's made an appointment to see you next Tuesday.'

'I've got to keep it quiet, not tell the press or anyone who he is. That's why I'm clearing these tombstones, so he can get a good look at our graves. He can see these for himself. There's nowt else I can tell him.'

'No family bible?' put in Mark.

'It got burnt years ago,' said Hartley. 'We've started another, but it doesn't go all that far back.'

'So you've never researched your own family tree?'

'Nay, lad, not me. I've allus had better things to do with my time. These are my family, buried here. I've no need to go raking around churches and libraries to find any more.'

'It's a big family, though, isn't it?'

'Big by some standards, I suppose,' agreed Mr Hartley. 'But we're Catholics, allus have been, right through the Reformation. And we've spread a bit, we've some relations living away from here, in Hull, Newcastle, Gloucester, Leicestershire, Wales and other spots, but we seldom keep in touch. Distant cousins, that sort of thing. They turn up at funerals, then you never see 'em again for years. We're just Yorkshire farmers, Mr Pemberton, and this is our home.'

'So you know nothing of his claims to be descended from your family?'

'I reckon he's made it all up. I'll bet some of his pals have been over here and have seen all those tombstones with Caleb Hartleys mentioned on them. They'll have gone back to America and told him, and because his name's the same, he's come to think we're relations of his. There's no other explanation, Mr Pemberton. We do get lots of Americans around here, looking up their families, then going back and bragging about ancient Yorkshire roots.'

'I suppose if they go back far enough, they might find a link. Now, do you mind if I look around at these graves?'

'Nay, lad, help yourself, it's a free country. Mebbe if you do turn up summat, you'll let me know?'

'I will, of course,' said Mark.

'Can we come and talk to you again if we have to?' asked Lorraine with one of her dazzling smiles.

'Sure,' he said. 'Especially if you find out he's rich! We're nobbut poor hill farmers, not high-flying politicians.'

Mr Hartley wandered off with his scythe as Mark and Lorraine began to inspect the rows of gravestones. This corner was devoted to Hartleys. There was a Caleb Hartley born in 1852 who died in 1922 — he had no other Christian name. His wife, Sarah, was buried in the same grave, having died in 1926. There was a Thomas Joseph Hartley born in 1884 who died in 1926, the Reverend Father Matthew Hartley born in 1888, died in 1961, and Private James Reuben Hartley, a casualty of the first World War. None had a Caleb name.

Private James Reuben Hartley of the 5th Battalion of the Green Howards died in 1916 aged thirty, and the inscription said, 'Death's rough call unlooses all our favourite ties on earth; and well if they are such as may be answered in yonder world where all is judged of truly.' Underneath, it said, 'Beloved son of Caleb and Sarah Hartley. Taken so suddenly. RIP.'

'If this chap was in the army,' said Mark, 'he might have founded a dynasty, eh? He could be the daddy of the America Hartleys.'

'I can't see that, sir — our soldiers didn't visit America or Canada during that war, did they? Besides, there's no mention of a wife or young family on his tombstone,' said Lorraine.

'I wish you'd not call me sir when we're alone. I do have a name. It's Mark.'

'It's not easy, sir...er ...Mark, me being a constable and you a superintendent. You're my boss...'

'Suppose I ordered you to call me Mark?' There was a twinkle in his eye. 'Then I'd have to obey, sir!'

'Precisely,' smiled Mark. 'Now, back to James. Perhaps he was a naughty boy when he was playing away from home?'

'So we need to know more about him?' Lorraine looked happy.

'It seems he was a hero, being lost in the war. Shall I ring the Green Howards at Richmond to see what their records show?'

'Good idea,' said Mark. 'Try the Green Howards Museum, I went there once, and they've got some useful displays and information about World War One. Names of medal winners, those killed on duty, the wounded and so on. I've a telephone in the car. There's no time like the present, is there?'

Directory Enquiries quickly produced the telephone number of the Green Howards Regimental Headquarters and Museum at Richmond in Yorkshire and Mark passed the handset to Lorraine, saying, 'Ask about privates killed on duty during 1916. There'll be a list, a roll of honour or something. We want to know where James was serving when he died, and we'd like to know more about his career if that's possible. Just think — the Hartleys might have a hero in the family!'

Lorraine called the number and waited, then said, 'This is Detective Constable Cashmore of the local police. I wonder if you can help me?'

'Yes, if possible,' said a woman's voice. 'I'm interested in a private of the Green Howards, 5th Battalion, who was killed in action during the First World War. It was in 1916. Private James Reuben Hartley is the name, he's buried at Wolversdale. I wondered if there was any information about him in your records? You know, where he died, where he served and so on. Yes, I can hold on.'

Lorraine waited and then the woman returned. 'He's not on our roll of members who were killed while on active service in the First World War,' she said. 'That list is very easy to find. But there is a reference in the Green Howards' Gazette of the period. He didn't die on active service, Constable. He was murdered while on leave in September 1916.'

CHAPTER FOUR

Lorraine was stunned. She stared at Pemberton almost in a state of shock with the handset clutched in her fist. She whispered, 'He was murdered, sir, she says Private James Hartley was murdered while he was on leave.'

'Oh my God,' he said. 'Let me speak to her.' And he took the handset from Lorraine.

'I'm Detective Superintendent Pemberton,' he announced. 'What's this about Private James Reuben Hartley being murdered?'

'That's what's in our Gazette, Mr Pemberton,' stressed the museum official. 'We've lists of personnel who were killed or wounded in 1916; the Green Howards' Gazette shows the casualties and Private Hartley is mentioned because he was murdered while on leave. It happened in September 1916, although the exact date is not given.'

'You've no more details?'

'Not in the museum or the Gazette. There might be something in the regimental records, but we don't keep them here. I can check, if you wish. I might be able to get a photocopy of whatever there is. If we have any information, I can't see there'd be a problem passing it to you in this case.'

'Could you? I'd be most grateful.'

'Is there anything in particular you require?'

'I need to know the exact date of his death and the full circumstances, along with his service record. I must know when he died and where he died and whether anyone was prosecuted for the murder. As much as you've got, in other words. I can come to the museum or any other office if necessary.'

'I'll check first, to see what we do have. I doubt if we'll have all that kind of detail, most of our World War One records have been destroyed. But I will check with the regimental HQ. It might take a while, but I'll call you. Where can I contact you?'

Pemberton gave her the numbers of two lines into the Incident Room, the fax number and the address of Thirklewood Hall. He also provided his office address at Great Halverton police headquarters but stressed the need for the utmost discretion. The lady, whose name was Mrs Preston, said she understood and would call him as soon as she was able.

'Well, blow me, Lorraine,' he said when he replaced the handset. 'That's a turn-up for the books, as they say. Who'd want to murder a humble private soldier who was coming home on leave before going off to fight for King and country?'

'A jealous rival?'

'You could be right!' said Pemberton.

'So, while we're out of the office and hot on the trail of a mystery, let's try the local newspaper. If he was killed locally, or even away from the district, the paper covering his home area would surely have carried the story.'

Again using his car telephone, he called the editor of the Rainesbury Gazette and asked if it was convenient to call within the next hour. The editor, Len Storr, knew Pemberton from previous investigations and readily agreed. By eleven forty-five, Mark and Lorraine were sitting in his office.

Mark explained his mission without any reference to links with the Vice-President and asked if copies of September 1916 editions were still available. They were; they were in the company's own library and comprised the actual papers, not microfiche copies. Mark and Lorraine were taken down to the musty basement where rows and rows of old newspapers were suspended in the gloom like drying sheets.

'Help yourselves,' offered Storr, a youthful man with a casual air. 'And might there be a story for me in all this?'

'I think there will be, Len, but not just yet,' Mark told him. 'I'll let you know, or you could ring me in, say, a month's time? Just to remind me.'

'Okay, the files are all yours,' and he left them to their work.

'Can you start at the end of the year and work backwards, and I'll start before the date of the murder and work forwards,' Mark told Lorraine. 'If we don't find anything, we'll meet in the middle!'

'Sure, but what am I looking for?' she asked.

'Any reference to Hartley's murder no matter how small. It should be headline stuff, at least in the early days of the enquiry. At that time, murder stories contained far more detail than the press are allowed to publish these days. So there should be quite a spread with a lot of useful background for us. They used to publish all the evidence before the committal hearing and trial — no wonder juries made up their minds even before listening to the case in court!'

Lorraine was first to find a reference. It was a paragraph in the 22nd December issue which said the police were no further forward in their investigation of the death of Private James Hartley of Pike Hill Farm, Wolversdale. There had been no arrest. There was a brief summary of the crime and a photograph of James Hartley, albeit not in army uniform. Well-groomed and dark-haired with a parting down the middle, he sported a fashionable bushy moustache, a short tweed jacket, knee breeches and leather leggings, and had a sheep-dog at his side. He looked like a gentleman farmer.

'OK, so we know it's true; we know it was our James Hartley

who was murdered. You push forward, Lorraine, keep looking to see if the story is elaborated; see if anyone was interviewed or whether any suspect was named. They used to do that, you know, in those days — the coroner could even name a suspect. Think of being publicly branded as a murder suspect by a coroner! Even if the case was never proved in court, the suspect had to live with that accusation.'

'I'm pleased the law has changed!'

'Right, well, keep looking, get as much detail as possible — I'll keep looking for the original story. It's got to be here somewhere.'

Mark found his story without any real difficulty because it tilled the front page of the issue dated Friday 15th September 1916. It was a weekly paper, published every Friday, and he read this edition carefully. The report told how, on the previous Monday, 11th September 1916, the body of Private James Reuben Hartley had been found on common land in the village of Rosen-thorpe. He had been shot through the head. The report went on to say that James Hartley had not volunteered for military service but had been conscripted in 1916 to serve in the North Riding of Yorkshire's own regiment, the Green Howards. He was one of two men from Wolversdale who had been conscripted at that time, the other being Eric Hall; Hall was an apprentice farrier aged nineteen. Both had undergone six weeks' basic training with the 5th Battalion near Richmond in Yorkshire and upon completion of that training, both had been drafted to France. Their ship was not due to sail from Folkestone to Boulogne until 13th September and so James had been sent home for one night, ie the night of the 11th, pending that departure. Eric Hall had gone direct to the port. James had been due to rejoin his colleagues on the night of Tuesday, 12th September at Folkestone.

To avail himself of the short leave, he had travelled home from Richmond in uniform and his journey had been by train. His brother, Luke, a veteran of the Boer War, had arranged to meet him at Rosenthorpe station with a pony and trap but had been delayed because his horse had shed a shoe. When Luke had arrived at the station, the train had come and gone, but there was no sign of James. The report went on to say that the station master, Maurice Proctor, had confirmed that James Hartley had left the train in uniform; being a local man, the station master knew most of the travellers. James had been carrying a kitbag, a back-pack and a rifle, and he had spoken to Mr Proctor, asking if Luke had arrived. Proctor had said he'd not seen Luke or the pony and trap, and so James had intimated that he would start to walk home. He expressed the hope that he would meet Luke somewhere en route.

When Luke arrived at the station sometime after James's departure, Proctor had told him all this, but Luke was adamant he had not seen James anywhere along the road. Luke had some shopping to do in the village and he had spent about an hour in Rosenthorpe, waiting near the station in case James turned up. Luke said his brother might have visited someone in the village, but after an hour or so, when James had not appeared, Luke had driven home to Wolversdale, a distance of about five miles.

Upon his return to Pike Hill Farm, Luke had been alone with the pony and trap, and had vowed there was no sign of James along the way. James had not arrived home ahead of him either. In short, James Hartley had not been seen or heard of since alighting from the train.

That same evening, James's body had been found by a game-keeper who was setting his snares. His kitbag and his regulation issue rifle were at his side and there was a very prominent bullet wound to the head. The newspaper report did not say whether his own rifle had been the murder weapon.

Detective Inspector Dawson and Detective Sergeant Ripley from Rainesbury police had been put in charge of the investigation. The report added that the coroner, Colonel Sidney Feltham, had conducted an immediate inquest which had delivered a verdict of murder by person or persons unknown, the cause of death being a bullet wound to the head. Pemberton was astonished at this — the inquest had been concluded without any evidence or statements from the police, other than the circumstances relating to the body at the scene. Certainly, no scientific evidence had been produced at the inquest. But that's how things were done at that time — coroners were virtually a law unto themselves. The subsequent post-mortem examination did, however, confirm that death was due to a single bullet wound in the head.

In reading the newspaper account, Mark realised that he must not rely entirely upon its coverage, although it did provide a good overall account of the crime. What he really needed was to find the original police file, if it still existed.

There followed a brief account of James's funeral at St Monica's in Wolversdale, with a photograph of the cortege leaving Pike Hill Farm. A horse-drawn hearse had been used; it was led by two strikingly handsome black stallions. The church had been packed for the Requiem Mass.

The Green Howards had been represented by a Major Brownlee and, from the report, it seemed as if the entire population of the dale had turned out to say farewell to James Hartley. Apparently, he had been a very popular man during his short life, although there was no reference to a regular girlfriend or a fiancée.

The Rainesbury Gazette carried the story of the murder hunt for several Fridays and when Mark asked Lorraine how she was progressing, she said she had found references well into November and December. Not one of them mentioned an arrest, however. It seemed that the murder of James Reuben Hartley had never been solved; and it suddenly dawned on Pemberton that he now had an unsolved murder on his hands.

'I reckon we might be using HOLMES and our Incident Room after all,' he smiled. 'So instead of trying to find out who killed Muriel Brown, we can find out who killed James Hartley.'

'Do you think we should?' Lorraine sounded cautious.

'I think it would be very fitting if we could discover the background to this murder, especially if an American relation is trying to find his roots among the same family!'

'There's no point in resurrecting such an old crime, surely?' Lorraine's pretty brow furrowed in thought. 'I mean, sir, er, Mark, what's the point? Whoever did it will be dead now.'

'Will they? Suppose it was a lad of sixteen who shot him. He'd be ninety-four now. He could be alive... Justice could still be done.'

'You're not going to reopen enquiries into this, surely?' she cried.

'Of course I am, it's my duty. Unsolved murder files are never closed.'

'But not after all this time. You'd really upset the Vice-President by raking up all this dirt.'

'There's no proof that this Hartley is related to the Vice-President,' he reminded her. 'But if they are related, think of the prestige if we, the British police, discover who killed our VIP's distant cousin all those years ago. So, young Lorraine, I am going to delve into this one! It'll give me something to think about in what is otherwise going to be a very boring period of work. And, in the preliminary stages at least, the Vice-President needn't know what we're doing, need he? At this early stage it's nowt to do with him or his minders.'

'But suppose the two men are linked, the Vice-President and the victim. The press would have a field day with that story.'

'There's no need to tell anyone at this stage,' Pemberton stressed. 'But I'll rethink the position if and when the Vice-President proves his links with the Yorkshire Hartleys.'

They took photocopies of all the newspaper reports and thanked Len Storr for his swift response to their request, Mark reiterating that there might be a story for the paper once he'd gathered all the facts. Then it was lunchtime. Mark found a charming harbourside pub where he treated Lorraine to a substantial if late bar snack.

'I intended going to the Big Bad Wolf in Wolversdale,' he said, 'but the food's good here. Then it'll be a case of back to work...'

'Sir, er...Mark, this isn't a current enquiry, you know. There's nothing urgent about it, you shouldn't be working flat out like this. Do as the Chief said. Relax a little.'

'I don't believe in missing opportunities or wasting precious time, Lorraine, and I want to get this one cleared up before the Vice-President arrives on Monday. We haven't much time, which means my next step is to find the old police records. If they're anywhere, they'll be here in Rainesbury.'

'What? From 1916?'

'The old generation of policemen never threw anything out, Lorraine. Everything was kept, just in case! It didn't matter whether it was a broken poker from the charge office hearth, an obsolete telephone handset or a file of lost purses dating from the Boer War, it was always kept — just in case. Police station lofts were always full of brown paper parcels containing old files and crime circulars; you could climb into the loft and scramble over old chairs, piles of ancient ledgers containing visits to public houses, examination of dog licences and visits to unoccupied premises from the last century. There were court files too, and the results of criminal enquiries together with the names of suspects and details of families' villainous behaviour. They were all neatly tied with string and labelled with their contents. An archivist would have a field day in the loft of any police station. Just think what secrets they must contain!'

'Surely, the police would want rid of old records — why don't they give them to somebody like the county archivist?'

'They'd never let anything leave the station, Lorraine, they wouldn't trust the archivist. Besides, the honest descendants of our best customers are still alive and kicking, and some are holding down very respectable jobs or positions in local society!

We can't let the public into all our secrets or let them be privy to our knowledge of criminals who are never caught.'

'I'll bet we could cause a few worries among the population if we did reveal those secrets,' she laughed.

'We could! The old policemen knew that — they liked to keep certain information on file, you never knew when it might be required, or be useful! I mean, dammit, it's important to know that the Red Lion Inn was visited by Sergeant Bloggs at 10.30pm. on Saturday, 7th May 1921 and that all was in order!'

'You're being facetious, Mark!'

'I'm being truthful, Lorraine!'

'So you reckon Rainesbury police will still have the file on Hartley's murder?'

'If the crime was never solved, the file would have been kept — just in case! And, as it happens, whoever made that decision was right. That file is now required, even if almost eighty years have gone by.'

'I can't believe they'd keep it all this time!'

'Want to bet on it? I say it's there, somewhere. If it's not, I'll buy you dinner tonight. And if it is there, you buy dinner!'

'You're on,' she smiled.

They drove to the police station at Rainesbury. It was a large modern building with lots of glass and external woodwork. Perched on a hilltop site close to the hospital, it overlooked the harbour and commanded fine views of the town beneath.

Access was via a steeply rising one-way street; half-way up that hill was a car parking area.

'That's where the old police station used to be,' he pointed to the car-park. 'It was a veritable Victorian pile built of red bricks and it was like a rabbit warren inside. It had been used since the creation of the force in 1856, but the new one was built just over twenty years ago. So they knocked the old one down and made it into a car-park!'

'And you say that old police station would be full of brown paper parcels all containing ancient files and papers?'

'Exactly, and when everyone moved into their posh new premises, they took all the old stuff with them, dust and all.'

'I would have thought they'd have taken the opportunity to throw most of it out.'

'You don't know how the minds of old-fashioned policemen worked! The Superintendent at the time said that everything must be taken to the new station, with the idea that, one day, someone would be instructed to go through the old papers and cast aside all the unwanted items. But who had the guts to make such far-reaching decisions? Who dared make the decision that a book of 1908 sheep dip records was no longer needed? Even when head-quarters said that all routine files more than ten years old could be destroyed, few of these old characters would do that. They just could not bring themselves to part with old books and files; hanging on to old records was bred into them. So they stuffed everything in the loft.'

'And you believe all that rubbish is still there?'

'I'm gambling that no clear-out was ever done. And once the rubbish got into the loft, there it would stay until somebody remembered it was there. Like me.'

'How do you know it all went to the new station?'

'I was there,' he grinned. 'I was a police cadet at the time. I lugged tons of brown paper parcels down from the old loft. Some of the younger lads tried to get rid of a lot of the stuff, but the old-stagers wouldn't allow it. It's all in the loft of the new building, Lorraine. And I'm gambling that the Hartley file is among it. Somewhere.'

'Why here? Why not another station? Rosenthorpe is quite a long way from here.'

'Rosenthorpe, the scene of the murder, was in the old Raines-bury division. Boundaries have changed now, of course, and new police forces have replaced the old, but Rainesbury's own divisional boundaries haven't altered a great deal. The files would have been stored in that old police station, the one that's now a car-park, and then brought here.'

By this time, Mark was turning into the car-park at the police station. He got out and Lorraine followed him to the reception desk.

'Hello, sir.' PC Mason, the constable on the desk, recognised them. 'Can I help?'

'Is the Chief Super in?'

'Yes, he's just back from lunch, sir. Shall I buzz him?'

'Please.'

PC Mason pressed the intercom and said, 'Detective Superintendent Pemberton and DC Cashmore to see you, sir.'

'Send them in,' was the reply.

Chief Superintendent George Ramsden was the tough but efficient commander of the Rainesbury Division and would want to know what Mark was doing here. Mark, however, was simply obeying a force courtesy — when you went into another man's patch to conduct an enquiry, you let him know of your presence — but not necessarily the whole purpose of the visit. Mark decided not to reveal anything, not at this stage. He would state just enough to gain Ramsden's co-operation.

'Well, what brings you here, Mark? And Miss Cashmore.' Ramsden pointed to two chairs.

Mark explained about Vice-President Hartley's forthcoming private visit and how he was responsible for aspects of security; he then led to the murder of James Hartley and said he wanted to examine the file, if it was available. He said he was sure it was in the loft.

'I can't see why a 1916 murder relates to the security of a modern VIP, but you CID fellows work in mysterious ways. Sure, have a look around, Mark. You know where to look?'

And so Mark and Lorraine found themselves in the roomy attic of Rainesbury police station. Dry and airy, it was fitted with electric lighting and there was easy access via a collapsible ladder.

Arranged in tidily positioned heaps upon the floor were scores of brown paper parcels all tied with string and adorned with tie-on labels which identified their contents. There were others in racks around the edge of the floor space. The place seemed to be full of them.

'What we're looking for,' advised Mark, 'is a parcel dated 1916 and marked either "Murders" or "Crime Reports" or "Unsolved Crimes". It might even be marked with some other title, but if it's here, I want it. I could have asked a constable to search, but I want to be sure, I want to do it myself, then I know it's been done properly.'

'I'm going to be covered in dust when I get out of here!' she grumbled. 'My hair will be awful…'

'Then we'll have to arrange a shower for you,' he grinned. 'And for me! So, Lorraine, isn't this a lovely way of spending your day off?'

'I could think of better ones,' and she sneezed violently.

CHAPTER FIVE

L orraine found the parcel. Clearly marked 'Crimes, Rainesbury Division, 1916', it was about two feet high, and the length and width of foolscap paper. Smothered in the dust of three-quarters of a century, it was wrapped in thick brown paper and tied with strong twine. Gingerly, she untied the knots to reveal the contents — scores of foolscap files in brown covers. Sitting on the top was a tattered buff file jacket marked 'Murder of James Reuben Hartley'. In red ink, it bore the word 'Unsolved' across the front and was held together with thin string. The Hartley file comprised a very thick sheaf of papers and was accompanied by several bulky brown envelopes. These had holes in the corners and they were fastened to the string which had been around the main file.

'I could kiss you,' beamed Mark Pemberton and so he did, planting his wet and sloppy appreciation on her dusty cheek.

'Sir, somebody might see us…'

'Who cares?' he smiled. 'So, you owe me dinner tonight!'

'I think you knew it would be here…'

'I didn't know that this particular file had survived, but, well, there was a fair chance it would be among the other stuff. So I'll buy the dinner because you found it. No arguments. Now, let's see if everything's here.'

He made a quick but thorough examination of the murder file, which was itself some six inches thick, and found it contained all the necessary reports — the examination of the scene, statements from witnesses and detectives, doctor's report, pathologist's report, coroner's report, details of the police action, results of house-to-house enquiries and an additional file of continuation sheets from the investigating officers. They were Detective Inspector Dawson and Detective Sergeant Ripley. Those sheets spanned almost a year, but it was clear, even from a casual glance, that no arrest had been made. No suspect had been named, consequently no one had been prosecuted or convicted of this murder.

The accompanying envelopes, of differing sizes, contained various exhibits including a selection of photographs. Although unprofessional by modern standards, the photographs did show the body at the scene, the service rifle and items of James's uniform such as his kitbag and back-pack. There were also pictures of the road leading into Rosenthorpe; the body had been found close to that road. There were pictures of a pony and trap taken from several angles and a sketch map of the scene of the crime. This showed the position of the body in relation to the road which passed by and in relation to two oak trees and a large boulder. Pemberton turned his attention to a thick envelope containing a small object and found it contained a used bullet. A note said it had been taken from the skull of James Reuben Hartley and was the cause of death.

'It's all here.' He smiled with happiness. 'What more can a fellow want? We'll take it with us, and our teams at Thirklewood Hall can start to program this data into HOLMES instead of the Muriel Brown case. It'll be interesting to see what a modern computer makes of a 1916 unsolved murder, won't it?'

'I didn't bargain for this when I left this morning, Mark,' she smiled, remembering to call him Mark.

'Me neither, but that's the way it goes. It means I've got something to keep me busy while I'm sitting around at Thirklewood Hall. And I'll have a go at linking our deceased JR Hartley with Vice-President Hartley. Having seen that Hartley chap in the churchyard and the Vice-President's photo, I'm convinced there is a family link.'

'But what good will it do, Mark, digging up all this old material? You might rake up some skeletons that have long since been laid to rest.' Her unease had not been appeased.

'That's precisely the point of a murder investigation!' he said. 'It might all lead to nothing, though, so let's see what develops, shall we? Then we'll decide what action to take.'

He refastened the string around the unwanted files, wrote upon the wrapping in ballpoint that he had taken the Hartley murder file, then dated and signed the note. Downstairs, he told PC Mason what he'd done and asked him to inform Chief Superintendent Ramsden.

Placing the file on the rear seat of his car, he said, 'Well, Lorraine, off we go again.'

'Where to this time, sir...er...Mark?'

'Where is the very first place a good detective goes when investigating a crime?' he asked.

'To the scene?' she replied.

'Exactly. So it is to the scene we shall go.'

THE MOORLAND VILLAGE of Rosenthorpe was set in the steep-sided valley of the River Bluewath. Once an iron-ore mining community, it was now a tourist centre with a steam railway, a folk museum, cafés and shops. Busy with trippers from Easter until September, it bore few signs of its fairly recent industrial heritage. The railway, however, was still operating, albeit in two distinct sections. One was a British Rail track running from Rainesbury to

Thornborough; this carried commuters and schoolchildren from the villages into either Rainesbury or Thornborough.

The second line was the Rosenthorpe Historic Steam Railway, Rosenthorpe station being the terminus. The line ran across the moors to the market town of Drakenedge. Rosenthorpe therefore hosted two railways: one a British Rail service hauled by diesel engines, the other a tourist attraction with steam trains. It was to this station that James Hartley had come shortly before his death, and at that time, both lines were operating with steam engines.

Prior to nationalisation, both lines were owned and run by the North-Eastern Railway. The village's iron-ore industry, which had led to the building of those railway routes in 1836, had ended around the turn of the century, but a thriving brick manufacturing works had appeared in its place. Its complex of ugly buildings had been constructed on the northern side of the railway station with rail links leading into the works. Mark was aware of this — when he was a child, those brickworks were still functioning, although they had now closed. Some derelict buildings remained while part of the old site now contained a modern housing development.

A range of stone-built cottages and fine houses adorned the hillsides while isolated houses and farms were spread along the bottom of the dale. Some tiny miners' cottages had been converted into larger homes and there was a fine Anglican church, a Methodist chapel, two pubs, a Co-op store, a butcher's shop and a garage. To the south of the village, there was a half-mile long tunnel which took steam trains away from the village.

'It's an interesting place,' said Mark. 'But if we park here, we can walk to the murder scene.'

He pulled into the car-park of the cricket ground where nets had been erected for both tennis and cricket practice.

A low dry-stone wall ran around the boundary to separate the ground from the undulating road. Opposite the cricket field, on the other side of the road, was some common land.

This was now thick with hawthorn trees.

Not long ago, this land had bordered the buildings, roads and railway lines of the brickworks and had been waste ground. Now it was a happy hunting ground for dogs going walkies, kids going exploring, lovers going courting and wild creatures going hunting.

'Hartley was found somewhere in there,' Pemberton pointed to a gap in the hawthorn hedge. 'Come along, let's look.'

He took the file of papers from his car and walked across the road into the common land, which covered several acres.

'We're looking for a boulder and some oak trees which were in one of the photographs,' he told Lorraine as he turned to the photograph in question. 'Even if the trees have gone, the boulder should still be there. It's quite distinctive — it reminds me of a frog's head. The trees and the boulder are shown in both the photograph of the scene and the sketch; they do pinpoint the precise location of the body.'

They refreshed their memories from several photographs and sketches, then began their search. It was far from easy — old paths had gone, and new ones had been formed; trees had grown where none had existed at the time of the murder and the disappearance of the brickworks and their waste products had surely led to some changes to the surrounding landscape. He and Lorraine wandered around for the best part of half an hour and he was about to call it off when he noticed the rock.

It was standing on the very edge of the modern road, almost completely hidden by the hawthorn hedge, but there was no sign of any oak trees.

'It's smaller than I thought.' Mark examined it. 'But it's definitely the one in that old photograph, there's a very distinctive mark or indentation there, to the right.'

One brown and slightly faded photograph showed the boulder in the left foreground, which made its size difficult to judge; the body of James Hartley lay behind it, his shoulders partially obscured by the bulk of that rock. The bottom of his legs, clad in puttees and army boots, protruded towards the right of the photograph and he lay on his back with his feet slightly apart and his arms outstretched. The background contained the two oak trees and they appeared to be growing out of a hedge. They were to the right of the photograph. The hedge contained other smaller trees and the ground upon which the corpse lay appeared to be covered with short grass.

Mark studied the photograph, puzzled momentarily by what it depicted, and then stood at the point from where he believed the picture had been taken.

'Got it!' he said. 'The corpse is lying right in the middle of what is now the road. Those trees must have been felled to make way for this modern and wider tarmac road; the earlier road, much narrower than this modern one, must have been behind that hedge. That places it roughly along what is now the edge of the cricket field.'

Lorraine looked at the area in question and tended to agree.

Mark continued. 'Now, in this photo, the old road must have run behind those oaks and therefore behind the hedge which grows under them. For us, looking at this photo, that old hedge obscures our view of the road, Lorraine. If that is true, it means the body was lying very close to the old road; in other words, it was hidden just behind the hedge. That hedge would bear thick foliage in September, so it would make an effective barrier. Passers-by would never catch sight of a body lying there. Now, are there any more useful pictures? There must have been some form of entrance to this land, a gate in the hedge, or just a gap. See the way the body lies? He was not shot there, I'll bet. I'll bet he was shot somewhere else and carried to where he was found, perhaps being rolled off a cart, which explains why he's lying on his back with his arms and legs apart. And see the rifle and kitbag? They've been placed beside the body, the rifle's close to his right hand. Was it put there to suggest suicide, perhaps? If so, it was a clumsy attempt — it's most difficult to shoot oneself in the temple with a rifle. We don't know what time the body was found, do we? The newspaper report didn't say. I'm curious to know whether anyone could commit this crime and dump the body in broad daylight.'

'There wouldn't be so many people around, no cars or tourists in those days,' Lorraine added.

'But people did go for walks and they did exercise dogs. Anyway, let's have a look at some more pictures.'

Lorraine searched the file to produce more photographs; there was one depicting the entrance to the common land. In this, the two oaks were on the right of the picture. To their left was a gap in the hedge without even a gate or fence; the lane, unsurfaced at that time, could be seen running directly past. The picture had been taken from the far side of the lane.

'It must have been so easy for a cart to fetch the body in here, eh? Or even drive it in here with him alive and on board, shoot him and dump the body over the side, making sure everything happened out of sight behind the hedge, and then drive off,' mused Mark.

'So you think somebody was lying in wait, even hiding here, to catch him as he walked past?' asked Lorraine. 'We do have a picture of a pony and trap in the file somewhere. It's obviously significant — was he shot in that trap and thrown out here? Luke, his brother, went to meet him in a pony and trap, didn't he? According to the newspaper, that was.'

'I reckon that's what those early investigators thought,' said Mark. 'Imagine the jealous suitor that you suggested — James wasn't a bad-looking chap, if that photograph of him is anything to go by, and perhaps he had upset a few of the local lads by stealing their girls? A handsome lad in uniform can always get the girls — or he could in those days.'

'I'm not as old as that!' chuckled Lorraine.

'Sometimes I feel as though I am,' he smiled. 'But look, suppose one of those jealous rivals didn't want James back in the area, even for a short time? He could have shot him. It would make sense — he'd know when James was returning, the whole district would know. In these tiny villages, everyone knew everyone else's business and a conscripted soldier coming home on leave would make local news. It would be easy to lie in wait and clobber him, then dump the body here.'

'Will his love life have been examined by those old detectives?' asked Lorraine.

'I sincerely hope so. That's the first thing we look into nowadays when we get a murder — the sex life of the victim is of paramount importance. I reckon they'd do likewise. We'll see what those old statements tell us. Now, is there anything else we need to inspect while we're here?'

'I doubt it, it's changed so much.'

'The road goes up and down like a roller-coaster!' Mark strode along it for a short distance. 'We used to call this kind of road switchbacks, they're lovely for cycling along. You free-wheeled down one hill and tried to get up the other side without pedalling.'

'It's only small peaks and troughs, though,' Lorraine said.

'They were mountains to a small lad on his dad's heavy bike,' laughed Mark. 'Come along, time to go. We can always come back if we need to. Now, what time is it?'

'Half-past four,' she said.

'Knocking-off time, I reckon. Well, by the time we get back to Thirklewood Hall, washed and changed, it'll be knocking-off time. Then I'm going to buy you that meal.'

* * *

MARK SLEPT WELL and alone in his uncomfortable room and next morning, Thursday, he called together his staff for a conference in the Potting Shed. He told them about his discoveries and suggested they abandon their reinvestigation of Muriel Brown's death in favour of the topicality of the unsolved Hartley murder.

'At this stage, I know of no proven connection with the Vice-President,' he stressed. 'And I want neither our American colleagues or the Scotland Yard officers to be aware of this enquiry. Not yet, anyway. It's confidential to us — highly confidential, in fact, and no one other than our own team must know about it. It must not take priority over our security duties, however, but I do regard it as very important even if, at this stage, it is nothing more than an unsolved murder of some vintage. But if the victim and the Vice-President are related, then it must be considered very important! So if the Americans come asking how HOLMES works, we can show them the Muriel Brown case.'

Mark then asked Barbara to arrange for several photocopies of the old file to be made so that DC Duncan Young could begin to program the salient facts into HOLMES and the others could be allocated their 'actions'. She'd need help with that work; it was a very bulky pile of paper. Detective Inspector Larkin would be in charge, as he would have been on a modern murder enquiry, and the men could operate in teams of two to alleviate the boredom of their current work.

Larkin smiled. 'TIE, sir,' he said. 'We can't follow that procedure very well, can we?'

'Trace, Interrogate and Eliminate, Paul? I reckon we might be able to trace and eliminate a lot of suspects after reading the file, and, who knows, maybe there are people still alive who remember the case. They can be interrogated — a chap in his eighties would have been around ten years old when the murder happened and might recall something vital.'

'It would be great if we could find some living witness!'

'We might well do that by tracing, interrogating and eliminating,' smiled Pemberton. 'And some memories must survive, surely? Village people would talk about the crime and it would become part of the local folklore. There must be some memories or suspicions lurking around the village.'

'Point taken, sir — I'll allocate actions as if it was a living enquiry — but I'll bet we don't arrest a suspect!'

'Perhaps not, but we might discover the guilty party, Paul, and that would please the Vice-President, eh? Perhaps the police of the time knew the killer but lacked the evidence to convict him? Think of that — a roots-type relative of Vice-President Hartley was murdered all those years ago and we find the killer to coincide with his visit. How about that for a public relations exercise?'

'Very good for Anglo-American relations, I'm sure, sir — that's if the two men are related. OK, we'll do what we can.'

And so the investigation into the murder of Private James Reuben Hartley was given a new lease of life. It took a long time for Barbara and her helpers to produce sufficient photocopies of the old file for all the teams. Upon receipt of his copy, Mark kept it in his office and, during quieter moments of that day, began to study it in detail.

By now, the business of running Thirklewood Hall in a manner able to cope with the VIP visitor was slipping into a routine. Of the seven doors, six were kept locked and all comers were obliged to use the front door, the main entrance to the Hall. A desk had been established there with a constable permanently on duty to check passes, enter names into a register and generally supervise all the comings and goings. Everyone working in the Hall had to inform the duty constable of his or her whereabouts, whether in or out of the building, so that messages could be passed without delay.

A new set of dedicated telephone lines had already been installed, with lines to the Americans, the Diplomatic Protection Group, Special Branch officers, Pemberton's teams, the reception desk, the Vice-President's suite, the Potting Shed and other places. Quite suddenly, Thirklewood Hall had been transformed into a busy but secure building. Mark was asked to attend a meeting with Lieutenant Shorhein, one of the White house officers, to discuss mutual security arrangements while the estate had been asked to padlock all perimeter gates, with the exception of the main entrance.

Meanwhile, the Americans began to establish their office system; a map of the area appeared on a wall, photographs of tourist attractions followed, a list of restaurants and village inns was displayed along with other local services like garages, churches, shops, supermarkets and so forth. The noise made by the Americans was unbelievable; all seemed to shout at one another and they seemed to be terribly busy, doing very little but making a tremendous fuss about it. Mark had not yet identified them all by name.

All had, however, been issued with passes and by the end of their short stay, he would know most of them. Many were loud and large, with booming voices and strong accents, hardly the sort to be overlooked. Mark's officers, by contrast, worked quietly and steadily among their computers, fax machines and extra telephone lines. In spite of the activity, Mark did find time to study the Hartley murder file.

His first priority was to establish the character of the deceased. James Hartley seemed to have been very popular with everyone, but he was not a ladies' man. There was no reference to any women friends and it did appear that he preferred to stay at home and live with his parents. Mark's first impression was that James Hartley was a wimp, a mother's boy.

For such a man, conscription to the army, followed by a posting to the front line in the trenches of the Somme, would have been terrible. It was enough to make a sensitive young man commit suicide. But in those days, suicide was considered a dreadful thing to do; it resulted in a terrible family stigma and in fact it was a crime, known as *felo de se*. In the so-called good old days, the bodies of those who committed suicide were not even allowed a church funeral but were buried at the crossroads. Thankfully, those days were long past, long before James's death in fact. But an additional factor was that James was a Catholic — and for a Catholic to commit suicide was unthinkable.

Then a curious thought struck Pemberton. Might someone have tried to disguise James's suicide as a murder? That was a real twist! Could someone have disguised it as a hero's death when in fact he'd been a whimpering coward? To fake a suicide so that it appeared to be murder was a very dangerous thing to do — the successful perpetrator might well lay himself open to a conviction for murder, a crime which carried the death penalty in 1916.

If that scenario was correct, who would go to such trouble to conceal the act of suicide? A member of the deceased's family, perhaps?

It was a thought that Pemberton could not ignore.

CHAPTER SIX

'Have you managed to produce anything like a victim profile yet?' Mark asked Detective Inspector Paul Larkin during their coffee break.

'I've concentrated on him for starters, sir. My first impressions are that James Hartley was a mother's boy. He wrote every day during his training. Detective Inspector Dawson seized the letters — the mother kept every one of his, and he'd kept every one he got from her. He'd carried her letters home with him; they were among his belongings when he was shot. The police seized them as evidence, but they were returned to the family once they'd been examined. We don't have copies, but we do have Inspector Dawson's interpretation of them. I'm sure James never wanted to join up, although to be fair, he did not appeal to the tribunal. Local tribunals were held so that men could appeal against conscription. His brothers were excused for various reasons — medical grounds, farming requirements and claims that they were running their own businesses. James was the only one of the Wolversdale Hartleys to be called up for the 1914-18 war. I can imagine the tears from his mother when she learned he was heading for the trenches in France. Awful rumours about conditions and the cruelty of the Germans had reached the UK — things were in a pretty desperate state, that's why conscription was started.'

'Is there any hint of a suicidal frame of mind in James? Do his own letters show that he was upset?'

'Dawson doesn't make that too clear, sir, but there is no direct reference to suicide in James's letters. If he hinted at it in any other way, no one mentioned it. I did see one statement from his CO which said he did well at training; he was always smartly turned out and was very capable with firearms. His instructors reckoned he would make a good soldier.'

'Girlfriends? Any sign of a romance? Was he knocking off somebody else's wife? Did someone in the village have a grievance against him?'

'Dawson went into that aspect pretty thoroughly, sir, but never found anything to suggest it was a motive.'

'So James had no enemies? Is that what we're saying?'

'That was the conclusion reached by Detective Inspector Dawson, sir. In and around Wolversdale, James was universally liked. He never got into bother; he was a regular church-goer, a devout Catholic, an altar server, and he helped the priest to look after St Monica's and its grounds, purely voluntarily. Mowed the grass between the graves, painted the exterior of the church, that sort of thing. Men and women liked him. He was a sensitive chap. Artistic in many ways but a good farmer at the same time; he was very skilled at working a sheep-dog and did win several local sheep-dog trials.'

'There's a photo of him with a sheepdog,' Mark recalled. 'It's in the file. So he was a happy man, Paul? What's your gut feeling about his general state of mind?'

'I think he was happy, at least until he got his call-up papers. His mother's statement says he was miserable at home from the day the papers arrived until the day he left to join the Green Howards, that was 1st August 1916. His parents never saw him alive again. His mother was devastated. I think she blamed Luke for James's death — if Luke hadn't been late arriving to meet James's train, James might have lived. That seems to have been her reasoning.'

'The reason for that late arrival was analysed, was it? By Dawson?'

'Yes. James went to the Gents after getting off the train; the station master, who doubled as porter and ticket collector, remembered him. Because Luke hadn't arrived, James started to walk home, but somewhere along the way, he and Luke missed each other. Luke did arrive later with a pony and trap, and he waited around the station, but James had already left for home. James was later found dead.'

'That means Luke had an opportunity to kill his brother. We must check timings, Paul. How is Duncan coping with programming this lot into HOLMES?'

'He's working steadily away, sir — he's not getting many interruptions, fortunately. It's a slow job but worthwhile because HOLMES might throw up something.'

'Good. Well, Paul, the sort of things we must check are: the time of arrival of the train — who saw James get off it? The time of Luke's arrival at the station — who saw him there? Who saw James walking to meet Luke? Who saw Luke with his pony and trap heading for the station?'

'Fine, I can do all that.'

'Good. Now, meanwhile our proper job continues! How are things going security-wise in this place?'

'We had one ripple of uncertainty from the US Embassy men, sir; one of them had found a skylight open on the upper storey and it seems the light shone through it into the sky. He thought we ought to close it and cover it with black-out material, just in case the Iranians flew overhead with helicopters and dropped bombs!'

'You're joking, Paul!'

'No, sir, I'm not. They seriously discussed putting black-outs against all the windows at night. Dunnock rejected that idea — he said it would only draw attention to the Hall if it appeared unlit during the hours of darkness. I tried to explain that the Iranians shouldn't know Hartley was living here anyway, but — well, they insisted. So we've blacked it out, just to keep him happy. Everyone's content now.'

'Any more wrinkles?'

'A minor one. We discovered one of the advance party hadn't been issued with a pass. There are two men with very similar names — one's a Wilbur Richards and the other's a Wilbur Rickard. That's been sorted as well.'

'What about our lads who are working nights? Are they getting enough sleep? Is the place quiet enough for them?'

'It's very early days, sir, but no complaints yet. Those with time on their hands are helping us with HOLMES and statement reading.'

'OK, that's a good sign, but we mustn't let the Hartley murder enquiry jeopardise the Hartley security arrangements!'

'It won't. It is a good idea, having this enquiry to keep us busy, it's going to be bloody boring just hanging about this house with nothing to do. How the hell anybody could be a security guard all day and every day beats me.'

'Thank God we're not! Now, we must remember this is a real murder enquiry even if it's doubtful whether the killer is still alive. So the next actions are to check those events at or near Rosenthorpe station. Tie in the victim with anyone who saw him. Trace, Interrogate and Eliminate!'

'Will do, sir — except the interrogate bit!'

'Right, but you'll know the sort of questions that should have been asked. Now, while that's being done, I'll see if we can determine where the other family members were that day. We know Luke went to the station, but where were Dad and Mum, and any other brothers and sisters? Do we know that?'

'That's something to keep you quiet for the next few hours,' laughed Paul Larkin.

And so Mark Pemberton settled down to study the statements. Detective Inspector Dawson had done exactly the same thing in 1916 and Mark discovered a table of timings in the file. James's father, Caleb Hartley, who was then aged sixty-four had been working all that day on the farm. It was a threshing day. Teams of men had mown the wheat and on that Monday in September 1916 it was time for it to be threshed. Some twenty men were working on that task at Pike Hill Farm. This was corroborated by his wife Sarah, whose maiden name was Hodgson; she was then aged sixty-two and she had been working all day, with other women, keeping the threshers supplied with food and drink. Neither she nor Caleb had left the premises.

Luke, who was then aged thirty-seven, had left the farm in the pony and trap at 2.30pm with a shopping list from his mother. She had requested that, while collecting James from Rosenthorpe station, he should call at the general stores to collect some provisions. With further days of threshing ahead, a lot of food was required. She would be baking and cooking and needed more ingredients. On that trip, Luke had obtained her shopping requirements — both his mother and the shop-keeper had confirmed that. The train from York via Drakenedge was due in at 3.35pm, giving Luke an hour and five minutes to cover the five miles between Pike Hill Farm and Rosenthorpe. That was ample time for a pony drawing a light trap.

Luke was married to Edith (née Brown) and they had two sons, Caleb James (eleven) and Paul (nine), and one daughter, Sarah (thirteen); they lived at the farm with their parents, a common family practice in the hill farms at that time.

As Mark scanned the statements from the family, which were numbered and indexed for quick reference, he discovered that another brother, George Stanley, aged thirty-five, also worked on the farm. He and his wife, Mary, lived rent free in a hind's cottage with their three children. The children had been off school, helping with the threshing. Mary had been helping her mother-in-law cope with the influx of hungry threshers while George had been working with the other men.

Samuel, aged thirty-four, had moved away from home upon marriage, and he ran a butcher's shop at Spelton, a market town some twenty miles from Rosenthorpe. Twins Thomas and Sophie, aged thirty-two had opened a furniture and carpet shop in Hull; Thomas was married with a family and lived in Hull while Sophie, then married to a man called Aiden Harland, had been unable to have children. Thomas and Sophie had named their shop Hartleys of Hull and Mark knew that it was still prospering. From those small beginnings, it had developed into a major department store.

The deceased, James, was next in the line of descent, while Matthew, aged twenty-eight, had become a Marist priest in 1913, being posted to Manchester. Jessica, aged twenty-six, had married a man called Henry Latimer and they had moved to Lincoln in 1913, while the youngest, Robert Alan, aged twenty-four, had been married in the April of 1916, and had moved to Newcastle with his wife. Her name was Freda, née Plews. Robert ran a haulage business in Newcastle.

Thus, thought Mark to himself, the only member of the family who was 'in the frame', as modern detectives would say, was Luke. Luke's movements must therefore be subjected to very close scrutiny; Pemberton realised that Inspector Dawson must have closely investigated Luke's movements, but how thorough had he been? Pemberton would repeat that action with the aid of HOLMES — after all, Luke seemed to be the only suspect.

Another good suspect was inevitably the person who found the body. In this case, it was a gamekeeper called Eddie Jackson, whose statement was in the file. Mark read it before going any further. Eddie Jackson had been a gamekeeper employed by Rosenthorpe Estate and on the night of Monday, 11th September 1916 had been setting his snares on waste land to the north of the village. The land was owned by the estate, but was treated as a common, the public having unrestricted access to walk, ride horses, have picnics or enjoy other legitimate activities, other than the playing of organised sports. The sports field opposite was for that purpose.

Jackson's statement went on:

I'd been among the bushes for about an hour and decided to walk along the lane to my next setting of sniggles. Sniggle is our word for a rabbit snare. As I was leaving the bushes I decided to go out of a gap in the hedge near the pair of oaks. I saw somebody lying there, between a big rock and the oaks. At first, I thought it was somebody having a nap and then realised it was a soldier because he was in uniform. I went to have a look and shouted something like 'Hey, wake up' but there was no response. As I walked past his feet, I looked at the face. I realised it was Jimmy Hartley, I've known him since we were children at school. I saw blood on the face. It had come from a hole in his temple, on the left side of the head, near eye level. It was dark blood and was congealed. I bent down to touch him and realised he was dead. I noticed his service rifle near his side, the right side I think it was, and thought he must have shot himself. I ran straight away up to the village to get PC Marshall. It would be about half-past seven in the evening when I found Jimmy's body and it was not quite dark. Other than touching his face and finding it cold, I did not touch anything else or move anything. I saw no one near the body. I then came back with PC Marshall to show him what I had found.

Attached to the statement was a further one from Detective Sergeant Ripley which stated that the gamekeeper's movements that day had been checked and verified. He had been on the grouse moor four miles from the village during that afternoon; three other men had been with him. Thus a prime suspect, the finder of the body, had been speedily eliminated from any suspicion. But had Luke been eliminated in this way? Mark turned to his statement.

There was the usual heading beginning 'Statement of Luke Caleb Hartley, born 10th March 1879, of Pike Hill Farm, Wolversdale, farmer.' His statement said:

I am the eldest son of Caleb and Sarah Hartley of Pike Hill Farm, Wolversdale and on Monday, 11th September 1916 I left home to collect my younger brother, James, from Rosenthorpe railway station. James had been called up for the army and was serving with the 5th Battalion of Green Howards at Richmond. He had finished his training and was due to go to France but had come home on one day's leave. He sent a telegram asking to be collected from the station at 3.35pm that Monday, 11th September. The tribunal exempted me from military service this time because of a heart condition; I was capable only of light farm work, so mother asked if I would collect James. She said it was a long walk home from the station, especially if he was carrying full kit, and because the others were busy threshing, I said I'd do it. I left home alone about half-past two with our pony and trap and went along the toll road which has a flat and well-kept surface. Half a mile on the far side of the toll bar the pony shed a shoe from her left foreleg and went lame.

I had to replace the shoe; I usually carry spare horseshoe nails with me on a long trip, and a hammer and other tools. I carry them in a hessian bag in the trap and so I replaced the same shoe. I've done farrier work before, so I knew what to do. It took about twenty minutes I reckon although I hadn't a watch with me, so I didn't really know. I continued and reached the station, but the clock said three fifty-five. I'd not seen James anywhere along the road, so I thought the train must be late, but Mr Maurice Proctor, the station master, told me it had come and gone. He'd seen James get off in his uniform and James had asked Proctor if I'd arrived. When Proctor said he hadn't seen me, James said he'd start to walk towards Wolversdale, and hoped he'd meet me somewhere along the way. Proctor said he went to the Gents before setting off. I waited around the station area for about an hour in case James had popped into someone's house and did my mother's shopping while I was waiting. I left the pony and trap outside the station so James would see it if he turned up. He would know it was ours. But when James didn't turn up, I set off home. I did not see him anywhere along the way. I got home about six, but James wasn't there. We were all very worried, although Dad wondered if Mr Proctor had been mistaken about James getting off the train. He thought it might have been another soldier. Mother was in tears, worrying herself sick, but I had the milking to do so I went into the shippen and got started.

Later that night, PC Marshall came to tell us that James had been found dead and it looked like suicide. James hadn't wanted to join the army and I know he was frightened about going to France, but I never heard him threaten suicide. He was too good a Catholic to do that. So far as I know, he had no enemies and I've never heard anyone threaten him.

Attached to this statement was one from the toll gate keeper who said she recalled Luke Hartley driving through on Monday afternoon about three o'clock. He was heading towards Rosenthorpe. She'd seen him again about five thirty heading in the opposite direction. The toll booth tickets obtained by Luke had been recovered and were pinned to the file. He'd paid three-pence for each journey, the rate being one penny per wheel and one penny for the pony.

The police had made strenuous efforts to find further corroboration of Luke's story but, other than a six-year-old girl, they had not found anyone who had used that quiet country lane at the material time. No one, not even that child, had seen Luke from the time he'd passed through the toll gate until the time he'd arrived at the railway station. There were no houses along the lane until the final fifty yards or so where it entered Rosenthorpe but enquiries there had produced nothing. The station master was the first person to acknowledge seeing Luke after he had passed through the toll gate — and the time taken to drive from the toll gate to the station would normally be around half an hour.

On this occasion, Luke had taken some fifty or fifty-five minutes — the explanation being the loss of a horseshoe. So Luke's story was not corroborated.

The police had interviewed the child, but her statement was in the form of question and answer and taken in the presence of her mother. The girl was Millicent Roe, born 19th February 1910, and she had lived at 3, Priory Cottages, Rosenthorpe. The interviewer was Detective Sergeant Ripley.

Ripley: You went shopping for your mother yesterday, Monday, didn't you?

Millicent: Yes.

Ripley: Where did you go?

Millicent: To Rosenthorpe shop.

Ripley: And what did you buy?

Millicent: Eggs and butter

Ripley: What time did you come home?

Millicent: Just before tea-time.

Ripley: What time is tea-time?

Millicent: Four o'clock.

Ripley: How long before that was it when you got home?

(*Mrs Roe interrupted:* She was home by quarter to four.)

Ripley: Did you see anybody along the lane?

Millicent: I saw a man in a horse and cart.

Ripley: Might it have been a pony and trap?

Millicent: Yes, I suppose so.

Ripley: Who was the man?

Millicent: I don't know.

Ripley: What was he doing?

Millicent: Sitting in the bushes.

Ripley: Which bushes?

Millicent: Near the cricket field.

Ripley: What time was this?

Millicent: Before I got home.

(*Mrs Roe interrupted again:* It's about five minutes' walk for her, from the cricket field home.')

Ripley: So you saw a man in a horse and cart about twenty minutes to four.

Millicent: Yes, I think so. I can't tell the time yet. We're learning at school.

Ripley: You weren't at school that Monday?

Millicent: No, it was holidays for threshing.

Ripley: Now, Millicent, this is very important. What was the man doing? The one you saw in the bushes.

Millicent: He was in the cart, sitting.

Ripley: Would you know him if you saw him again?

Millicent: I don't know.

Ripley: How many men were there in the cart?

Millicent: Just one.

Ripley: Did you see anybody else walking along the lane? A soldier?

Millicent: No.

(*Mrs Roe:* She left the shop before the train came in, Mr Ripley. James would have followed her along the lane).

Ripley: Millicent, you are very small, and I think you would walk slowly. Did you see a soldier behind you? Catching up to you?

Millicent: No.

Ripley: The man in the bushes, did he stay there?

Millicent: Yes, all the time I was walking past, he just sat there.

Ripley: Did he see you?

Millicent: I don't think so. He was facing away, he never said anything.

Ripley: What did you think he was doing?

Millicent: I thought he was having something to eat or having a rest.

Ripley: Why did you think he was having something to eat?

Millicent: He was looking down at his hands, at something he was holding. I couldn't see what it was. I thought it might be his tea.

At this point, Ripley had concluded the interview, and the question/answer sheet had been signed by Mrs Roe.

As a consequence of this statement, Luke Hartley was interviewed again but denied he had been stationary in the bushes. He maintained he had driven directly from the toll gate to the station, stopping only to replace the shoe at a point along the toll road; after replacing the shoe, he had relieved himself behind a hedge. He had driven past the two oak trees but stated he had not seen any person or a horse-drawn vehicle in the bushes, nor had he seen the schoolgirl.

Pinned to this part of the file was a short additional statement by Detective Sergeant Ripley. It said, 'On Wednesday, 13th September 1916, I accompanied Millicent Roe, aged six, and her mother, Alice, to the point where she claimed to have seen the man sitting in the horse and cart among the bushes. I identify that location as the place where the body of James Hartley was later found.'

CHAPTER SEVEN

Pemberton felt sure Luke had been lying. If he had driven a pony and trap along that lane between the times he'd stated, the lane that he and Lorraine had examined, then Millicent Roe must have seen him — unless he'd been hiding. And the only place to hide was among the bushes — which was where the child had seen a man in a horse and cart, as she described it. Pemberton's instinct was that Luke had not told the truth and that he must surely have been Dawson's prime suspect.

Mark then realised that he himself must establish that the death of James Hartley was a genuine murder and not a suicide, however unlikely the latter seemed. That had not yet been done to his satisfaction. A ballistic examination of the bullet, if it had been done, should determine that issue. Furthermore, if this had been a modern investigation, Luke would have been subjected to the most intense questioning about his precise movements during that journey to and from the station and there would have been a determined effort to find more witnesses, even if they themselves had something to hide. If the man in the bushes had not been Luke Hartley, then who had he been and why had he been there? Why had he not come forward to help the police?

Pemberton left his office and went over to DC Young.

'Duncan.' He sat on the desk beside the detective. 'From what I've read so far, Luke Hartley's very much in the frame. If we'd been doing the investigation, Forensic would have gone over his clothing with a fine-tooth comb, we'd have given that pony and trap a real scientific examination, the scene would have been meticulously searched by the task force and we'd have been turning that farm over to find the murder weapon — assuming it is not that rifle. So do we know whether the bullet was examined to see whether it had been fired by James's army rifle?'

'I've not had time to go through the whole file, sir, but I'll check now for that. Luke's top of my suspect list too, by the way.'

'Fine, and I'll look as well. What we need are further sightings of him. I can't understand why nobody reported seeing him between the toll gate and the station on either journey. If he stopped for twenty minutes or thereabouts to fix a shoe on his pony, surely somebody must have seen him? I'm sure Dawson would have tried to find more witnesses. If no one saw him, where was he? Did the police check that the shoe had been replaced? Was that possible? New nails in the hoof, say? Did anyone, other than that child, use the lane that afternoon? Did anyone else use the toll road? When you're going through the files, can you concentrate on those elements too?'

'Sure, yes, sir.'

Mark walked around the mansion at this point, chiefly for a little break from his spell of intense reading but also to show his staff, and the visiting teams, that he was taking an active interest in his official duties. He had words with the detective on the desk, who assured him there were no problems, he spoke to the uniformed constable who was on patrol duties within the hall, and he spent time with the Americans to assure them that, so far as the internal security of Thirklewood Hall was concerned, all was progressing smoothly. There were still three clear days before the great man arrived. He was told that the suite to be used by the Vice-President was undergoing a quick but thorough redecoration, with new curtains and soft furnishings as befitted a man of his eminence. Mark made a mental note to have the entire suite re-examined for listening devices and planted bombs, although he felt sure the dangers of bringing in new furniture and craftsmen at this stage had been considered by all concerned. It was something he must check, however. A job for Paul Larkin, he decided.

It was during his perambulations that he saw Lorraine Cashmore emerging from the dining-room. This large, ornate room had been used by the schoolgirls as their refectory and it was now the canteen for the resident officers.

Lorraine had been enjoying a morning coffee.

'Morning, sir.' She used the formal style of address on this occasion because other officers were around.

'Hello, Lorraine. Are you managing to occupy yourself?'

'I'm on half-nights, sir. I shall be manning the desk from 6.00pm till 2.00am, so I thought I'd pop out for a while.'

'I might have come with you, but I want to plough through the Hartley murder file, and besides, I'm supposed to be on duty here!'

'Is there anything I can do for your Hartley enquiry? I need something to occupy me, so I thought I might go to Wolversdale again and do some more investigating of the Hartley family.'

Mark felt she could help and told her of his gut feeling about Luke Hartley, suggesting she might like to revisit the scene of the crime. He asked her to try to ascertain whether Luke's story would stand up in a modern court, referring her to the various statements in the file. He drew her attention especially to the one given by Millicent Roe — her sighting of a horse and cart at the very place the body was found must surely carry some credence. And the toll road might still be there, for example. Perhaps Lorraine could establish distances between the key points, and the times required to cover those distances either on foot or by pony and trap.

'But if you do all this, Lorraine, it's classed as duty, remember. This is not a hobby, it's work!'

'I might remember that if I want any time off for a special reason.' She smiled and left him.

Mark returned to his office and resumed his study of the Hartley murder file.

His priority now was to examine the pathologist's report and the police examination of the scene. Had the murder weapon been found, for example?

The pathologist's report was couched in terms which were similar to those in use today. It described the body of James Reuben Hartley as that of a thirty-year-old man in good physical condition, clean and well nourished. Other than the wound in the temple, there were no suspicious marks or bruises on the body. He was now clean-shaven, the army having removed his moustache. The fingers of the right hand were stained, and the forefinger bore a very rough tip, the signs of a pipe smoker. Examination of the internal organs showed no heart disease or other malfunctioning of organs like the kidneys or liver which might have contributed to James's death. Those organs, and the lungs, were all in first-class condition, as one would expect in a healthy and active young man. Examination of the skull, however, did reveal a .45 calibre bullet which had lodged in the brain. Mark knew that .45 bullets were almost certain to have been fired from either a pistol or a revolver; few rifles, if any, were of .45 calibre. Beyond all doubt, that bullet had caused his death. So what make and model was the army issue rifle?

In the opinion of the pathologist, the bullet had been fired from fairly close range and had entered the brain via the left temple. The bullet had been recovered for scientific examination.

Pressed to be more precise, the pathologist expressed an opinion that the weapon had been fired from a range of about twelve inches, this assessment being given because particles of gunpowder had been found in James's hair, but there had been no scorch marks on the skin. Had the muzzle been within a mere inch or two of the head, then there would have been scorch marks on the skin.

The pathologist believed the wound had not been self-inflicted. One reason for this hypothesis was that the deceased was known to be right-handed. To fire a bullet into one's own temple from a range of about a foot while holding a rifle was highly unlikely but not impossible. It could have been done with a pistol or a revolver. If James had committed suicide, the pathologist argued, the muzzle of the weapon would have been pressed against the temple to guarantee its effectiveness, not held away at a distance which could result in a miss. And for a right-handed man to discharge a handgun into his own left temple was highly unlikely. In the opinion of the pathologist, therefore, the wound was not self-inflicted. Death had resulted from the actions of another person — murder, in other words. The only weapon found at the scene was James's service rifle and expert examination showed it had not been fired.

More importantly, the calibre of the rifle was not the same as that of the .45 bullet.

The rifle was known as an SMLE — a Short Magazine Lee Enfield, Mark III. This was a .303 calibre rifle and thus it could never have fired the fatal bullet; besides, when privates of the Green Howards returned home on leave, they never brought any ammunition, even though they did bring their rifles. Mark now realised that his earlier assumption had been wrong. This was not a suicide dressed up to look like murder — beyond all doubt, it was murder. It now seemed to be a murder which had been clumsily dressed up to look like suicide, but the killer had not paid due attention to the finer details which were required to ensure an efficient cover-up. Those old policemen had done their job with customary thoroughness.

In the mind of Mark Pemberton, this put Luke even higher in the frame of suspects — but had he had access to a .45 weapon of any kind? He began to peruse the file for statements from anyone other than the toll gate keeper who might have seen Luke on that fateful journey between Wolversdale and Rosenthorpe.

* * *

ARMED with her copy of the Hartley file, Lorraine returned to the scene of the crime. She stood on the side of the road with the boulder on her left as she tried to visualise the area as it would have been in 1916. To her left in the distance was Rosenthorpe railway station and the village with its shops and cottages. She could not see the station from here, although there was a bridge over which one of the branch lines ran. But there was a long, clear view towards that bridge.

As she gazed towards the bridge, a car was coming towards her; as it moved beneath the railway bridge, it almost vanished from sight, only its roof being visible. But as it approached her, it was evidently climbing a very slight incline because it gradually materialised in full. This disappearing trick was due to the bumps and hollows that Pemberton had described as switch-backs. She wondered if all those inclines had been there in 1916. And as she pondered that, she thought of little Millicent Roe walking that same road. Is that why she'd not seen the approach of Luke in his pony and trap? Had she, or the pony and trap, been concealed in one of the dips at the crucial time?

To her right, the road curved slightly away towards a corner; from the corner, a lane branched off to the right into what was called Priory Fields, the site of an ancient monastic establishment. Continuing its route, the lane turned sharply left, with a link with the old toll road near the river, and then it climbed high on to the hills to vanish over the horizon. Although the modern road, at this point, did not follow the earlier one with one hundred per cent accuracy, Lorraine believed their routes were very similar. A person standing forward from this boulder by, say, twelve feet or so, would have stood in the middle of the old lane and would have been able to see the railway bridge. That was a good half-mile away. How long would it take for a pony and trap or a small girl to walk that distance?

Surely someone must have seen Luke upon this lane? Or was there a conspiracy of silence? If people had seen him in the lane at the material time, had they kept quiet? If so, why? Why would anyone shield a murderer? She knew that villagers could keep secrets; they did not like outsiders prying into their affairs, but surely there must be a stronger reason for not providing the information which would bring a murderer to justice? As Lorraine stood at the scene of the murder, deeply engrossed in her thoughts, a middle-aged man with a spaniel on a lead approached from her right. He had come from the area of Priory Fields and looked about sixty-five. A retired gentleman, she felt.

'I wouldn't stand there too long,' he said without a smile as he neared Lorraine.

'Why not?'

'Young Jimmy Hartley was found dead there. It's unlucky to stand there,' he said.

'I don't understand.' She pretended to be vague.

'You on holiday, then?' he asked, for the area was popular with holidaymakers.

'No, I'm gathering information for a book,' she lied, knowing that villagers loved to air their knowledge about spooks and weird occurrences. 'Ghost stories from the moors.'

'There used to be a ghost here,' he said as if on cue.

'You're joking?'

'Not me. It was the ghost of Jimmy Hartley, so they said. Wandering this lane in his uniform. A soldier's uniform. It haunted this place because there was a murder here, in 1916.' He was in full flow now, having found an interested audience. 'That rock was where the body was found, it was Jimmy Hartley, one of the Hartleys from Wolversdale. Nice folk, nasty thing to happen to them. They still live there, you know, up at Pike Hill Farm. Decent people, very hardworking and honest. The police never did get the killer, but folks don't talk about it nowadays. The family never mentions it. Afterwards though, folks would never walk this way after dark; some said Jimmy's ghost haunted the lane. They moved the lane a bit, to make this new road. When they moved it, in the 1950s it would be, there were no more hauntings.'

'Right here, was it?' she asked, hoping as if she sounded astonished. 'The murder, I mean.'

'This very place.' The man was clearly keen to air his local knowledge. 'Come back from the army, he had, getting ready to go to France to fight for King and country, and somebody shot him. It was in all the papers. Before my time, of course, but when I was a lad we were told all about it by our parents. We even sang a song about it.'

'A song? What sort of song?'

'It was a nursery rhyme sort of thing. All the school kids would sing it.'

'Can you remember it?' she asked.

'Oh, aye. The tune was Bobby Shafto — you know, Bobby Shafto's gone to sea, silver buckles on his knee...'

'I know the tune,' she said.

'Well, this was it,' and to the tune of Bobby Shafto, the man sang:

> Jimmy Hartley's gone to hell,
> And his brother's gone as well;
> Jimmy Hartley's gone to hell,
> Tainted Jimmy Hartley.

'Those are very strange words,' Lorraine said. 'What do they mean?'

'No idea, I wasn't born till 1929, but we sang that as kids.

Mind, we had no idea what it was all about.'

'They're not very flattering words, are they? You'd think if Jimmy was from a good family, the song would have been nicer. You know, a sort of memorial.'

'They do say that there was a lot of nasty things going on up at that farm, secret things, you understand,' and he winked in what she regarded as a conspiratorial manner.

'Nasty things?' She was puzzled by this remark, but when she pressed him to elaborate, he shook his head. 'Best leave things alone,' he nodded. 'Let sleeping dogs lie, isn't that what they say?'

'Perhaps you're right,' she agreed. 'But who'd shoot a soldier who was about to go to war?' she continued, hoping some gossip or folk memory had survived down the years.

'You'd have to ask old Millie,' said the man. 'She saw him.'

'Saw who?'

'The killer, he was just where you are now. In his pony and trap or horse and cart. Only a lass she was then, of course.'

'Millie? Who's Millie?'

'Old Millie Roe at Priory Cottage, across two fields from me. She's in her eighties, mind, but as wick as they come. She knows all about it, she saw the killer.'

'She saw the killer?' Lorraine cried.

'So they said. She reckons she did.'

'But not the actual murder?'

'No, I don't think she's ever claimed that much. Mind, her story gets better with every telling. But she does say she saw him hiding in the bushes, right where you are now.'

'And you say she's still living there?' Lorraine was amazed. 'At Priory Cottage?'

'Oh, aye. It was her mother and father's house before they died. Millie was the youngest of a big family — she never got wed, you see, and lived with her parents. She stayed on when they died. Worked on the brickyard for years, she did, clerking. She's still hale and hearty and she loves a chat — we send all the reporters and writers down to her. Folks still write about the murder and she loves to tell 'em a tale or two.'

'I might just pop and see her,' smiled Lorraine.

'She'll be capped to bits. Tell her Arthur Harland sent you,' he said.

'Thanks,' smiled Lorraine.

'Well I must be getting along. I'm off to the post office for a postal order for my pools. One day, I'll win a fortune, you'll see if I don't...'

'You live locally?'

'Oh, aye, at Ford End Cottage, not far from here, just around a corner or two.'

'Did there used to be a toll road here?' she asked him.

'Yes, it started near our house, where the ford crosses the beck. It belonged to Rosenthorpe Estate and was used well into the 1960s. Then they closed it, it needed loads of repairs and was too costly, but you can still walk along to the old toll gate. It's there, still got its list of charges up.'

'And are there any ghost stories about the toll road?'

'Some said there was a phantom stage coach with four black stallions that used to gallop down that road just before a death in the Rosenthorpe family. But I've never seen it, and no one's seen it for years.'

'It'll do for my collection.' She smiled her gratitude.

'It allus showed up the night before a Rosenthorpe died,' he said. 'Galloped right along the toll road and vanished near that ford. There's allus some good tales around if you get talking to folks.' He beamed and went on his way.

He was right, of course, and so Lorraine decided to visit old Millie Roe. She'd continue her pretence of being a writer — people were far more forthcoming when talking to an author than when being quizzed by a police officer.

Millie lived in a hovel. It was a small, stone-built house with a honeysuckle-covered porch, and the door was standing open. The dark interior reminded her of Victorian times; a log fire smouldered in the grate where a kettle was singing on the hob, and the stone-flagged floor was covered with clip rugs. There was dirt everywhere.

'Yes, who is it?' A small and stooped old lady answered her knock. She wore carpet slippers, an old flower-patterned apron and a ragged brown woollen cardigan.

'Arthur sent me,' Lorraine began. 'Arthur Harland. He was telling me about the ghost along the lane. He said you knew the story behind it.'

'Aye, lass, I do. I knows all about it. It was a murder, you see...'

And leaving Lorraine standing at the door, she launched without any prompting into the story of James Hartley's death.

Lorraine listened. It was a fairly faithful but somewhat elaborated account of her childhood statement and she dwelt at some length on her sighting of the man with the pony and trap. Lorraine noticed she did refer to a pony and trap now, although as a child she'd said it was a horse and cart. Did such discrepancies matter?

Millie went on to say she was adamant the man had been sitting very still just off the road, on precisely the spot where the body was later found.

'Who was it?' asked Lorraine.

'Now I've never said who I thought it was. I mean, some things is best left alone. I was only a bairn, you see, and didn't know the man then, but well, later, mebbe I began to realise who it was. But I never can tell. My lips are sealed.'

'I know the verse they used to sing,' said Lorraine, singing it in her soft musical voice.

'Aye, we sang that at school,' said Millicent.

'I thought Jimmy was a good man,' said Lorraine. 'I thought he wasn't the sort to get himself into trouble? He was the sort who'd go to heaven, not to hell. And what a funny word to use — tainted.'

'That's because he wasn't as pure as folks reckoned,' said Millicent, who then added, 'Neither him nor his brother. I reckon that Luke went to hell an' all. But how did you know about them, then?'

'It's just what people said, people I've talked to about my book of stories...Arthur...'

'Arthur never knew him, he was dead and buried long before Arthur was born. He's just passing on tittle-tattle.'

'So what had Jimmy done?' Lorraine persisted.

'I think I've said enough,' said Millicent.

'The man you saw in the bushes, Millicent, when you were six. Was it Luke Hartley?'

'You ask some very direct questions, young lady,' said Millie. 'Not the sort a normal visitor asks.'

'I'm a policewoman, but I'm off duty, visiting the area,' Lorraine said. 'I suppose I'm trained to ask questions.'

'Then you'll get nothing more from me!' and Millie closed her mouth, folded her arms across her breast, turned away from Lorraine and slammed the door.

CHAPTER EIGHT

While Lorraine was in Wolversdale that Thursday afternoon, Detective Superintendent Pemberton remained at Thirklewood Hall. There were always minor details to attend to, but the American contingent did not interfere. They were too busy decorating the suite and making the final plans for the arrival of their Vice-President. Their last-minute work was keeping them very busy. This allowed Mark to study an account of the search of the scene of the discovery of Hartley's body.

As it was September, the ground had been dry, but very faint wheel marks had been found. The wheels had formed shallow depressions in the one or two areas of softer ground and had been identified as the tracks of a pair of wheels such as those on a light cart or gig. The marks lacked any identifying characteristics, other than that the wheels were slightly dished; the tracks were sixty inches apart. In other words, the tracks could have been left by almost any two-wheeled horse-drawn vehicle, although they were probably from a lighter type, such as a gig, a governess cart or a light market cart rather than a heavier four-wheeled vehicle such as a hay-cart or farm waggon. The report added that the wheels of Luke's trap had been compared and did match the width of those found at the scene, although that width was standard on many types of light cart.

Similarly, the marks suggested that the wheels had worn solid rubber tyres rather than iron rims; Luke's cart had rubber tyres. Rubber tyres did not crush the smaller grains of stone as steel would have done. Mark examined the photograph of Luke's cart; it was lightweight and built of wood with large wheels and high sides. To the rear there was a low door above a step which hung low, while the high sides bore wooden mudguards. Inside were two seats which faced each other across the narrow floor, not facing the front like some. These carts were fast and light, often being used by women or governesses taking children on outings. They were easily hauled by a single pony and were sometimes called traps. So Millicent would be right calling it either a cart or a trap.

Similarly, hoof prints had been found, but the hardness of the earth had rendered any detailed comparison impossible. Mark sought a paragraph which might say that the shoes of Luke's pony had matched any marks found at the scene but found no such entry. There were no photographs of either the wheel marks or the hoof prints, the impressions being too faint to register on the film of that time.

There was no indication of when the vehicle in question had made those impressions — it could have been the previous day or even earlier. The only fact to emerge was that the child witness, Millicent Roe, had probably been correct in her statement that there was a stationary pony and trap or horse and cart at the scene on the afternoon of the murder.

There was nothing to suggest who that vehicle belonged to, nor was there any real evidence to link it to the crime. It was good circumstantial evidence, however, although enquiries had failed to substantiate Millicent's tale — no pony and trap or horse and cart, other than Luke's, and no man other than Luke, was known to have passed that way around the material time. Mark knew that assumptions could be drawn from those facts, but as a piece of hard evidence, such assumptions were almost useless. Besides, it was doubtful if the child's story would withstand a sustained cross-examination in court.

It was clear that the police had done a thorough job in searching the scene. They had found a penknife, rusty and broken, which had been eliminated; they had found an old leather shoe, size nine, which had been eliminated; and they had found a half-crown which could not be associated with the murder. The locations of those items were marked on a sketch. No spent bullet had been found, suggesting that there had been only one shot aimed at James, the one which had lodged in his head. The bullet casing had not been located either, suggesting the killer had taken it away, and no other firearm had been discovered in spite of an extensive search. A note said the murder weapon had never been found; in addition to the immediate surrounds of the murder scene, Pike Hill Farm had been thoroughly searched for a murder weapon or any weapon of .45 calibre. Several shotguns and two .22 rifles had been found, but all were legitimately held. Nothing else was found. None was the murder weapon, and all had been eliminated. There were photographs of all the weapons and other objects found during those searches.

So far as the discovery of James's body was concerned, the report was very detailed. Dr Herring, the village general practitioner, had examined the body in situ to certify death and said that, in his opinion, death had occurred some six or eight hours prior to his examination. He could not be any more precise. He refused to certify the cause of death and so the post-mortem had been arranged. Mark had already studied that report.

The body had been lying on its back with arms and legs outstretched, albeit not to their fullest extent. The rifle had been lying with its butt about ten inches from the index finger of the victim's right hand. There was a wound in the left temple with congealed blood. The body was clad in the military uniform of a private soldier, a 2 ½ inch square red flash at the top of the sleeves identifying the uniform as that of the 5th Battalion of the Green Howards. A uniform peaked cap lay some distance from the body, closer to the lane; a tin hat was fastened to the top of the back-pack which was still worn by the deceased on his back. A kitbag, also unopened, lay nearby, some four feet from the body.

The uniform on the body comprised black boots, puttees, belt and webbing, trousers, tunic, underwear, socks and shirt, all of which were present.

His back-pack was complete and in position; when opened, it was found to contain his army greatcoat and some smaller items of spare clothing like socks. It also contained letters from his mother and some family photographs. His other small side packs contained items such as iron rations, a 'housewife' (needle, cotton, scissors, etc), ear-plugs, a trench pipe (which could be smoked upside down) and a trench tea-making outfit comprising fire-lighters, water purification tablets and tea tablets. Among his equipment were his knife, fork and spoon, a billy can, a tin mug and a book of orders about his posting. A check with his unit confirmed nothing had been stolen from his kit. Theft did not therefore appear to be the motive.

His pockets had contained £1.15s.7d cash, a rosewood pipe, a tin of tobacco, a box of matches, a handkerchief, a wallet and rail ticket for his posting, a comb, a penknife, an apple and some sweets. A detailed search of his belongings revealed no letters other than those from his mother and no indication that there was another woman in his life. There were no letters from eager girlfriends awaiting his return to Wolversdale and none carrying threats from jealous rivals. It was all innocuous stuff with nothing to hint at any enmity from any quarter. Pemberton realised that James was something of a mystery man and he decided he must learn more about him. Surely Dawson had researched his background in greater depth?

From his reading of the papers, however, it was clear that Dawson had also done some careful research into Luke's background. The file contained a fairly comprehensive biography. Luke Caleb Hartley was born on 10th March 1879 at Pike Hill Farm, Wolversdale, the eldest son of Sarah and Caleb Hartley. He had attended St Monica's Catholic school in Wolversdale, leaving at the age of fourteen to work on his father's farm. He had never undergone any form of further education.

He had married Edith Brown in 1900 and shortly afterwards had had a brief overseas encounter as a private in the Boer War; he'd embarked late in 1900 and had returned in May 1902 at the end of hostilities. He then produced three children, Sarah Jane born in 1903, Caleb James born in 1905 and Paul Simon born in 1907. Discreet enquiries by the police had shown that Luke was considered a very good and protective father who was very serious in his outlook. He had very little sense of humour; when away from the farm, he always dressed smartly and would never enter the village in his working clothes in the way that many of his contemporaries did, nor did he spend his evenings in the inns drinking beer. Although born a Catholic, he had lapsed, never going to Mass or receiving the sacraments, although he did insist that his children went to the Catholic school and followed their faith. He was very strict with his children and did not even let them play with others in the village. They had, therefore, a rather sheltered upbringing.

The police knew nothing against Luke, however; he had no convictions and his marriage seemed happy. He owed no money to traders in the district and appeared not to have any enemies. In short, he was a dull, hard-working and very honest Yorkshire moorland farmer who assisted his ageing father in the family business. It seemed that his few months in South Africa had been the only excitement in his mundane life.

In his capacity as the eldest son, he would naturally inherit the farm. That was the moorland custom at that time, farms always passing from father to eldest son. The farm was owned by the Hartleys and thus there was no tenancy problem to worry about. Locally, these small moorland farmers were known as yeoman, a name signifying they were not landed gentry but landowners in their own right, albeit in a minor way.

In 1916, at the time of James's death, Luke was thirty-seven and his father was sixty-four; there was no such thing as a retiring age for farmers at that time, but old Mr Hartley and his wife would one day decide to move into a cottage, the move symbolising the shift of power from father to son. From that day, Luke would occupy the farmhouse and would be in charge. In some cases, the change-over was long awaited — some old farmers worked well into their eighties.

But this file was incomplete. It did not record events after 1916 and so Mark had no idea what had become of Luke and his family, nor did it reveal the date of the decease of Caleb and Sarah, the parents.

The file did, however, itemise the other members of the family, as Mark had already discovered, and he realised that this would provide Vice-President Hartley with a very accurate start to his search into the family roots. It would eliminate the chore of searching through masses of old records and ledgers. He wondered if the current family realised that these old police records existed? Probably not. But did they know of James's murder? That was something to ask George.

Mark had already examined the whereabouts of family members at the time of the murder and all could be eliminated. Except Luke. If Mark was to prove Luke guilty of murdering his brother, he'd need more factual information and more witnesses.

He wandered out of his office to speak to DC Young.

'Duncan,' he began, 'has anything else turned up?'

'I've found a statement here, sir, one I think will be of interest,' and he indicated the one he was working on. 'It's number 42, cross-referenced to number 18.'

'What's all that mean in English?'

'Number 18's from a woman living next door to the general stores in Rosenthorpe, sir, a Mrs Hutchinson; she confirmed that Luke Hartley had passed her cottage at the time he claimed. She saw the pony and trap go past and remembered it because when she looked out of her window, she saw the linesman at the same moment. He was doing his stuff on the railway bridge.'

'Doing what stuff?'

'Tapping the wooden chocks that hold the railway lines in position on the sleepers. Linesmen walked down the line by using the ends of the sleepers as a kind of stepping stone; as they walked, they swung a big hammer and tapped any loose chocks back into their shoes.'

'And this lady saw him?'

'Yes, sir.'

'So why is that important, Duncan?'

'Well, if he was working on the line in the region of that bridge, he'd have a high, long and unobstructed view along the lane towards the cricket field and Wolversdale. He'd be able to see who was using that road because the bridge crosses the road that Luke would have used.'

'Good stuff! And?'

'Well, he did see Luke, sir, in the pony and trap, heading towards the bridge. And better still, sir, he saw Millicent Roe walking away from Rosenthorpe. He claims he saw them walking towards one another, yet neither Luke nor the child say they saw each other.'

'So what can we deduce from that, Duncan?'

'There could be a conflict of timings, sir. I think the timings are crucial. According to the linesman, whose name was Joseph Lapsley, he was working his line on Monday, 11th September 1916, walking down the line towards Rosenthorpe station. He was due to finish there at 4.00pm. He didn't live in Rosenthorpe, his home was at Lington, two stations up the line. He always caught a train home after work. I ought to add that he was not working on the same branch line as the train carrying James — that came in from Drakenedge, whereas Lapsley was on the other line. That's the one in from Thornborough. Both lines met at Rosenthorpe, as we know — it was a junction. From there, the lines merged and went towards Rainesbury. Anyway, sir, Lapsley was on the bridge at 3.20pm. He stopped work for a few minutes to light his pipe and as he was looking over the parapet, towards the cricket field, he saw Luke approaching in the pony and trap. Luke was a long way off, but Lapsley was positive it was him. He was approaching Rosenthorpe and was beyond the far end of the cricket field, about ten minutes' drive from the station.'

Mark thought for a moment. 'So if he'd kept going in that direction, he'd have got to the station around 3.30pm, just in time to meet his brother?'

'Yes, sir.'

'But that doesn't agree with Luke's own statement, does it, Duncan? According to Luke, he was delayed along the toll road for about twenty minutes which means he would have come past the point where Lapsley saw him about 3.40 or 3.45pm.'

'That's right, sir. If Lapsley is correct, Luke was lying. I checked with the girl's statement, Millicent, that is. If she was right, and if she did see a man in a pony and trap in the bushes, it must have been Luke. It couldn't be anyone else. Lapsley said there were no other ponies and traps or horses and carts on that stretch of lane while he was working on the bridge. The man he saw must have turned into those bushes within minutes of being noticed by Lapsley and it must have been Luke. Lapsley goes on to say that he noticed a chock missing from a shoe on a nearby length of rail and found it lying on the track; he went over to pick it up and tapped it back into position. When he returned to the bridge parapet to continue smoking his pipe only a couple of minutes later or less, Luke, pony and trap had vanished. Lapsley could not see him — the police did ask whether he would have noticed him sitting among the shrubs beside the lane and Lapsley said not. The bushes were too thick; viewed from the railway bridge, they formed an almost impenetrable barrier. But Millicent was still walking away from the village, heading towards the cricket field.'

'Did the police take this sighting seriously?'

'Yes, sir, it seems so. But Lapsley's timings were open to argument because he hadn't a watch with him. He based his timings on the passage of the trains — and the 3.37pm from Rosenthorpe to Thorn-borough had passed him just before he got to the bridge. It was on time, too; it came in at 3.30pm and always waited in Rosenthorpe station on Platform 1, for the one from Drakenedge to come in. That was the one carrying James. James's train came into Platform 2 at 3.35pm; the Thornborough-bound train always waited a few minutes so that passengers could make the connection if they wished.'

'I think I would have accepted those times from Lapsley,' said Mark.

'Dawson quizzed him at length about the accuracy of his claims, sir. Lapsley said he was ninety-nine per cent sure his timing was correct because he did that stretch of line once a week and never needed a watch. And he'd never been late booking off duty — he could time his route to the minute, he claimed, what with passing trains, village church clocks striking and so on.'

'But in court, a good defence lawyer would have shot down any such claims to be accurate without a watch,' said Mark. 'So what's Lapsley say about Millicent?'

'He saw the girl walk under the bridge while he was smoking his pipe on top. She was heading away from Rosenthorpe, heading towards the cricket ground and towards Luke and his trap. He felt sure they would have met.'

'But they didn't, and she said she never saw Luke on the road.'

'That's right, sir. But there is an explanation. Between the bridge and the far end of the cricket field, there are several rises and dips in the road. Lapsley reckoned the child might not have seen Luke if she'd been in one dip while he was in another. Each would be out of sight of the other, if only for a few moments; after all, she would not be a very tall person.'

'Well done, Duncan. That's a very astute piece of deduction — and it confirms the child's story. It means we can accept her timings as accurate.'

'But it doesn't put Luke in hiding, does it?'

'So where else was he? I reckon this does put him in hiding, waiting for his victim to come along. You know what I think, Duncan? I think Luke set off to meet James with the firm intention of murdering him. He made his plans very carefully. I think the tale of the pony shedding a shoe was a lie; he told that to account for the delay in arriving at the station. In fact, he was early and drove off the lane to hide in the bushes to await James as he walked past. As James strode past, following Millicent along the lane, Luke called for him to enter the bushes. It would be an easy thing to do — perhaps by asking for some kind of help. James would have responded, and I reckon he climbed into the trap. Perhaps there was a conversation, a heated argument even. Then Luke shot him, and he would probably have fallen out of the trap. Luke tried to make it look like suicide. James's worries about going to fight in the trenches were well known to the family and so his suicide might not be out of place. Then, having shot James, Luke continued to the station ostensibly to meet him, and thus established a kind of alibi. I think he had a .45 hidden in the trap, perhaps among the tools he mentioned. It would be easy to conceal a revolver or pistol in a hessian tool bag. In the village, he did a bit of shopping and made sure he was seen about the place, especially at the railway station — he spoke to the station master and generally made people aware of his presence. Then he drove home, passing James's body along the way. I wonder if Lapsley heard the shot? Perhaps he was too far away, perhaps he was making too much noise hammering his chocks home. But I'm convinced Luke is the killer, Duncan.'

'But why would he murder his own brother, sir?'

'That's what we must find out.'

CHAPTER NINE

Following her abrupt dismissal by Millicent Roe, Lorraine decided to revisit the Hartley family graves at Wolversdale. There, she reasoned, she might find some clue to the origins of the curious verse that had circulated after James's death. If James had been such a fine, pure young man, why did the verse say he and his brother had gone to hell? And why call him 'tainted' Jimmy Hartley?

Clearly, there was a good deal more to this murder than had ever reached the ears of the investigating officers or the press of the time; it was odd, she felt, that the local people, even today, would not talk freely about it.

When she arrived at St Monica's churchyard, she found that further efforts had been made to tidy the grass around the Hartley tombstones. Here was the starting point for any research into one's family tree, and it was to this family burial ground that the Vice-President would be brought.

Lorraine returned to James's grave and studied the inscription anew, but it failed to provide her with any further clues about his 'tainted' taunt. Then she began to hunt for Luke's grave. She found the grave of George who had died in 1951 aged seventy, Samuel who died in 1955 and Father Matthew Hartley.

Father Matthew was the priest who'd died in 1961 aged seventy-three, his body being brought back from Lancashire for burial with his family. She remembered that other members of the family, of that era, had moved away, Robert going to live in Newcastle, Jessica in Lincoln, and Thomas and Sophie in Hull. Thomas was buried here, however, doubtless wishing to return to his own roots. Lorraine found the double grave of Sarah and Caleb. Sarah, the daughter of Alice and William Hodgson, had died in 1926 ten years after the death of her beloved son, and Caleb predeceased her in 1922.

There were several more recent family graves too, those of younger generations, but she could not find a grave for Luke. She returned to her car to check the precise name in her file — it was Luke Caleb Hartley, born 10th March 1879. No date of his death was given simply because he'd been alive at the time of the murder investigation. And so she returned to the tombstones to conduct a detailed search, moving from one to the other in strict sequence as she worked her way among them. Eventually she was convinced that there was no tombstone for Luke Caleb Hartley. Puzzled, she began to search the rest of the graveyard, a mammoth task, but she worked methodically. She did find other Hartleys, perhaps distant cousins, but there was no Luke among them. She did find a Caleb, eldest son of George. This Caleb had died in 1975; and she remembered the man she and Mark Pemberton had met here yesterday.

He was called George Caleb, she recalled. The grandson of this George and the son of this Caleb, perhaps? She wondered how many Calebs there were in the family. The Vice-President was also Caleb — Caleb Hodgson Hartley — and Hodgson was the maiden name of the matriarch of this family. It was an old Yorkshire moorland custom to name sons after their mothers' families, and so a lot of Yorkshiremen have borne Christian names which are really family surnames — Readman, Hodgson, Yeoman, Preston, Strickland, Latimer... And so, if Vice-President Hartley wanted to claim some Yorkshire ancestry, he had the right names if nothing else! But, she mused, he also had a more than passing likeness to the George Hartley they'd encountered in this very place.

Lorraine did consider that he could be buried in an unmarked grave, but for the one-time head of the Hartley family, this was most unlikely. If Luke was not buried here, then he and his family must surely have moved away, she concluded; so was this Luke, the murder suspect, the man who had emigrated? Was he the ancestor of Vice-President Hartley?

It was an intriguing thought. Lorraine remembered that the George she'd met here now lived at Pike Hill Farm, albeit not in the actual farmhouse. According to what she'd heard from Pemberton at the outset, this was the family farm and Luke, as the eldest son, should have occupied the farmhouse in succession to his father, but it seemed he had not wanted to inherit it.

His brother George Stanley had taken over the farmstead — so the George seen tidying the graveyard was his grandson.

Having established that Luke had apparently disappeared, she decided to return to base to prepare for her 6.00pm — 2.00am shift on the reception desk at Thirklewood Hall. Before leaving, she decided to examine the War Memorial. It stood outside the churchyard, in a neat square of stone-flagged ground with iron railings around it. There, under the title 'Killed in Action 1914-1918', she saw the name of Eric Hall, a comrade of James Hartley, who had been killed in the battle of the River Aisne on 28th May 1918. But there was no mention of James Reuben Hartley. These were the only two men from Wolversdale who had fought in the First World War. It seemed very few, but out of a population of only seventy or so, it was a considerable number — especially as neither had survived.

As she was leaving the churchyard, she noticed the parish priest entering the main door of his church. She called out to him.

'Excuse me, sir, er, Father.' She was not accustomed to speaking to Catholic priests and was not quite certain of the correct form of address.

'Yes?' He was a man of medium height with a shock of jet-black hair, dark eyes and a ready smile. There was more than a hint of Irish in his accent as he said, 'Can I help you now, miss?'

'I was looking at the Hartley graves.' She was speaking as she approached him. 'And there is no Luke. I wondered if you knew anything about him? He was the eldest of the family, around the turn of the century, that was...'

'And why would you be interested in him?' was the question put to her.

She decided to admit her identity and said she was involved in the security arrangements for the forthcoming visit of Vice-President Hartley. She knew the priest must be aware of that visit, as the Vice-President was clearly going to visit the family graves. But she made no mention of the murder link.

'So I'm occupying my time looking up his family history,' she concluded. 'It makes my work much more meaningful.'

'I'm fairly new here, my girl.' He smiled. 'Two years it is since I arrived. I'm afraid I don't know the family background, other than that one of them was killed in the First World War, when he was in the army. Fighting for his country. Some of the Hartley's still come to this church, I'm delighted to say, but a lot don't.'

'James,' she said, as if to give credence to her presence. 'James was the one who died during the war. I wondered if there was any record of Luke's death in your parish registers.'

'If he's not in the graveyard, my girl, he won't be in my register. There's a stone for every Hartley.'

His manner was somewhat dismissive and so Lorraine did not pursue the matter at this point. She could always inspect the parish registers at some future date if it was really necessary. She returned to her car and drove back to Thirklewood Hall.

* * *

MEANWHILE, Mark Pemberton had re-examined the statement made by Maurice Proctor, the station master of Rosenthorpe, to see if he could glean any further clues about the precise timing of Luke's arrival at the station. But the statement was not sufficiently precise. It did confirm that Luke had arrived sometime after the departure of the train from which his brother had alighted, but Proctor could not be precise. He guessed Luke arrived about twenty minutes or half an hour after the train had gone.

Proctor had also mentioned the fact that Luke had then hung around the village and the station for an hour or so, just in case his brother turned up. When James failed to arrive, Luke had set off upon his return journey and, upon departing, had said he hoped to catch up with James along the way. But, reasoned Pemberton, this was by no means an alibi.

Mark also found statements made by Mr and Mrs Hartley, the parents of Luke and James. They confirmed Luke's departure from the farm in the pony and trap at 2.30pm on Monday, 11th September 1916. Luke had said he wanted to set off in good time so as not to be late, and that he'd be back with James around half-past four. Luke had returned to the farm much later than he'd expected because of waiting for James.

James's mother had stressed in her statement that James was unhappy about going to France but did say he had never shown any sign of being suicidal. One of the factors which had increased concern in both James and his mother was the reports in the English newspapers about the struggle in the Somme. In a battle on 1st July 1916, eleven British divisions had left their trenches to fight the Germans and more than 57,400 had become casualties. Major Stewart Shand of the 10th Battalion had won the VC for his bravery near Fricourt; he was killed in action on 16th July while helping his men to climb out of the trenches under machine-gun fire. Reports of this kind had upset Mrs Hartley, making her worry even more about James's future. Then there'd been reports of trench fever, of men fighting and sleeping knee-deep in mud, of lice-ridden clothes, rotting corpses lying every-where... And Mark thought that Mrs Hartley was being a normal mother worrying in a normal way about her son going off to fight.

While he was re-examining the old file, Lorraine returned. It was about four thirty and she popped into Mark's office looking excited.

'You look as if you've just won a raffle or something!' laughed Mark.

Over a cup of tea produced by Barbara, Mark's secretary, Lorraine told Mark about her day. When she reached the stage of referring to the road beneath the bridge, he laughed and said, 'Don't tell me! The child was in the dip in the road and couldn't see the pony and trap...'

'Sir! You let me work that out... I went all the way to Rosen-thorpe and you knew all the time...'

'No, I didn't,' he said. 'Duncan worked it out — or guessed it. But I'm delighted you have confirmed that it is a distinct possibility. But you've found more?'

She told Mark of her conversation with Millicent Roe, referring to the peculiar rhyme she had discovered and the tale of the ghost of James Hartley. When she had concluded this part of her story, Mark nodded in agreement.

'There's something bloody odd about all this.' He sighed. 'I've a feeling that if we dig much deeper, we're going to turn up a lot of nasties from the past.'

'Should we call a halt, sir?' She used the formal term auto-matically for this was, at least for the moment, a discussion between a subordinate and her boss. 'Perhaps we should not pursue it any further — you know, let the family rest in peace. It's going to be traumatic enough for the Hartleys having to cope with all those Americans. They're going to start digging too, aren't they?'

'Let us suppose there is some muck to unearth, Lorraine.' Pemberton smiled. 'Suppose the Vice-President himself decides to dig deeper. He might find something nasty. Imagine that — what a shock for our VIP visitor.'

'But that is surely his problem, not ours.'

'I appreciate that, and I am the first to realise that these people might not be related to him. But if there is something dirty awaiting discovery, I think we should be the ones to find it. In fact, we must find it, if only to stop him mouthing off all over the place. Assuming we do find something awful, we can then decide what further action to take. We might be able to smooth things over, if you see what I mean. Knowledge is power, don't forget, Lorraine! I don't want him blabbing all over the world's press about skeletons in the cupboard of a decent, hard-working English family — which he might do if he's anti-British. Imagine these decent folk having to live with that, just so that he can score some obscure political point. It would be especially awful if they were not related to him.'

'You're very wary of his so-called Yorkshire bluntness!'

'It could be worse than that Yorkshire bluntness!' laughed Mark. 'So, if there is something lurking in the woodwork, I want to be the first to find it. And there is something lurking, I'm sure, and I'm positive it's linked to James's death.'

'Fair enough. I can see the sense of your argument.' She smiled. 'But Millicent clearly knows something. She's not senile by any means and I believe she's come to realise precisely what she saw when she was only six.'

'I'll try to find time for a chat with her,' Mark said. 'But first, I think we should glean every scrap from this old file. It does keep throwing up surprises. It might produce more questions that

Millicent could answer I'll bet she's the only surviving witness from the murder investigation.'

'And I must go and get ready for my desk duty.' Lorraine realised it was almost time for work as she hurriedly sipped the last of her tea. 'But before I go, there's another puzzle.'

'You have been busy.'

She smiled. 'I'm like you, I can't bear sitting around getting bored! So after Millicent told me her story, I went back to Wolversdale churchyard. They've done more work there, clearing the Hartley graves for their important visitor.'

'And?'

'Luke's not buried there, sir,' she said. 'Out of the brothers and sisters mentioned in our file, those who were alive in 1916, several are buried in St Monica's. But Luke is not. If he was head of the family, you'd think he would have been buried with the others.'

'The file doesn't say when he died?'

'No, there's no mention of his death.'

'What about the continuation sheets? Have you gone through those in detail? I believe they contain a potted version of the enquiries which were pursued for several months after the murder. There might be some reference to Luke there — you know the sort of thing: he might have gone to live in another area, he might have died, taken another farm or something. Duncan won't have got that far yet in programming HOLMES — it'll mean a physical search of the file.'

'I never thought of looking there, sir,' and she blushed as if admitting an error.

'I haven't read them either. I was leaving them until the very end, as a sort of summing up. I thought they might round off the file, for us as well as for that old team. But it might be worth a look if Luke did disappear for any reason. So did Luke emigrate? Do you think our Luke could in fact be the Vice-President's grandfather? And a murder suspect to boot!'

'There are certainly a lot of uncanny coincidences,' Lorraine said. 'It's just odd that George did not agree, that he knew nothing of Luke. Anyway, I'll plod through the files again while I'm on reception tonight. Now I really must go and get ready.'

He watched her lithe figure disappear from his office. She had a most alluring walk, sensuous and flowing, smooth and even stately. She was lovely.

* * *

EVENING DUTY at the reception desk kept Lorraine very busy. The Americans and the officers from Scotland Yard and the local Special Branch seemed to be coming and going all the time, some walking in the parkland, others walking down to the little town to sample the hospitality in the local inns and others going for drives in the surrounding countryside. There seemed to be even more of them now and Lorraine found herself checking passes in and out, making entries in ledgers and answering questions about everything from how old the church tower was, to whether the Lord of the Manor wore a coronet and why Yorkshire people hunted foxes and grouse but hated badger baiters. She told them where to find good food, books about the area, maps of the moors and details of places like Castle Howard, Duncombe Park, Nunnington Hall, the moors steam railway and the coastal villages like Staithes and Robin Hood's Bay.

After finishing his daily stint at 7.00pm, Mark went to his room, washed and changed, and came down for his supper in the canteen. He joined Paul Larkin at his table and ordered soup followed by a ham salad, then ice-cream as a sweet. During the meal, they deliberately avoided talking about the Hartley enquiries, partly because each felt it unfair to 'talk shop' when off duty, and partly because they might be overheard.

Larkin said he fancied a walk into the town for a pint of real ale and invited Mark to join him. Mark agreed. It would be a very pleasant excursion.

They checked out at reception, showed their passes to Lorraine and watched her enter their names in the ledger.

'Is the system working, Lorraine?' Mark asked.

'Yes, sir, it's simple but effective. If anyone fails to return without reason, we can tell fairly quickly just by checking down the right-hand column. And everybody who goes out knows the system now, so it's working well. We've even got the decorators into the system!'

'Great. Well, Paul and I are going to sample the quality of the ale at the Brockton Arms. See you when we get back.'

As the two detectives drank their glasses of real ale in the comfort of a friendly Yorkshire inn, it was inevitable that they discussed their current work. They were in a quiet corner near the fire where there was little chance of an eavesdropper over-hearing them. Mark found himself explaining to Larkin some of his recent thoughts about the feasibility of continuing with his Hartley investigations and he found Larkin agreeing with him. He knew Paul well enough to know that he would not express his agreement if he did not believe they were doing the right thing. Mark found this reassuring. In delving into the background of the Hartleys, it seemed he had already turned up more than he'd anticipated. But, as he had said before, murder was murder, whether it had been committed last night or nearly eighty years ago.

And an unsolved murder file was never officially closed, even if it was stored in an attic for decades and even if the chief suspect might turn out to be an ancestor of the Vice-President of the USA.

Their conversation ranged over the facts which had so far emerged, Mark expressing his professional opinion that Luke Hartley was by far the most obvious suspect. The fact that he had not been arrested for further interrogation remained something of a puzzle because the circumstantial evidence against him was sufficient to justify an arrest, if not a trial in the Assizes. Careful and systematic interrogation could have followed while he was in custody. He might have 'coughed' if he'd been incarcerated for a week or two. At that time, there were none of the restrictions which are imposed on modern police interrogations; restrictions of the kind enforced by the Police and Criminal Evidence Act 1984 had never been thought necessary.

Paul Larkin highlighted the nagging fact that no motive had been found; there had not even been a hint of one. There was no family animosity, no jealous rival — nothing which would amount to a motive of any kind, let alone one for murder. And without a motive, it was difficult to understand why anyone would kill the returning soldier. And so, after talking shop over several pints, the two detectives walked back to Thirklewood Hall.

It was eleven thirty when they entered, and Lorraine's face was a picture of happiness.

'Sir,' she said, 'you were right. Luke was mentioned in those continuation reports.'

'Was he? So what happened to him?'

CHAPTER TEN

'He emigrated, sir, to Canada, in 1916,' Lorraine told him.

'Canada? Are you sure?'

'Yes, according to Inspector Dawson. It was following Dawson's initial enquiries. You remember the railway linesman, Lapsley? He claimed to have seen Luke and Millicent Roe near the scene of the murder and we wondered why that evidence didn't result in Luke's arrest. Well, Lapsley wasn't interviewed until Friday, 13th October — we didn't check the date on his statement when we read it. He lived away from Rosenthorpe and the police didn't realise he'd seen something until later — but by then, Luke had left the country. Lapsley hadn't come forward earlier because he hadn't realised how important his evidence was. There's a note among the continuation sheets which says that this statement confirmed Dawson's belief that Luke was guilty, and he decided to re-interview Luke about the facts revealed in Lapsley's evidence. But when he got to the farm to confront Luke, Luke had already left, and his family had gone with him. Wife and kids. They had sailed from Liverpool on 6th October — Dawson checked with the shipping line. Neither Luke nor his family told a soul they were leaving — it was all done with the utmost secrecy.'

'Had he run away? Does it say anything about him running from justice?'

'No, but it does look as if it was planned. There's nothing to say he'd fled from the police, there's just a note to say that he'd gone to start a new life in Canada.'

'Canada? Not America?'

'Yes, lots of people from this district did that — Canada was full of English families from this part of Yorkshire who'd left to seek their fortunes.'

'Do we know when Luke made those plans? In other words, did he plan to leave England before or after James was killed?'

'We don't know when he started thinking of going, but does it matter? He might have wanted to get away from the farm anyway; he might have blamed himself for James's death. If he didn't kill James, he probably dwelt on the notion that if he'd been on time at the station, James would have lived. And I can't see him having an easy time with his mother once James was dead — she seems to have been neurotic or at least to have had a fixation with James. I'm sure she'd blame Luke for James's death even if he was innocent. I can't see that his departure can be regarded as a sign that he murdered his brother even if it was a form of personal guilt for his death.'

'That's not how I see it!' Mark told her. 'I reckon he killed James and then left the country before he could be arrested. He must have known that, sooner or later, the truth would emerge.'

'I agree he must have had some feeling of personal responsibility, whatever happened.' She spoke softly.

'I think he realised he was the main suspect and that he'd be questioned at length if more evidence came to light. So he went somewhere beyond the reach of the local constabulary.'

'But,' said Lorraine, 'if Dawson really thought Luke was guilty, and Lapsley's statement was the clue he'd been waiting for, wouldn't he have pursued Luke to Canada?'

'I doubt it. In spite of everything, there was no real evidence, no firm proof of his guilt, certainly not enough to justify a policeman crossing the Atlantic to arrest him. And I'm not sure what extradition procedures were in force at that time — although they did go after Dr Crippen! Murder was almost certainly an extraditable offence but without the necessary proof I doubt if Luke could have been brought back for trial. You can't extradite suspects unless you've got some fairly strong evidence.'

'So if he had murdered James, he would be able to begin a new life overseas without anyone knowing his past?'

'Exactly — unless there was some very positive evidence against him. In this case, the evidence was all circumstantial and very weak.'

Pemberton was now struggling to assess the implication of the Vice-President's grandfather being a suspected murderer. But was this Luke really the Vice-President's grandfather?

'Lorraine, I've a nice job for you. Try to ascertain whether our Luke Caleb and the Vice-President's grandad really are one and the same person. We don't know for sure that they are, do we? We need more evidence, more links, something positive.'

'Where do I start on that, sir?' She looked slightly flustered at the task he'd given her.

'Well, the Americans have some information which they've produced from somewhere. They've already provided us with a little of it, so have words with that boss chap of theirs from the White House. They probably have a lot more detail about Hartley's claim to be of Yorkshire descent.'

'You mean Mr Dunnock?'

'That's him. I've seen him eyeing you from time to time — exercise your feminine charms on him! Tell him we need to complete our files for security purposes. And then, having established what you can at the other side of the pond, give the Maritime Museum at Liverpool a ring. They keep emigration records and might even have passenger lists from that period. And photographs? Does the Vice-President have photos of his ancestors? Any relics which might have come from Wolversdale? Surely Luke must have taken some precious family heirlooms with him. The Vice-President might still have some family treasures which can be linked to Pike Hill Farm.'

'But if our Luke and his Luke are one and the same person, it's not going to be very pleasant for the Vice-President to learn of his grandfather's guilty secret.'

'At this stage, Lorraine, we're not sure whether his grandad had a secret, are we? It's speculation on our part. And I would never reveal anything that was grossly embarrassing without consulting the Chief Constable first — and he'd have to have words with someone in high places before we presented any unsavoury facts to the great man.'

'When shall I make those enquiries, sir?'

'In duty time, Lorraine! What are you doing tomorrow?'

'I'm on standby, sir. Just hanging around here, in other words.'

'Find yourself a quiet office, then charm Mr Dunnock into telling you all about the Vice-President, and follow it up by ringing a few people, starting with the Maritime Museum in Liverpool.'

'Thanks.'

'Well, I'm off to bed and then, tomorrow, if there's nothing to keep me here, I'm going to visit George Hartley at Pike Hill Farm. It's time I talked to him at length. I'm sure he must know something about his family's past.'

* * *

NEXT MORNING, Friday, 8th July, Detective Inspector Paul Larkin assured Mark Pemberton that he was quite capable of coping with any matter which might arise at Thirklewood Hall. Mark therefore drove out to Wolversdale, having first telephoned the Hartleys to make an appointment. George said he would be around the farm buildings all day and told Pemberton he could come at any time during the morning. Half-past ten was suggested because that was 'lowance time, when the farmers and their staff take a break for their allowance of sandwiches and cakes with tea or coffee. Alark arrived at twenty-five past ten. He drove into the well-kept and very spacious yard, noting the rugged stonework of Pike Hill farmhouse ahead of him. To his left, however, was a brick-built bungalow standing on land which had once been a paddock at the west end of the house. This was now the home of George Caleb Hartley and his wife. Mark went to the kitchen door where he was met by Mrs Hartley, a stout happy-faced lady with red cheeks and short grey hair.

'He's in the sitting-room,' she said, 'waiting. I'll fetch your 'lowance through, Mr Pemberton.'

'Thanks.'

The spacious sitting-room was sumptuously furnished with a pair of matching three-piece suites, a thick carpet rich in autumnal shades and lots of original watercolours around the walls. As Mark entered, his eye caught one of the paintings and Hartley spotted his interest.

'Our Maria did those,' said George. 'Sold a fair lot, she did, and had exhibitions. She liked the moors, you see, Mr Pemberton, and allus painted scenes with heather in.'

'They're good.' Pemberton found them attractive. 'She's captured the feel of the heather.'

'Aye. She got the purple just right — not many folks can do that. They either make it too red or too blue, but not our Maria. She was good with her purple.'

'Who was Maria then?' asked Mark. 'A sister of yours?'

'Nay, lad, a lot older than that, a great aunt. My grandfather's sister.'

'You're a big family?'

'Aye, we are that. Spread all over t'country now, and doing well most of 'em, especially t'youngsters. You'll have heard of Bartholomew Caleb Preston?'

'The Member of Parliament?' said Mark. 'That's him. Conservative. Junior Minister for summat or other. Well, he's descended from the Hull Hartleys, my Great Uncle Thomas. Then there's the Latimers from Lincoln, they're in business down there, doing very well.'

'I've heard of the Hartleys of Hull,' acknowledged Pemberton.

'Aye, it's a famous store, make no mistake, and then there's Great Aunt Jessica, who married Henry Latimer, well, she started the Latimer branch off. And we had one who was a priest, Father Matthew, he's buried down the village.'

'You're obviously proud of them all.' Mark settled in one of the easy chairs as George waved him to be seated. Then Mrs Hartley brought in a tray containing their 'lowance. It bore two massive mugs of hot coffee, a plate of biscuits, a sponge cake already sliced into enormous V-shaped chunks, some scones and two rounds of ham sandwiches.

'Good heavens, are we expecting somebody else?' Mark eyed the food.

'Nay, lad, this is our 'lowance,' said Mrs Hartley, putting the tray on a low table. 'It'll just put you on till it's dinner time.'

Dinner time on these moors was around noon, when another huge meal of cooked meat and three vegetables would be consumed by the hungry farm workers. She gave Mark a plate and told him to help himself, then left.

'I am proud of them all,' said George, resuming the earlier part of their conversation. 'It's allus said hereabouts that a Hartley's not frightened of hard work and that no Hartley has ever been out of a job. We've never been on the dole and we've allus fended for ourselves.'

'It's a pity other people can't say the same.' Mark did not really know how to respond.

'Too reliant on other folks, too reliant on state hand-outs, most of 'em,' he grumbled. 'Anyroad, Mr Pemberton, you've not come to talk politics. Is it summat to do with that American chap.'

'Yes, it is.' Mark knew that what he was about to say would be very difficult indeed and he really did not know how to broach the subject of the death of James or the departure of Luke. But he knew that, when in doubt, you started at the beginning and you told the truth.

He continued. 'Mr Hartley, you know that Vice-President Hartley claims to be descended from your family?'

'Aye, we 'ad a chap from t'Embassy came weeks ago to tell us. Drove all t'way up from London just to say so.'

'And it was news to you?'

'It was that! I've never come across that tale before and, well, I was taken aback by it. I mean, some of the Hartleys have done very well in life, but, I mean, being Vice-President of the United States! I never thought he'd be one of ours. I mean, that's flying a bit high for us Hartleys, Mr Pemberton. We're nobbut yeoman, Yorkshire hill farmers.'

'So you don't reckon it's true? About the Vice-President's ancestors coming from here? From this farm?'

'Nay, lad, nobody's ever said owt about that. If we'd had American cousins, you'd think somebody would have known, wouldn't you?'

'So you've never delved into your family background?'

'No, never. We're not that way inclined, Mr Pemberton, we're not academics, we're too busy earning our living on the farm, working on the land, day in and day out. We've no time to go delving into old records or scratching around churchyards.'

'It's very popular these days, especially with the Americans,' he said.

'Mebbe so, but what's past is past, I reckon. Families get spread about, but I've never heard owt of an American branch of the Hartleys.'

'And the other family cousins? They've never referred to an American branch either? They've not bothered to research their family roots?'

'Nay, not to my knowledge. If they had, I think I would have known. After all, this farm was where it all started with my great grandfather Caleb Hartley. And we're all buried down the village in St Monica's. But, well, I'm getting on for seventy now and nobody's ever come to me asking about bygone Hartleys — until that American Embassy chap turned up.'

'How do you feel about it now? If it was true, for example, would you be pleased?'

'Well, I'm a bit of a realist, Mr Pemberton, I must say I'd be right proud if we were related, but sometimes it's best to leave things unsaid. Now, if this fellow starts investigating our family, well, he might turn summat up that's best left alone.'

'Are there some family secrets that should not be publicised?' Pemberton put to him.

'I don't know of any, but if folks start delving, you never know what'll turn up. Every family has a skeleton or two in its cupboard, as they say, even if we don't know what they are. Mebbe it's best to leave things as they are. I can't say I would welcome these Americans digging into our background. That hardly seems right.'

'But you know of no skeletons?' Mark asked.

George shook his heavy grey head. 'Not me, not among the Pike Hill Farm Hartleys. We've allus been law-abiding and religious, never got into debt or left bills unpaid. We've allus done what's right, Mr Pemberton, so I don't reckon we've any skeletons to worry about. But the snag is you never know what our cousins or half-cousins have got up to over t'years, especially them that's moved away. You can pick your friends, Mr Pemberton, but you can't pick your relations. You're stuck with them!'

'Suppose there was some hidden secret? What would you do?'

'Do?'

'Yes, with this American interest in your background. Would you hide it?'

'Is that why you're here, Mr Pemberton?' The old farmer's

shrewd eyes looked directly into Mark's face. 'I thought there must be summat important bringing you here, a policeman, I mean. Are you saying there is summat I ought to know?'

'We've been doing a bit of background research of our own, Mr Hartley,' Mark began. 'I — by that I mean myself and a team of detectives, we are responsible for the security of Mr Hartley when he arrives. So we did a little bit of checking…'

'You're not saying some of my cousins are likely to have a go at him, are you?' George looked horrified. 'Attack him or summat?'

'No, I'm not. At least I hope not! But, well, we thought there might be a hero in the family…'

'You mean James? Him that died in World War One? He was a soldier, you know, Green Howards, 5th Battalion. My grandfather's brother. He's buried down the village, but I've never thought of him as a hero. The Embassy chap asked about him, he asked what had happened. He must have looked round our churchyard before coming here.'

'As I did. I thought it would be nice to discover how he died too,' said Mark gently. 'So that we could tell the Vice-President — that's if he is linked to the family, of course.'

'Oh, and did you find summat?'

'You don't know how he died? The family haven't said?'

'Well, tales did come down from my grandfather. As a lad, I heard that Great Uncle James was shot when he was coming home on leave, he never got to the trenches, that's why his name isn't on our War Memorial. No one ever did find out why he got shot — there was tales hereabout that it was a German spy.'

'A spy?' Pemberton asked.

'Aye, but I reckon it was just tales, village gossip. Nobody was ever caught for shooting him, I do know that, and folks said the lane was haunted, they said a ghost haunted the spot where he was shot. I've had all sorts of folks asking for details, for books and things, but I know nowt about that carry-on, Mr Pemberton. All I said was that James was an ancestor of ours, but I knew nowt about ghosts and things. A load of rubbish is all that. But he died before I was born, and nobody ever said what really happened. Having heard things as a kid, I just thought the Germans had got him, summat to do with him being a soldier. There was a tale he'd stumbled across a spy doing summat very secret and got shot for his trouble.'

'That's all news to me,' admitted Mark. 'I've never come across that story, it was never considered by the police. The investigation never included that angle, and it is very well documented.'

'Well documented?' asked George.

'By the police of the time. They made very exhaustive enquiries,' said Mark, seeing that George was listening intently. 'James came home on leave and got off the train at Rosenthorpe. He was supposed to have been met with a pony and trap, because he was carrying all his kit, but the person who was supposed to pick him up didn't get to the station in time. Later that same evening, James was found dead. His body was found lying beside the road on some common land.'

'Down near Rosenthorpe cricket field — I've been there,' said George.

'That's right. When he died, he was in full Green Howards uniform — and he had been shot, as you say.'

'Suicide, you mean? Had he done it himself?'

'No,' said Mark. 'That was the first suggestion, but he had been shot by someone else. He was murdered, Mr Hartley, there's no doubt about that.'

'Well, I appreciate knowing the true story. How come you know all this, Mr Pemberton?'

Mark explained how he had acquired this knowledge, emphasising the fact that the Rainesbury Gazette had the story in its files and saying the police investigation did not mention anything of spies or military assassinations. This was a straightforward case of civil murder.

'I thought you should know the facts before your guest arrives,' concluded Pemberton.

'Aye, you're right. It's best we know what happened if those Americans start asking. So Great Uncle James was murdered in 1916? He wasn't shot by a spy or owt like that?'

'No. He wasn't a hero, Mr Hartley, although he did complete his training with the Green Howards and his CO said he had the makings of a very good soldier. He got good reports.'

'Well, I'll be damned. I don't know what to say about all this. But, Mr Pemberton, who'd want to kill my Great Uncle James?'

CHAPTER ELEVEN

Mark had anticipated this question but decided it was unwise to reveal his deepest suspicions at this stage.

'We don't know,' he answered. 'The murderer was never found, no one was arrested, and no motive was ever discovered.'

'That's bloody terrible, Mr Pemberton.'

George almost whispered the words. 'In a small community like this, especially in them days, you'd have thought somebody would have been caught. It was a hanging offence then, wasn't it? Mebbe it was a German spy after all? A hit and run killing?'

'I doubt it, honestly I do. What it means, Mr Hartley, is that we have unearthed an unsolved murder. I'd like to delve a bit deeper and find out all I can before the American contingent arrives. I'd like to get answers before they come, which gives me only two clear days. It's Friday now and the Vice-President comes on Monday — and there's a weekend in between. I need to know as much as I can before then — and the Americans might not be quite as discreet as my officers.'

'But this chap who's coming, he's not going to blab it all over t'papers, is he?'

'He does have a reputation for speaking his mind, Mr Hartley.

Yorkshire bluntness is what he calls it, but because this is a private visit, the press will not be told of his presence.'

'Well, that's good news. I was told to say nowt about it.'

'And I have no intention of informing the papers, whatever we find out about his family, or yours. Everything will be kept confidential. But I doubt if we can stop him speaking out if he wants to — after all, if he does find his Yorkshire roots he might want to tell everybody about it even if it is embarrassing for some.'

'A Hartley failing, Mr Pemberton. Some of us have opened our mouths a bit too much at times. Said things that mebbe we shouldn't. So he's like that, is he? Mebbe he is my cousin!'

'He does it all the time, so I'm led to believe, but the snag is that when he opens his mouth, he's speaking for the entire United States of America. And people do listen; he has said some fairly antagonistic things about this country in the past.'

'Well, I wouldn't want him blabbing on about our family, Mr Pemberton, especially if there's summat wants keeping quiet.'

'My own view, for what it's worth, is this,' said Mark. 'I'd like to find out as much as I can about the links between your family and his, and I'd like to do so before he gets here, and I haven't much time left. If there is anything to be kept quiet, we might be able to persuade him not to shout about it either here or in the States. That's assuming, of course, that he really is a relation of yours.'

'Now, that's a point,' said George. 'Mebbe he's not connected at all!'

'T think he is,' said Mark quietly. 'I think the Embassy man who came to see you was right.'

'Oh my God… You've discovered summat else?' George sighed. 'After all these years of thinking I knew my family. I thought I knew every one of 'em, well, the Wolversdale Hartleys anyroad. But I never knew about yon murder.'

'You know that Vice-President Hartley claimed to be

descended from a Luke Caleb Hartley who emigrated to America?'

'Aye, that's what the chap from the embassy told me. But I'd never heard of a Luke who'd emigrated. He said the Luke chap was his grandfather.'

'It seems that was his grandfather's name and certainly, there was a Luke who emigrated,' Mark told him. 'He was your grandfather's brother.'

'Was he, by God? Are you sure? I never knew about him, Mr Pemberton. Mind, I never knew much about my grandfather's family. You don't, do you? Most of us know nowt about our grandparents' brothers and sisters, do we?'

'That's true.' Mark realised he knew so very little about his own family of that generation.

'So, Mr Pemberton. Are we talking about the same Luke? Who was this Luke chap?'

'It's very possible it is the same man but at this point, I have no confirmation of that. I am trying to establish any possible connection. Our Luke, the one who emigrated, was the eldest son of your great grandparents, Sarah and Caleb Hartley. As you know, they lived here, in this farmhouse.'

'Eldest son? But I allus thought my grandfather was the eldest. He was George Stanley, he died in 1951.'

'Luke was born in 1879,' said Mark. 'His full name was Luke Caleb Hartley.'

'Well, I'll be damned!' said George. 'That explains it.'

'Explains what?'

'Summat that's been puzzling me for years. It's why my dad was not called Caleb. You see, Mr Pemberton, we Hartleys have allus given the eldest son the name of Caleb, mebbe not his main name, but allus as part of it. My dad was a Caleb and I'm George Caleb, being his eldest son. And we called our eldest lad Alan Caleb. But you see, my grandfather was *not* a Caleb, he was

George Stanley. I've often wondered why he wasn't a Caleb. I allus thought he was the eldest son of Sarah and Caleb.'

'Well, now you know. Your grandad wasn't the eldest son, he was the second son. The eldest of that generation was Luke Caleb and he was the man who emigrated to Canada. Then he moved down to America. I'm having enquiries made to establish his movements, but I must admit I'm pretty certain that he is the Luke Caleb who left this farm.'

'And did he start the American side?'

'I think so. I think he is the grandfather of the current Vice-President of the United States.'

'So that makes the Vice-President a cousin of mine, of us, of the Hartley family?'

'It does indeed, if it's true. And when you meet him, you'll see the family likeness. He could be your own brother if his photo's anything to go by. Now, I've no idea how much background information the Vice-President has managed to unearth for himself, but I am having enquiries made at Liverpool to see if we can trace any emigration records for 1916 — the year Luke left. I want to know if and when Luke Caleb actually sailed, who went with him, when he went and where he went.'

'I don't know what to say, Mr Pemberton. Two shocks in one day. All that about Great Uncle James and then finding out we've got cousins in America after all this time! I never dreamt of anything like this. Mind, I did wonder just a bit when that chap from the Embassy turned up. Caleb Hodgson Hartley, well, they're all family names. That Vice-President has got all the right names, my great granny was a Hodgson... By gum, but if this is true and we've got famous American relations, well, I just don't know what to say...'

'There's no family bible, didn't you say the other day?'

'There was, years ago, but it got burnt, so I was told. My grandad started a new one. We've got that.'

'But it doesn't mention Luke?'

'No, not a mention, not a word.'

'Can I see it, please?'

'Aye, of course, I've got it ready for when Caleb Hodgson Hartley comes here.'

George went off to find the bible and returned with a huge black leather-bound volume. The centre pages were marked by a blue ribbon and he flicked it open, then laid it on the coffee table before Mark.

'See,' he said, 'it shows Sarah and Caleb who lived at this farm; he died in 1922 and she died in 1926. And their family, according to this, were George, the eldest, that's my grandfather, then Samuel who was a butcher and Thomas and Sophie, the twins, who went to Hull. Then there was James the soldier, Matthew the priest, Jessica, who married a chap called Latimer, and Robert, the youngest, who went to live in Newcastle after marrying Freda Plews.'

'But no mention of Luke?' noted Mark. 'Nay, not a reference. Why do you think they've missed him off, Mr Pemberton?'

'I wonder if he left under some sort of a cloud, Mr Hartley? Had he upset the family, I wonder? Did he do something very wrong so that his father wanted nothing more to do with him?'

'Well, mebbe so. But there's nowt in our family gossip to hint at that, Mr Pemberton. Mind, my own dad might have known, he'd have been around in 1916 when Luke left home. He'd have remembered summat but he died in 1951.'

'I wonder if there was a concerted effort by your grandfather's family to eradicate every reference to Luke?'

'Now why would they do that, Mr Pemberton?'

'They might have blamed him for James's death,' Pemberton heard himself say.

'Bloody hell! He didn't kill his own brother, did he?' For George this was the third awful shock of the day.

Mark sighed. 'I don't know, but I rather suspect the family blamed him to some extent.'

'Now why would they do that, Mr Pemberton?'

Mark told George about Luke's movements that day and George listened intently.

'If he'd got himself to t'station on time, he'd have picked James up and he wouldn't have got shot? Is that it?'

'That's what the family might have thought,' agreed Mark. 'It's very possible they blamed Luke for what happened to James, so he might have decided to begin a new life in Canada. If his family blamed him, then the locals might have done the same. Maybe he couldn't tolerate their suspicions. Besides, it wasn't all that unusual for farmers to emigrate to Canada. Lots of them from this area did emigrate to Canada after the First World War, they did it to find work and start afresh.'

'But this was during a war, Mr Pemberton.' George was shaken by what he was hearing. 'I'm beginning to smell a rat here. Are you saying that Luke might actually have killed James? You used the word "suspicions". Did Luke murder him — that's different from just letting him get shot by somebody else?'

'It's a possibility. He was strongly suspected,' Mark had to admit. 'I didn't really want to suggest that to you, but, well, you've asked, and I cannot lie to you. Luke was a very strong suspect and, having read the files myself, I'm inclined to believe he was the killer.'

'So he ran away before they could catch him, is that what you're saying?'

'I don't know. If he did kill James, we do not know the reason. I need to learn a lot more about the family.'

'It would explain a lot, wouldn't it, Mr Pemberton?'

'You mean the lost family bible? The absence of any reference to Luke in your family history?'

'Aye. All that.'

'Yes, it would. It does suggest that efforts were made to keep Luke's existence a secret — until this Vice-President arrives on the scene and begins to trace his family roots.'

'I'm shocked, Mr Pemberton, honest I am. But I must thank you for discovering all this before the Vice-President comes here. Just think if he'd told me all this… So, what'll I tell him?'

'That's going to be difficult. If his aides are any good, they're bound to want to know more about James who died in the war; his grave shows the date of his death.'

'So they could check up from that?'

'Yes, just like I did. It's easy to find a copy of the local paper with the murder story in it. They can't find the actual murder file because I've got that, and so, in their minds, it'll probably go down merely as an unsolved murder, without any hint of Luke's part in it. But it wouldn't take much to unearth the links with Luke.'

'I'll play dumb, Mr Pemberton. I'll tell 'em I know nowt about the family history. And I'll keep this to myself, at least for the time being.'

'Thanks, I think that's wise. I'll keep you informed of what I discover; let's hope we learn more before Vice-President Hartley arrives.'

'Thanks — I hope we can get summat sorted out. Now, Mr Pemberton, answer me this, are you sure you don't know the reason why James was murdered?'

'Truthfully, I don't know. I was hoping you might have heard something within the family that might help. If we can establish that, it might help us to decide whether Luke was involved.'

'I've heard nothing, Mr Pemberton, not an inkling.'

'There was an old verse the kids used to sing. It started after James died. I was told that the children of this dale, in the neighbouring villages, would sing it.'

Mark then sang the words to the Bobby Shafto tune which accompanied them:

> *Jimmy Hartley's gone to hell,*
> *And his brother's gone as well;*
> *Jimmy Hartley's gone to hell,*

Tainted Jimmy Hartley.

'Aye,' George acknowledged. 'That song was being sung when I was a lad at school. I sang it myself.'

'Did it mean anything to you?'

'Not really, not when I was five or six.'

'Was it used by the other kids to tease you with?'

'No, not really, I don't think they knew what the words meant. It was like those nursery rhymes, they sang the words and danced around never really knowing what it was all about.'

'Did you ever think it might be your great uncle they were singing about?'

'Well, I did wonder if it was summat to do with the ghost they sometimes talked about. And Great Uncle James being shot by a spy — as a growing lad, I did wonder if he'd been a spy himself, even. Working for the Germans or summat nasty — tainted, you see. But I never gave it much thought — really, it meant nowt to me. Mind, once I sang it at home and Dad told me to shut up, but he never said why, never explained.'

'I think it does refer to James,' said Mark. 'And I wonder if the brother referred to was in fact Luke — it said he's gone as well. It said Jimmy had gone to hell.'

'Some said going to fight in the Somme was like going to hell,' commented George.

'James never got there,' Mark reminded him. 'But if James was a wrong 'un for any reason, it would explain why the word "tainted" appears in the verse, and why they said he'd gone to hell when he died. That's if we can rule out the spy business.'

'Sorry, Mr Pemberton, you've baffled me now. So far as I know from family gossip, Great Uncle James was a lovely lad. He was an altar server at church, good with kids and helpful to his parents. A real decent young fellow, by all accounts.'

'The police file also says he was a decent man,' Mark agreed. 'Then, as now, the police always delve into the character of the victim and they found nothing against James. He had no criminal record and they found nothing to suggest he had made enemies. And that makes his death more of a mystery.'

'And it still is?' said George.

'Yes, and it still is,' agreed Pemberton.

'So what are you going to do now, Mr Pemberton?' asked George Hartley.

'I want to find out just what happened all those years ago,' said Mark.

'I'll help in any way I can' said George. 'I want to get this thing sorted out.'

'If we can find a motive for his death, we'll be more than halfway to solving the puzzle as to who killed him. Now, are there any family heirlooms or anything that might provide a clue? Did James leave anything behind? Great Grandad Caleb? Did he leave anything?'

'There's a trunk of Great Uncle James's belongings, things his mother kept after he died. We've still got that, it's somewhere in the farmhouse. I'll have a look for it, Mr Pemberton. You'll be interested in it?'

'Certainly — it might contain something of interest.'

'I'll ring you when I've found it,' promised George, and so Mark left his Thirklewood Hall number, exhorting George to ring at any time. 'And if I find anything about links with America or Canada, I'll let you know that.' He paused and said softly, 'If the family have clammed up about Luke and James ever since 1916, there must be a reason, mustn't there, Mr Pemberton?

'Exactly,' said Mark, getting up to leave the house. 'And I reckon you need to know what it was before your American cousin finds out.'

'Leave it with me, Mr Pemberton,' said George Hartley.

CHAPTER TWELVE

While Mark was chatting to George Hartley at Wolversdale, Lorraine was in conference with Mr John T Dunnock of the Vice-President's staff. Upon learning that the tall and glamorous plain-clothes officer wished to speak to him, he had organised coffee and biscuits in his suite; he was clearly enchanted by the young detective. He had a large green file on his desk upon which she could see the legend 'Operation Roots'.

'Hi,' he began in his distinctive drawl. 'You are an English lady detective, is that so?'

'Yes, I'm a detective constable. Lorraine Cashmore is my name.'

'And I know you are working here, in Thirklewood Hall, for the duration of the Vice-Presidential visit. I've seen you around the place.'

'I am, sir, yes. I'm engaged on internal security and am a member of the local force.'

'Lucky old local force is what I say!' He beamed at her as his secretary organised the coffee. 'So you want to ask me about Vice-President Hartley's family roots? Is that so?'

'Yes. I'm working with Detective Superintendent Pemberton and, as you know, we are responsible for internal security.'

'And a very good job you are doing, all of you!' He beamed again. 'So what is it you wish to know?'

'Superintendent Pemberton is anxious to know more about the Vice-President's relations in the UK.' She smiled. 'We need to know their background and location so that we can carry out a full security check. I understand the Vice-President will be going to the homes of the people he believes to be his relations. We'll need a list of all the venues and people involved — we'd like to give them all a security check, through our own network.'

'That figures. You might have some local information on them that isn't known nationally by the DPG in Scotland Yard. So, well, why don't I give you a copy of our own details? It's confidential material but we're all in this together, aren't we? Although, Lorraine, you know it's never been confirmed that he actually does have relations in the UK? That's why he's coming here, to find out if the local Hartleys are part of his family.'

'Yes, I know that, Mr Dunnock, but I believe that some preliminary research has been undertaken? Some links have been suggested but not yet established?'

'Sure, Vice-President Hartley has done a little himself, but, well, time's in rather short supply for a man of his position and to be honest with you, Lorraine, that sort of research is hardly the kind that the White House staff could undertake on his behalf. It's a private matter, you see. He wants to come here to find out as much as he can. In three days, though, he's not going to discover a great deal.'

'Quite.' Lorraine flashed her smile at the American. 'Now, I believe he claims that Luke Caleb Hartley settled in the States after emigrating from the UK in 1916. He was from Yorkshire and originally settled in Brockville, Canada, before moving to Utica in the State of New York.'

'Right,' smiled Dunnock.

'I'm interested in details of the actual emigration, Mr Dunnock, so that I might be able to link Luke with existing people here. Then we can do our checks on them. I understand that immigration and emigration records show details of next of kin, for example. There are lots of Hartleys in this part of Yorkshire, you see, and we don't want to waste time checking on them all if only one family is of interest.'

'I do know that your city of Hull was mentioned by the Vice-President — he has some relations there, I believe. He's going to visit them, store-owners they are, Hartleys of Hull. And the main ones are, as I'm sure you know, the Hartleys of Wolversdale. Now, let's see what the file says.'

As she sipped the strong coffee, he scanned the file before him, refreshing his memory.

'I did study his papers before coming here, but as one gets older, one's memory gets poorer.' He grinned. 'Now, Vice-President Hartley was hunting through his father's belongings some years ago when he found a letter from his father's Aunt Sophie in Hull, Yorkshire, England.'

'She founded a big store in Hull.'

'Sure. Now, that letter, it was addressed to the Vice-President's Aunt Sarah but the Vice-President's father — that's Caleb James Hartley — had kept it for some reason. I think our Vice-President felt it was quite important, from a family point of view.'

'Do we know anything about the Vice-President's Aunt Sarah? I know nothing of her.'

'She was quite a lady, it seems — she founded the James Hartley Foundation, a children's home in the US. I think the letter prompted him to find out more.' Lorraine wondered if the Foundation had been named in honour of the deceased James but did not refer to that at this juncture. Instead, she asked, 'So he regarded the letter from Sophie as important?'

'I don't see why. It wasn't much; it consisted of a very short note. It was dated 1924 and said that Patrick had made his first

Holy Communion. It didn't say anything else, except to wish everyone luck in their new life.'

'Maybe Patrick had come to England from her Foundation in the US?' suggested Lorraine. 'I've not come across that name before — Patrick, I mean — but I do remember reading about Sophie. She was one of twins, brother and sister of Luke Caleb, we think.'

'Right, well, the Vice-President found that letter to his Aunt Sarah — she died in 1991 in New England, by the way. By then, she was Mrs Walter J Swinburne and was eighty-eight years old. She had no family, her husband was a college lecturer, and he'd retired long ago. Anyway, Lorraine, when the Vice-President found that letter, he vowed to trace his roots. Till then, you see, he'd never even thought he might have English ancestry. He started to enquire in Hull and found a big store called Hartleys of Hull.'

'It's still operating.'

'It sure is. Well, the PRO for the store sent a booklet over to him. It contained a potted history of the Hartley family of Hull and said the family originated at Pike Hill Farm, Wolversdale. It told how Caleb Hartley had married Sarah Hodgson in 1877 and how they had had eight children. And with our Vice-President being called Caleb Hodgson Hartley, well, that really set him thinking. We learned that Thomas and Sophie were twins and together they had moved to Hull in 1910, when they were only twenty-six years old, to establish a store which grew into the highly successful Hartleys of Hull. No one at the store knew anything in detail about the Hartleys of Pike Hill Farm, but our Embassy did establish that Hartleys continued to live there.'

'The Hartleys are still living at Pike Hill Farm,' confirmed Lorraine.

'Sure, we've checked that out. When our agents went to interview the oldest member there, George Hartley, he claimed to know nothing about a Luke Caleb, although they did know of the

Hull connections. But the Vice-President felt sure the secret of his family roots lay in Wolversdale at that farm. And so he decided to visit the farm at the first opportunity. Well, when he had to come to England on government business, it seemed that Providence was being kind to him. He decided to stop off a while and check out his ancestry.'

'He won't have much time to delve into family records,' said Lorraine. 'Researching a family history can take months.'

'He appreciates that. He just wants to see the graves of his ancestors in Wolversdale, Sarah and Caleb in particular. And, of course, he wants to establish that his grandfather, Luke Caleb, was born at Wolversdale and lived at that farm.'

'There is no grave of a Luke Caleb in Wolversdale,' Lorraine pointed out. 'The family graves are in the Catholic churchyard there. He'll find the other graves without any trouble; George Hartley has been cutting the grass around them to make them tidy!'

'You British cops take your duties seriously, eh?' He smiled. 'So, have I helped?'

'There is a little more. Do we know when Luke sailed from England or when he arrived in Canada? Where he sailed from, for example?'

'Sure. Hang on, it's all here somewhere.'

From the files, Dunnock was able to tell Lorraine that, from records held in the National Archives of Canada, it was known that Luke Caleb Hartley, along with his wife Edith, daughter Sarah and two sons Caleb James and Paul Stephen, had arrived in Quebec on 4th November 1916, having sailed from Liverpool, England. The ship was the *Montcalm* which, during the earlier stages of the war, had been disguised as the HMS *Audacious* in an attempt to fool the German fleet. It had reverted to a passenger vessel in September 1915, not long before Germany began her spring submarine campaign in the Atlantic. German U-boats had torpedoed several passenger ships — indeed, in March 1916 the passenger vessel Sussex, crowded with passengers heading for Dieppe, had been sunk by German submarines.

There was considerable risk in sailing the ocean at that time, but passenger vessels did continue their work. Passenger manifests of the time contained a lot of genealogical information, and the one bearing Luke's particulars included the destination of the passengers, which in Luke's case was Brockville on the northern banks of the St Lawrence Seaway, some 120 miles to the South-West of Montreal. There the Hartley family intended to establish a livestock farm comprising cattle and horses. Luke was fairly successful, but after ten years decided that his future lay in America. He then moved to Utica in the State of New York where he and his sons established a successful business in real estate, housing and property dealing.

'The thing is,' said Mr Dunnock, 'that from 1907, the law changed so that every ship's manifest had to contain additional information about emigrants. It had to include details of their health, whether they could read and write, who paid their passage, the amount of cash they carried, whether they were anarchists and, more important for us, the names of next of kin back in the UK.'

'So the Canadians weren't accepting everyone who wanted to enter their country?'

'Not by any means. They were aware that there were draft-dodgers in the war and so they were very careful who they allowed into their country. Luke was accepted, even though he had a slight heart problem. The manifest does contain the names of his next of kin — and they were given as Sarah and Caleb Hartley of Pike Hill Farm, Wolversdale, Yorkshire, England.'

'That's fairly conclusive, I'd say!' said Lorraine.

'Yep, sure is. So you can imagine what the Vice-President felt when the present Hartleys of Pike Hill Farm said they knew nothing of his grandfather! It made him even more determined to find out exactly what lay at his family roots — so he's coming all this way to find out.'

'It's kind of you to take the time to talk to me,' smiled Lorraine. 'You really have been most helpful.'

'Glad to be of assistance, Lorraine. I'll get a photocopy of the Vice-President's family background for you — with details of the ship's manifest and so on. Contact me again if you need more. Perhaps we could have a drink together sometime?'

'I'd like that,' said Lorraine, lying through her teeth.

But she walked out of his office with everything she needed, including a copy of the letter sent from Hull all those years ago. And she'd done it without making a long drive across the Pennines to Liverpool. She made a mental note to buy Mr Dunnock a drink — but that was all!

* * *

BACK IN THE POTTING SHED, Lorraine began to check her newest information against details she'd abstracted from the murder file. Certainly, Luke's twin brother and sister had gone to Hull and certainly they had established a thriving retail business. But during her previous reading of the file, the name of Patrick had never cropped up and so she turned to that part of the murder file which referred to Luke's brothers and sisters. Dawson's old system was easy to follow, and she quickly found details of Thomas and Sophie.

Thomas Joseph Hartley, born in 1884, had married Catherine Taylor, aged eighteen, in 1902. At the time of James's murder, they had four children, Caleb aged thirteen, Sarah aged eleven, George aged nine and Robert aged seven.

Thomas and his family had left Wolversdale in 1910 to establish their business in Hull and, at the time of the murder, were still living there. Thomas's twin sister, Sophie, had left home at the same time as her brother; in 1912, after arriving in Hull, she had married Aiden Harland, a local man. At the time of James's death, both Aiden and Sophie were working hard alongside Thomas to establish Hartleys as a major store in the city. There had been no children to the couple at that point and so Patrick must have been born after the file had been compiled in 1916.

Lorraine spent an hour or so plodding through the heavy file in an attempt to glean any snippet of information but was unable to discover anything else of relevance. She wrote up her discoveries, therefore, in the form of a statement and passed it to DC Duncan Young to be entered into the HOLMES data bank.

'I'll do it after lunch,' he said. 'Come along, let's share a table.'

As they ate their meal, Duncan was grumbling. 'I can't see why the boss is bothering with this old crime, Lorraine. I mean, it's not as if the killer will be alive, is it?'

'He could be!' she retorted.

'Or she!' laughed Duncan. Duncan Young had served for eight years, three of them as a member of the CID. With a civilian background of computers and data processing, he was the ideal man to supervise the operation of HOLMES. A pleasant young fellow with dark wavy hair and brown eyes, he had a young wife at home and a baby girl aged two. Firmly set on a police career, he often said he wished to spend more time on the beat or making crime enquiries, but his skills with the computer had been considered important enough for him to be seconded to HOLMES.

'It would be grossly boring here unless we had something to do,' said Lorraine. 'I'm enjoying it. I know that Mark Pemberton wants to close the file — he'd love to find the killer just for the hell of it. You know how he hates to leave any murder undetected.'

'We'd be better off concentrating on the Muriel Brown murder — that's only eight years old! At least her killer should still be around, and he could still serve his sentence if we find him.'

'But there's no immediate pressure to clear up that one, is there?' Lorraine reminded him. 'Just think of the prestige if we solve this crime before the Vice-President arrives!'

'If I was him, I'd be far from pleased to learn that snoopers had discovered my murky family secrets before I knew about them,' laughed Duncan. 'Besides, we're not sure that the two Hartleys are linked, are we?'

'It's almost certain. The details are in those papers I've just given you.' She produced one of her devastating smiles.

'You're as bad as Pemberton — you never stop!' he grumbled.

'It's fascinating. The Luke who's in our frame for killing his brother is almost certainly grandfather of the Vice-President of the United States. Think of that, Duncan, think what the press would make of that story, both here and overseas!'

'Bloody hell!' smiled Duncan. 'I'd better keep that under wraps.'

'The boss doesn't know that yet,' Lorraine warned him. 'So keep it very much to yourself. He does suspect, but he asked me to get confirmation and I got it from Mr Dunnock.'

'So where is Pemberton now?'

'He went over to Wolversdale to interview the senior member of the Hartley clan. I can't see they'd welcome the news that a great uncle or something similar was a killer!'

'We'll never prove that, surely, not after all this time?'

'All we need is a motive.'

'I've not found one, not even after wading through masses of statements and papers. That James seemed to be a really nice guy, never a trouble-maker of any kind. His mother doted on him. If Luke did kill him as our boss and you seem to think, then I haven't found any motive, not even anything remotely like one.'

'You think it could be someone else?'

'HOLMES has thrown up one gap.'

Duncan's expression showed signs of a minor triumph.

'Really? What?' Lorraine was excited by this news.

'Thomas, Luke's brother in Hull. The initial enquiries showed he lived in Hull, but a detective was asked to check that. His report said Thomas was away from home when he called, away on business, but nobody found out where he went. Nobody checked that story, nobody bothered. The police of the time relied on the statement from his sister, Sophie, who simply said he was away on business but confirmed he lived and worked in Hull.'

'Surely somebody checked it out?' she cried.

'Why should they? If he wasn't anywhere near the murder scene, why bother to find out where he was? Dawson would have relied on the local force to make those enquiries and if they were satisfied, then there was little Dawson could do.'

'So what are you doing about Thomas's whereabouts?' Lorraine asked.

'I'll see if HOLMES produces anything that might help us decide where he was. Now, on to another subject. This verse they've discovered. Is it important? I mean, do I have to log it in HOLMES?'

'I think you should,' said Lorraine. 'It uses a funny word — tainted. I've never come across that in such a verse before, so why was James tainted? Tainted with what? Or how? How was he tainted? What's it mean? The word might crop up in some of the statements and reports, mightn't it? Can HOLMES find other references if they're there?'

'Sure, if I ask it to search for tainted, it'll do so, provided the word's been entered. It's just like looking for references to red cars or ginger-haired men. I'll stick it in, then. But I'll bet this is the first time that HOLMES has been used to store the words of a nursery rhyme!'

'It's not a nursery rhyme, Duncan — people often used to sing verses like this after a murder. I've come across quite a few of them, especially relating to Victorian killings. Murders had considerable impact in those days, particularly upon a small and isolated community. And remember, this is a historic crime; we've got to think like the people of Britain would have thought in the 1914-18 war.'

'It's not easy,' admitted Duncan Young. 'But it's fun,' smiled Lorraine.

'Hello, the boss is back!' said Duncan, looking towards the door. 'I'd better return to my chores!'

'He looks quite pleased with himself,' said Lorraine. 'I wonder what he's discovered.'

CHAPTER THIRTEEN

'You're looking rather pleased with yourself, sir!' was Lorraine's comment as Pemberton approached her table. DC Young was making his exit, but Mark halted him.

'How's it going, Duncan? Anything useful turned up yet?'

'One small thing has cropped up, sir,' replied the detective. 'It's probably nothing, but the whereabouts of Thomas Hartley, the Hull brother, were never checked. His sister, in business with him at Hull, did confirm he wasn't in Hull on the day of the murder. She said he was away on business, but no one knows where he was. The statements don't say.'

'Didn't the Hartley murder detectives check?'

'They didn't go to Hull, sir, like we would have done nowadays. They passed the enquiry to Hull City Police, probably by telegram; I think there was a lack of information in the communication. They asked Hull to find out if Thomas was at the shop at the material time, and the answer came back that he was not. And his sister confirmed he wasn't, saying he was away on business. But no one bothered to ask where he was. But in all fairness, I must say there's no suggestion he was anywhere near the scene of the crime. His name never cropped up among the local witnesses.'

'Oh, bloody hell! Thomas isn't in the frame now, is he?'

'He could be the brother who's mentioned in that funny verse, sir,' put in Lorraine. 'After all, that brother, whoever he was, wasn't named in the verse, was he? It just said he'd gone as well, without saying where. And we assumed it was referring to Luke.'

'OK, Duncan, pass the word around the team; we must examine the file minutely to see if we can find out where Thomas was that day. I'll be very surprised if Dawson let that one through the net. Now, anything else of interest?'

'No, sir, we're just plodding along and abstracting data from those old statements. Apart from Luke, there's no other real suspect — I'm not sure that I would put Thomas in the frame at this stage.'

'I agree, I can't see him as a genuine suspect, but think of it in modern terms — in a modern enquiry Thomas would be the subject of a TIE, so we'll put him through that procedure, as much as we can, that is. But congratulations, you've done well.'

'Thanks, sir,' smiled Duncan.

'Well, sir, what's making you look so pleased with yourself?' ventured Lorraine.

'I've just come from an interview with George Hartley,' Mark said. 'I wasn't looking forward to meeting him at all.'

'You've discovered something?'

'I've discovered he's easy to get on with and I'm pleased because I'm so relieved about that! Old George was a real gentleman, most helpful and co-operative.'

'That makes a change these days!'

'Well, these old Yorkshire farmers are full of common sense and they do respect their police officers. I must admit I thought he wouldn't want to talk to me, especially as I was busily stirring up the family mud. Although I didn't learn a great deal, I did get his co-operation and that's important. He said there was a trunk of James's things his mother had kept and he's trying to find that for me. In all, it was a very refreshing interview. I'll dictate my statement to Barbara after lunch, Duncan, then you can have it for processing.'

'Thanks, sir. Well, I must be getting back to my machine, it frets when I'm away,' laughed Duncan, leaving Mark alone with Lorraine.

'Let me get something for my lunch, Lorraine, and then you keep me company and tell me your news. Can I get you anything? A drink?'

'I've eaten, but coffee would be lovely.'

Minutes later, sitting with his soup, sandwich and coffee, he asked how her day had been so far. And she was able to provide him with her positive news about Caleb and Sarah being named as Luke's next of kin in the ship's manifest. Pemberton listened carefully, proud and pleased at her success.

'That's great news, Lorraine. I was thinking on the way here, we've got a signed statement made by Luke, the one in the police file, and if there's a signature among the stuff the Americans have got, we could make a comparison. If they matched, it would add strength to the matching of the two Luke Hartleys.'

As Lorraine continued to outline her discoveries, Mark listened intently and then asked, 'These links with the Hull Hartleys — have any enquiries been made there? It's odd that Hull should crop up twice in such a way — first with Duncan Young's discovery about Thomas and secondly with that curious letter about Patrick. Have we been plodding the wrong trail, Lorraine?'

'I don't think so. But Hull will have to be looked at, eliminated from our enquiries.'

'Trace, Interrogate, eliminate!' he laughed. 'Yes, we must TIE Hull!'

'When Vice-President Hartley discovered the letter from Sophie, the one referring to Patrick's first communion, his staff contacted the Hartley store in Hull,' Lorraine told him. 'They got a publicity leaflet back, saying that the Hartley dynasty began at Pike Hill Farm in Wolversdale. No one at the store knew anything about the Pike Hill Hartleys, other than what they'd published in the store's official history.'

'They didn't provide any clues about Patrick?'

'Apparently not. But you know what some PR people are like — they answer a letter by shoving a leaflet in the post and they never read the precise request.'

'So who is this Patrick? We must find out who he was. We need to TIE him too! Why write overseas from Hull to tell Luke's family about him? I find that rather odd. And why keep the letter?'

'It might have been kept accidentally, sir; it might have got lost or inadvertently tangled up among some other correspondence. It could be one of many letters received over the years.'

'Or it might have been kept for a specific reason!' He shook a finger at her. 'That's something we can't ignore.'

'So that's two new puzzles for us,' she mused.

'If I remember correctly from reading the file, Sophie was unable to produce children, so he can't be one of hers. Unless she produced one later? That sometimes happens, doesn't it? Women go for years without having children and then, in later life, become mums.'

'I'll have to read the statements again, sir, to be sure of that.'

'Right, do that. Go through them in fine detail — the answer might be there somewhere. Then I'll come and see you in, say, half an hour?'

'You're a hard task master, Mark Pemberton!' She laughed, draining her cup. 'But yes, come and see me then.' But when Mark returned to the office where she was working, she said, 'Sir, Duncan was right about Thomas Hartley. None of the other statements show where he was. The enquiring officer, who was a detective sergeant, either didn't ask or he was satisfied with the answers he received. So the whereabouts of Thomas were never checked.'

'That's bad.'

'I've found a little more. It seems Sophie said she could

confirm he was meeting business acquaintances, some of them regarding matters which were confidential. The detective was satisfied with that and Dawson didn't send the enquiry back for further investigation.'

'He slipped up there, didn't he?' cried Mark. 'I'd have had that sergeant's guts for garters! He didn't do a proper job — damn it all, it was a murder enquiry.'

'Dawson might have been satisfied with the outcome. Perhaps the sergeant did a local check and perhaps Dawson was content to let him make the decision as to whether Thomas was in the clear. Maybe Dawson knew more than we know.'

'Then it should be written down and entered in this file. That slip might have been a very bad error! He could have let Thomas get away with murder.'

'Bloody hell! You're not seriously putting Thomas in the frame now, are you?'

'But he is in the frame now, Lorraine! He's a suspect simply because no one knows where he was on the day his brother died. So, let's think it through. Hull's not all that far from Wolversdale — he could have got there that day, couldn't he? By train?'

'No one reported seeing him, sir.'

'Millicent saw somebody in the bushes beside the road, right on the murder scene. She didn't know who it was. She was a local kid — you'd expect her to have known Luke, but not Thomas if he was living away from the area.'

'Do we really think Millicent saw Thomas in the bushes? It's a long way by road, and there were no cars in those days.'

'But there were trains. He could easily have got to Rainesbury and that's not far away.'

'There's no way we can check that now, is there, sir, unless there are further clues among the statements.'

'If this was a modern enquiry, we'd have to find out his movements, and we'd have to find out who Patrick was. As you know, every person named in a murder enquiry has to be traced, interrogated and eliminated. I'm very interested in this Patrick. Who was he? Why has he suddenly materialised?'

'He was mentioned in the Vice-President's own file, sir.'

'But he wasn't mentioned in our police file, was he? He's not a relation, is he?'

'I did wonder if he'd come over from the James Hartley Foundation in America, for a long holiday or something. But I can't answer that without referring to the file.'

'It was a nice touch that, Sarah naming a foundation after her Uncle James. Obviously, she thought a lot about him, like everyone else did.'

'His death must have meant something to her,' Lorraine said wistfully.

'So Patrick is our mystery man now, and we must find out about him, Lorraine. Another nice job for me! I want words with the Registrar of Births and Deaths in Hull to see if Sophie produced a child and I want to have a chat with whoever is now running Hartleys of Hull.'

'What about, sir?'

'To see if they keep business records dating back to 1916. Some companies do keep records, you know, so that the company history can be written up from time to time. And they might know who the mysterious Patrick was. Right, I'll get Barbara to ring Hartleys to make an appointment. I fancy a drive down to Hull.'

'Very good, sir,' she said most formally.

'And you're coming with me.'

* * *

THE REGISTRAR OF BIRTHS, Marriages and Deaths at Hull was a Mrs Julie Tyndall and she explained that it was impossible to make a search for Patrick's birth at such short notice.

Such a search could not be completed in such a short time.

Much more detail would be required, too; she suggested that Pemberton visit the Consolidated Index of Births, Marriages and Deaths at St Catherine's House which was on Kingsway in Central London. It would mean a lengthy search by Pemberton or one of his staff. Once the relevant entry had been found, application could then be made for a copy of the birth certificate. She did say that the Consolidated Index was now on film and that a few copies had been made available to reference libraries. She added that the County Reference Library at Great Halverton had a copy — so Pemberton could inspect it there rather than make the trip to London. She stressed it would mean a long and diligent search. It would be even more difficult without a precise date or place of birth — checking to see if Mrs Sophie Harland had given birth in Hull between, say, 1916 and 1924 would undoubtedly require hours and hours of painstaking research. Mrs Tyndall also suggested that Pemberton search the local parish church registers, but he'd require details of date and place of birth if he was to avoid a long, boring search.

He thanked her and drove to Hartleys where his appointment was with a Mr Hurworth at 4.00pm.

Promptly at four, he and Lorraine were ushered into a plush first-floor office where a tall, smart man of around forty welcomed them. Slightly balding with dark hair, he wore dark, heavy-rimmed spectacles, expensive cuff links and a gold tie-pin in the shape of the letter H. He exuded an air of total confidence as he welcomed them.

'Detective Superintendent Pemberton? I'm the managing director of Hartleys, Donald Hurworth is the name.' And he extended his hand in greeting. Mark introduced Lorraine who also shook hands, and they were then settled into comfortable chairs and offered tea and biscuits by Hurworth's secretary.

When the introductions and formalities were over, Hurworth said, 'Well, I'm intrigued by this visit. Your secretary said it was in connection with a visit by the Vice-President of the United States? Mr Caleb Hodgson Hartley.'

Mark did not wish to tell this man the entire story, at least not at this stage, and so he said he was in charge of local security arrangements, including those for the Vice-President's visit to Hull. Mr Hurworth was aware of the proposed visit. Pemberton added that he was also endeavouring to discover some details of the family history in readiness for the Vice-President's arrival at Thirklewood Hall. He explained that he knew of the links between the Hartleys of Pike Hill Farm and those in Hull, then told of Vice-President Hartley's past contact with the store, adding that he'd been sent a small booklet about its history.

He also said there was every reason to believe that Luke Caleb Hartley, who'd lived at Pike Hill Farm until 1916, was in fact the Vice-President's grandfather.

'Really? Well, I'll be damned!' beamed Hurworth, who blushed with pride. 'The Vice-President did say he wanted to visit the store and of course we agreed, but I never really thought there was any link with our family.'

'Did he suggest there might be?'

'Well, it was one of his aides who contacted me; the name of Hartley was clearly of interest and all he said was that Vice-President Hartley was seeking his roots. We've had this sort of thing before with other Americans thinking they were connected. They weren't, of course. But I said I would welcome Mr Hartley and help in whatever way I could. But you say he wrote to us for information?'

'Yes, some time ago, apparently. Before he was a VIP! He got the standard PR response — a leaflet in the post. At that time, he'd have been regarded as just another American trying to sort out his family roots.'

'I'm a Hartley too,' said Hurworth with some pride. 'Donald Caleb Hurworth. My mother was Maureen, the eldest granddaughter of Thomas Hartley who founded the business.'

'You'll be the eldest of her children?'

'How do you know that?' smiled Hurworth.

'The name Caleb is given to the eldest son,' Mark said. 'Mr George Hartley, of Pike Hill Farm, told me that.'

'That's true, and my son is Stephen Caleb. And so the name continues.'

'The Vice-President is very keen to learn about his relations, but we've a gap around 1916. I know that Thomas Hartley and his twin sister, Sophie, came to Hull in 1910 to establish this store. Thomas went away on business in 1916, and I'm anxious to discover where he went — just to fill a gap. I wondered if he'd gone home to Wolversdale for any reason.'

'Wolversdale is the family home,' said Hurworth.

'Yes, I've already talked to Mr George Hartley at Pike Hill Farm. Now, the period around 11th September 1916 is the one which interests me. I know that some companies keep very detailed records for historical purposes and wondered if, by any fluke, you had a record of what Thomas was doing at that time.'

'We do have the minutes of every meeting, Superintendent, all filed and dated. I can get the 1916 file within seconds — we have files for every year since our foundation,' and he buzzed his secretary on the intercom. 'Georgina, bring me the 1916 minutes, will you?' While they were waiting, Hurworth outlined the development of Hartleys of Hull since its earliest days, giving due praise to both Thomas and Sophie; Thomas, it seemed, was the hard-headed businessman while his sister had a flair for fashion and design. She selected much of the early stock, especially the soft furnishings, and seemed able to forecast future fashions.

'Do you ever visit Wolversdale?' Mark asked Hurworth eventually.

'We've been to funerals and weddings,' he said. 'We try to keep in touch, but we've no real contact with the Pike Hill Hartleys now. We're too far removed from the present generation. For example, I had no idea we had a possible American branch of the family although I do know about the family hero.'

'James?' smiled Pemberton.

'You know our history! He was shot in the First World War. A very nice man, by all accounts.'

'I'm sure the Vice-President will be keen to visit his grave,' Mark added, not wishing to relate the story of the murder at this point. 'His links with Wolversdale have surprised a lot of people,' and then Georgina entered with a file. Hurworth thanked her and opened it.

'September 1916,' he muttered to himself. 'Here we are... Yes, Thomas was travelling then, meeting suppliers and customers. Minutes of a meeting dated Monday, 4th September 1916 — Mr Thomas will be absent from his office between Wednesday, 6th and Wednesday, 13th September 1916 because he is travelling to meet suppliers. His itinerary is given so that telegrams can be sent in case anything urgent arises. 7th, he'll be in Scarborough, 8th in York, 9th in Thornborough where he will stay overnight. 10th, a Sunday, he would remain in Thornborough, 11th travel to Rainesbury, 12th a meeting in Rainesbury with the accountants, home on Wednesday, 13th. So, Superintendent, that was his itinerary!'

'Brilliant! Does it say where he was staying? Hotels and so on, and the companies he was calling upon?'

'Yes, he intended staying overnight in Thornborough and overnight in Rainesbury. It's all here, minuted so we could contact him in an emergency. He'd do day journeys by train to Scarborough and York.'

'I'm amazed!' Pemberton complimented Hurworth. 'Clearly, you had a very efficient system in those days.'

'And it continues to this day!' beamed Hurworth.

Pemberton wondered if the detective sergeant who'd made the murder enquiry all those years ago had seen this itinerary; if so, he'd have been satisfied about Thomas's movements because there was no reference to Rosenthorpe.

'Thanks.' He smiled at Hurworth. 'I wish I could produce information as quickly as that. So, on his trip from Thornborough to Rainesbury, he could have called at Rosenthorpe, that's the station for Wolversdale. It's on the Thornborough to Rainesbury route.'

'Is it? I'm not too sure of the railway's geography in that area. But it doesn't say anywhere here that he intended to call at the family home.'

If this man did not know the geography of that railway, thought Pemberton, then neither would that Hull detective. He'd been satisfied with the answers given at that time, answers which suggested that Thomas had never been near the scene of the murder. But in fact, he could have been right at the scene without any member of the family realising!

'If Thomas travelled from Thornborough to Rainesbury, he would have passed the family farm,' Pemberton said. 'I wonder if the National Rail Museum has got the old timetables from pre-nationalisation days? The line was run by the North-Eastern Railway in 1916 — their timetables might exist. I wonder if, by any chance, he got off the train at Rosenthorpe for a family reunion, hoping to see James before he went to the trenches? He could have done that quite easily on that itinerary; he could have spent an hour or so at the farm, then resumed his journey on another train.'

'Thomas might have done that, Mr Pemberton. He was always keen to maintain links with his family,' said Hurworth. 'That is part of the tradition of Thomas and Sophie — they were very strong believers in the sanctity of family life. In fact, Thomas wanted to be buried in the family corner at Wolversdale.'

'I've seen his grave there. So can I take a photocopy of these minutes?' Mark asked.

'Sure, Georgina will see to that,' and he buzzed her once again.

She took away the file for photocopying while Mark explained that the Vice-President would be in Yorkshire and Humberside for only three days.

'I'm sure he'll be interested in seeing your business, especially because of the links with Patrick,' said Pemberton, hoping for some reaction. He got it.

'Isn't life awful!' said Hurworth. 'Poor old Patrick died only last year. He was seventy-seven. He'd have been thrilled to bits to meet the Vice-President.'

'So who was Patrick?' asked Lorraine, who had been sitting quietly at Pemberton's side during this interview.

'He was Sophie's son,' replied Hurworth.

CHAPTER FOURTEEN

'Sophie's son?' Lorraine echoed the words. 'She must have had him quite late in life?'

'Yes, she was thirty-two. He was the only child; Sophie died in 1952 and her husband, Aiden Harland, followed in 1959.'

'And was Patrick involved in running the store?' asked Pemberton.

'Oh yes, very much so. He was a brilliant mathematician and had been a university lecturer for a time, that was before joining the company. He had a breakdown in his early days — he was a very intense young man, and quite brilliant, and things got too much when he was lecturing at Crumbleclive College. We were never quite sure what caused his breakdown, but he left lecturing and for a time went to live in a monastery. He felt it was the right place in which to recover. He did recover, but never returned to his old job. In his late thirties, when he left the monastery, Patrick came to us and apparently found happiness and great success in looking after our financial affairs. He had a flair for the business.'

'And was he a Caleb too?' asked Mark. 'Er, no, he wasn't, now that you ask. He was just Patrick, with no second name.'

'With Sophie being such a family-orientated lady, I'd have

thought she would have given her eldest son the Caleb name,' commented Mark. 'Anyway, you say Patrick died in 1993?'

'Yes, from a heart attack. He was never very robust, but always kept himself busy. He worked with us until the last moment, he never thought of retiring. Hartleys was his whole life, Mr Pemberton. Other than his church, he had no outside interests.'

'And has he any family?'

'No, he never married. He was a bachelor throughout his life, never showing any inclination towards the opposite sex, but he wasn't homosexual. He was strict Catholic, very prudish in many ways, a regular church attender, a member of his parish pastoral council and so on. We're all Catholics, by the way, we kept the faith right through the Reformation and are proud that it continues in the family, even if some are a bit casual about it. Patrick was an example to us all. He went to the same church all his life, St Ignatius in Hull. He is missed by them and by us.'

'Is that where he made his first Holy Communion?' asked Lorraine.

'Yes. He had a certificate for his first Holy Communion and a picture of the Last Supper as a memento of his Confirmation. They hung on the wall of his home. The church was very much a part of his daily life. I remember seeing the certificate and picture — they were from St Ignatius' church.'

'If the Last Supper was a memento, would it contain a date of his confirmation?' asked Lorraine.

'Yes, it would. I have a similar one, but I can't remember what date was shown on Patrick's,' said Hurworth.

'And its whereabouts now?' asked Pemberton. 'What happened to his stuff when he died?'

'Sorry, I've no idea. When his home was cleared, most of the things were disposed of, except for those he had specifically willed to his relations or the church. I would think small stuff like those certificates would have been thrown out.'

'I'm interested because Sophie wrote to the Vice-President's

Aunt Sarah to tell her that Patrick had made his first Holy Communion. Clearly it was an important stage of his life. The Vice-President has got that letter. It was posted here in Hull.'

'Really? You mean it's survived all these years? It's amazing what turns up after all this time,' smiled Hurworth. 'That letter must be all of seventy years old!'

'Do you know whether Patrick maintained any form of contact with the Canadian, later the American, branch? Luke wasn't his godfather, was he? Or something like that?'

'I've never heard him refer to the Canadian or American Hartleys at all,' said Hurworth. 'He would sometimes refer to Pike Hill Farm and once went there as a child, with Sophie, but I've never heard him talk of any overseas relations, not at all. Not once.'

'It's odd that Sophie would make an effort to keep in touch with Luke's family about Patrick,' Mark mused. 'Anyway, if he made his first Holy Communion at St Ignatius' church, he'd surely have been baptised there too?'

'Almost certainly. Children made their first communion when they were seven or eight, so I guess it would have been at the same church. Sophie lived in the same house in Hull all her life. I never saw his baptismal certificate though — I never had cause to look for it — but I expect it would have been there. His parents always attended Mass at that church. Sophie and her husband kept their faith right to the end.'

'So Patrick was the last link with Sophie?'

'Yes, he was. With his death, there is no longer any link with Sophie, our joint founder. My family is the only branch which is linked to the original Hartleys, but we do have other directors now. And Thomas's other descendants did not join the company. Those of my generation are spread around the world, one in Norway, one in Australia, and there's another famous cousin, he's an MP, a rising star in the government.'

'Bartholomew Caleb Preston?' smiled Mark.

'You have done your homework,' complimented Hurworth, and then Georgina returned with the photocopying.

'This information is most useful,' said Mark, accepting the file. 'I don't suppose you would keep the more detailed stuff, like accounts from the period, Thomas's expenses for train fares and so on?'

'No, we've never seen any reason to hang on to the minutiae of the business; all that kind of stuff would have been destroyed years ago. We tend to have a clear-out of old stuff every ten years, but we do retain the minutes of all our meetings. They're the stuff of history.'

'Well, I appreciate this help. I might be in touch again before the Vice-President arrives,' said Mark.

'You'll be most welcome,' said Donald Hurworth. 'Goodbye.'

* * *

'So, WHERE TO NEXT?' asked Mark once they were outside.

'St Ignatius' church,' smiled Lorraine. 'I think we ought to inspect Patrick's baptismal record.'

'Do you? Why? We know who he is.'

'Do we?' She produced one of her enigmatic smiles. 'I thought Sophie couldn't produce children? Isn't that what we learned from the early police enquiries?'

'Yes, but women do have youngsters later in life — she was thirty-two when he was born.'

'But he's not a Caleb, sir; he's Sophie's eldest male child yet he's not called Caleb. I'd have thought a strongly family-orientated woman like Sophie would have given her eldest son the Caleb family name. But she didn't. I ask why.'

'What are you suggesting, Lorraine?' asked Mark.

'That he was not her natural son,' and she smiled again. 'It wouldn't surprise me if he was adopted.'

'You could be right, and it would answer a few questions. Yes, you could well be right!' He looked thoughtful. 'Come along, then, to the church we shall go!'

The Catholic church of St Ignatius was a late Victorian building set in a spacious churchyard surrounded by elms and holly trees. Its somewhat ornate exterior of dark stone, with saints and angels adorning the upper walls, hinted at what the interior would be like. It was heavily gilded inside, more like a French or Belgian church than an English one, and candles were burning in a side altar. Mark and Lorraine padded quietly down the aisle, admiring the beautifully carved Stations of the Cross while seeking some sign of the priest. They found him outside, weeding a patch of garden on the south side of the building.

'Good afternoon, Father,' Mark greeted him, and the stout priest straightened up with a groan, putting a hand to his aching back.

'Good afternoon. Really, I should delegate this task to a young parishioner but they all seem so busy these days. So I do it myself, even if it does make me ache all over. I tell myself it's God getting his own back on me for my fifty-five years of imperfections!'

'He'd have a whale of a time with me then!' grinned Mark who then introduced himself and Lorraine.

'So how can I help the law?' asked the priest, who said he was Father Simmons.

'I'm interested in checking your baptismal register for 1916,' said Mark. 'We're in charge of security for the forthcoming visit of Vice-President Hartley of America he's coming to England to look up his roots.' Mark embroidered his tale by saying they were filling some family gaps before the arrival of the great man. 'He's very interested in Patrick Harland. The Vice-President's grandfather, Luke Hartley, emigrated from Yorkshire to Canada and then America, and Sophie kept in touch about Patrick. There is a letter telling of his first Holy Communion, for example.'

'Yes, it was a sad day when we lost Patrick. He's buried here — that's his grave, the one with the flowers on.'

'He was born in 1916,' said Mark. 'I wondered if he was baptised here? It's the sort of question the Vice-President might ask, and if so, he might wish to pay a visit.'

'Oh, well, come into the presbytery. I'll have a look at the old records — they're all on my shelves, from the date the church was consecrated.'

Father Simmons took them into the presbytery and showed them into his simple study. As the priest pulled the register from the shelf, Mark asked, 'He'd have been baptised very soon after birth, wouldn't he?'

'Oh yes, especially at that time. He'd have been baptised within three days of being born, not like the Protestants, who waited weeks. Do you know his actual date of birth?'

'Sorry,' said Mark. 'We've just come from Hartleys and they said he was seventy-seven when he died in 1993. That makes his birthday around 1916. That's as near as I can get.'

'We'll check from late 1915 right through to the end of 1917,' said the priest. 'There were not too many entries at that time. I've been through these registers time and time again looking up family births and so forth. Now, Patrick Harland. Let me see when he was baptised.'

Before beginning his search, Father Simmons produced a bottle of sherry from a cupboard and offered them a glass; both accepted. While they sipped the fine dry sherry, he waded through his register, muttering the names as he turned the pages.

'Harland, Harland, Harland... There's a Harrison here... mmm...' But as he turned the pages, he failed to find any reference to Patrick Harland.

'It doesn't seem he was baptised here,' said Father Simmons. 'Sorry.'

'Perhaps it was done at another church?'

'Possibly. It would mean checking at every one. We have quite a number of Catholic churches in Hull — eighteen including this one. But knowing the family, Patrick would certainly have been baptised somewhere. I'm surprised it wasn't done here. Everything else was, this was his family church.'

'Thanks, Father.' Mark shook him by the hand. 'I hope the other priests are as helpful.'

'Maybe they will be. I wish you success and will pray for the Vice-President when he visits. I wonder if he'll come to this church?'

'I don't think the final itinerary has been drawn up, but he might want to see where Patrick made his first Holy Communion,' smiled Mark, draining his glass. 'Well, we'll be off. Thanks for your help.'

'It was my pleasure,' said Father Simmons, returning to his weeding as Mark and Lorraine left the premises.

As they drove away, Mark asked Lorraine, 'Well, what do you make of that?'

'It makes it even more likely that Patrick was adopted,' she said. 'The signs are all there. In 1916, Sophie was unable to produce children, and suddenly there is Patrick who doesn't have the Caleb name. So he's clearly not the eldest son of a Hartley. If he'd been Sophie's own child, he'd have been baptised in the family church, surely?'

'So we can forget him, can we?' Mark teased her.

'No, we can't, sir! We must find out where he came from, especially as his mother saw fit to keep in touch with Luke about him.'

'I agree! I was just teasing you. So how do we find out who Patrick really was? Who were his parents and why was he adopted? Where do we start that kind of enquiry?'

'Official adoption did not start until 1926,' she said. 'Therefore there'll be very few records.'

'Does it really matter who his parents were?' Mark was thinking aloud. 'Is he of any real importance to our murder enquiry?'

'Trace, Interrogate and Eliminate, sir? We must eliminate every name that comes within the scope of our enquiry, and that includes Patrick, surely. We have traced him to Hull and to Sophie who felt Luke should know about his progress, but the Pike Hill Hartleys froze Luke out of their lives. They tried to hide Luke's very existence from the younger generation. So I reckon we must find out more about Patrick before we eliminate him from our enquiries.'

'And that means a trip to St Catherine's index, does it? That'll be one almighty chore, searching through those records.'

'Don't forget, sir, that Luke is our chief suspect and he is also the Vice-President's grandfather. Our enquiries are taking us all the way back to Luke without our knowing why. Can you imagine the chaos this would cause Vice-President Hartley if he was searching his own roots?'

'I'm more concerned with an unsolved murder than family roots, Lorraine, but I daren't tell too many people about that! And what about Thomas, eh? Is it just coincidence that he might have been passing through Rosenthorpe station on the very day that his brother died? And surely a man like that would not pass so close to his old home without calling in? I know he didn't have a car and that people relied heavily on trains; it wouldn't surprise me if in those days there was a train every two hours or so between Thornborough and Rainesbury. So two questions arise, Lorraine. One: if Thomas was so close to home, why did he not call in? Two: if he did call in, why wasn't his visit mentioned to the murder team?'

'Do you think the family was covering up something, sir?'

'It looks very much as if they were, but what? To answer that, I think we need to go back to Wolversdale, Lorraine, and I need to talk to George again.'

'And what about that rhyme, sir? I mean, could the word hell be a corruption of Hull? *Jimmy Hartley's gone to Hull and his brother's gone as well.* The words might have changed over the years. And it's possible that the brother referred to could be Thomas. So did James ever go to Hull for any reason? Do we know that?'

'That's one for Duncan Young and HOLMES to answer for us, but it's another interesting theory.'

'And you'll need to find train times for 11th September 1916, won't you, sir.'

'You keep calling me sir, even when we're alone! I do have a Christian name, you know, and it's not Caleb!'

'Force of habit — I'm sorry. Ignore me when I do that — but it is a mark of respect, Mark! If I call you sir for most of the time, I won't be disrespectful in public, will I?'

'I know, I'm sorry. Rank is a bloody nuisance at times. It means you can't be friends with whoever you want just because they're of a different rank. I hate it, to be honest.'

'But I don't mind calling you sir, sir!'

'I do. I hate it...really I do.'

'I'll try to remember to call you Mark, sir, when we're alone.'

'Like now?'

She grinned, having teased him, and slipped her hand through his arm.

'Where to now?' she asked.

'Back to Thirklewood Hall, I think. I want to check Luke's signature if that's possible, but without the Americans realising why I have one of his statements on a murder file! I wonder if anything else has happened while we've been away?'

CHAPTER FIFTEEN

After the Detective Superintendent had left Pike Hill Farm that morning, George Hartley had called his wife.

'Christine,' he'd shouted into the kitchen. 'When we were living in t'farmhouse, can you remember what happened to Great Uncle James's stuff?'

'That old trunk, you mean?' She'd come into the lounge, drying a cup that the men had been using.

'Aye, a big brown tin trunk it was. My dad told me to take good care on't, not to throw t'stuff out, it used to belong to Great Uncle James.'

'Well, it was there when we left, in that box room at the back of t'house, upstairs. Under a lot of other things, old boxes of this and that, stuff that had been there for years.'

'Our Alan knows not to chuck it out, doesn't he?'

'You told him not to,' Mrs Hartley had said. 'You explained it was heirlooms, stuff that had belonged to James before he died, and Alan said he'd not have it removed, not ever. It'll stay there for when Paul Caleb takes over t'farm and he'll hand it down.'

'I never did have a look inside yon trunk,' George had told her. 'I've no idea what's in there.'

'Me neither,' she'd admitted. 'It was sort of sacred, if you know what I mean, I'd have felt dirty if I touched anything of his. I would have felt I was trespassing, interfering with his belongings, so I never looked inside either. Anyway, why do you want to know all this?'

'You know that Vice-President chap who's coming, well, the police are looking after his security and they're checking on all t'family, helping him to trace his ancestors. That detective chap reckons the American will be interested in Great Uncle James, him being shot in t'first war. So I thought I might check his things over, just in case there was summat that would interest those Yanks. Heirlooms and things, personal bits and pieces to look at.'

'Does that mean we are related to the American?'

'I reckon we could be cousins — we should find out for certain before too long. The American's dad went to Canada from York-shire in 1916, they called him Luke Caleb Hartley. Now my dad never said owt about a Luke Caleb and there's nowt in our family bible, but the police reckon he did come from here. They're doing a bit of checking up, you see, ready for when t'American gets here.'

'I can't say I want a lot of American tourists tramping over our land checking their family roots,' Christine had remarked.

'Our graveyard at St Monica's should keep 'em happy,' he'd laughed. 'Great Uncle James is there, and there's the grave of Sarah and Caleb and some others.'

'So you don't intend selling things from James's trunk?'

'No! 'Course I don't. I just want to see what's inside. There's no harm in that — it might help us to trace our relations from t'past. I don't know anyone else who's looked inside, do you?'

'Your dad always said he'd never looked, he said the trunk had to stay with the farmhouse so long as Hartleys lived there, and so, apart from dusting it once a week, I never looked inside either. It was allus locked, anyway. Mind, I can't remember anybody saying we shouldn't look.'

'Right. Well, I've got t'key, it passes from father to son, and I reckon this visit by an American Vice-President who might happen to be a distant relation of ours is a good enough reason to open it up. Come along, I'm going over to t'farmhouse to find it.'

'You go without me, I've enough to do without stirring up a lot of mouldy dust. Let me know what you find.'

And so George, a heavy-footed man, had stomped across the yard to the house where Alan's wife, Jennifer, was sweeping the flagstones. The key to the trunk was in his hands.

'Hello, Dad,' she'd smiled. She was a solidly built woman of thirty-five with a scarf around her fair hair and a smile on her handsome pink cheeks. She wore a pair of green Wellington boots, jeans and a colourful sweater. 'What brings you here this morning?'

'That chest of Great Uncle James's stuff. It's in the loft, isn't it?'

'Yes. Alan said it was best there, better than being in the house. He felt the kids wouldn't be tempted to try and open it and use whatever's inside for playing with.'

'Does it contain clothes, you reckon?'

'Well, it might hold some army uniform, him being a soldier, and if it does, they'd be in there nicking the stuff for fancy dress parties or whatever. So it's safe, Dad, if that's bothering you.'

'I want to have a look inside,' announced George. 'It's to do with that American chap that's coming.'

'Well, we might find out at long last exactly what's in there, so help yourself. You know the way.'

He tramped up the first flight of stairs in the spacious house which had been his home since childhood, the memories stirring as the familiar sights, sounds and scents assailed him. Then he clambered up the narrow flight of wooden stairs into the loft. Years before, the loft had been equipped with a stout wooden floor so that it could be used for storage and even serve as sleeping accommodation if required. George had installed electric lights and central heating, so it was now a cosy, dry and comfortable room, large enough to sleep half a dozen guests if necessary.

There were roof windows too, and they boasted stunning views across the moors.

Here were disused beds, mattresses, chairs and curtains, boxes of childhood toys, some of which would be worth a fortune for collectors, old paintings, fire screens… The loft was the repository of family belongings spanning a century at least and probably longer. As George stood and looked at the bewildering array of objects, he realised that if ever the farm required an injection of capital, then a useful sum could be raised by auctioning some of these items as antiques.

But that was not of immediate concern. Right now, his objective was the tin chest of Great Uncle James. He found it with no trouble; it had been pushed into a convenient space against a wall and on it rested an old ironing board, two deck chairs and the top of a kitchen table, recently used as a board for cutting and preparing wallpaper. Shifting these oddments, George revealed the old trunk. In rough handwriting on top, done in whitewash or paint, was the name 'James Reuben Hartley'. The trunk, some four feet long by two feet wide, stood about two feet high and had a rounded lid. A clasp fastened the lid and it was securely padlocked.

As he stood above the trunk, George now felt a distinct unwillingness to open it. After what the policeman had told him, he felt that it might reveal something unpleasant.

Already, his family traditions had been jolted by the truth about James's death, but there was the additional mystery of Luke. Why had the present generations not been told about Great Uncle Luke and his emigration? George, approaching the end of his own life, was wise enough to realise that he was under no obligation to tell anyone what he might find here; he could allow the family traditions and legends to continue. He could let everyone continue in the belief that James had died an honourable if mysterious death, and he considered there was little need to inform them that there had once been a Great Uncle Luke who was master of Pike Hill Farm. But, at the same time, George was astute enough to see that if these Americans did begin to delve very deeply into the family background, then they would surely uncover the truths — just as the policeman had done, so very quickly. And perhaps that policeman knew more about Luke? After all, Luke was the founder of the American branch of the family so somebody overseas must know a good deal about him. There were bound to be some facts that had been obscured since his departure from Pike Hill Farm in 1916.

It was with mixed feelings, therefore, that George Hartley brushed away the dust, unlocked the clasp and raised the lid of James's trunk. It was very dark in this corner and he was unable to see the contents, so he gripped one of the handles at the end and hauled the trunk a few yards.

Once it was nearer the centre of the floor, the light was above it and now he could carry out his inspection. The first impression was that it had been neatly and systematically packed. The contents appeared to have been carefully handled and positioned; an old army blanket covered the top, and underneath everything was neat and tidily stored. George did not feel like disturbing the contents. But, as the senior member of the Hartleys, facing what might be a family crisis centred upon James, he felt that he must go through the trunk.

As he cast aside the old blanket, he saw a pile of books in one corner and lifted them out to inspect them; they comprised children's books of the last century and early years of this one. Slipped among them was a rosary, a statue of St James the Great and some medallions of the Blessed Virgin Mary and St Christopher. There were some juvenile religious books, a child's missal, a First Communion book, a catechism, a picture book of the gospels and another about the life of Jesus. There were novels too: he found an 1877 edition of *Black Beauty* which said inside, 'Sarah, her book, Christmas 1877'. Sarah would be James's mother, George's own great grandmother — George felt sure she had packed this trunk as a memorial to her beloved son.

She had included *Cranford* by Mrs Gaskell with coloured pen-and-ink sketches, and among several books of poems were the works of Burns, Cowper and Milton, the last being a school prize awarded to Sarah in 1864. From this, he deduced that James had liked reading.

There were some photographs of James as a child, James as a growing boy and later as a teenager with a sheep-dog at his side. One taken of him in his early twenties showed him with a central parting in his dark hair and a bushy moustache, the fashion of the time.

There were the letters that James had sent home during his training with the Green Howards, all tied in a parcel with a piece of pink ribbon, and mementoes of his formative years such as his First Communion certificate, a confirmation picture of the Last Supper and a handwriting prize for winning a schools hand-writing competition. There were some small and childish wooden creations — a cross, a bookrack, a toothbrush holder, all apparently made by James in woodwork classes at school because they were among his arithmetic exercise books. There was one of his essays too, written when he was nine. It was called 'Our Farm' and revealed an almost idyllic lifestyle: James spending time exploring the woods and moors, finding barn owl nests in the barn or helping to feed the hens. There were some watercolour paintings too, the artist being 'James Hartley, aged 8 ¾'.

George also found two toys, a battered wooden railway engine painted green and a box of lead soldiers, Coldstream Guards by the look of them. His army issues were here too — his tin hat, his webbing, his socks, his tunic, trousers and puttees, all neatly cleaned and pressed where necessary. His boots were beneath the kit; they were clean and looked almost unused.

In a tin box, George found James's peaked cap complete with Green Howards badge. Gingerly and with the utmost care, he lifted out each of these items, one by one, and placed them on the blanket which he had spread across the floorboards. James's backpack and its contents were next to be lifted out. The huge greatcoat occupied most of the backpack, but other oddments here included a trench pipe, matches, the housewife, the cleaning materials, iron rations, tea-making equipment, water purifying tablets, water bottle, billy can, knife, fork and spoon... All were still here, just as James had left them. His kitbag now contained two army blankets, some woollen gloves and spare socks and a heavy military issue woollen sweater.

In a brown envelope, George found a number of Mass cards. Printed on sturdy white high-quality paper, they sported black edges and black printing. These announced James's death and the date of his funeral, and would have been sent to friends, relations and villagers to inform them of the Requiem Mass and interment.

The cards bore the same verse as his tombstone and these were clearly the spares. James's mother had kept them. He found himself reading some of the paperwork, scanning the novels, looking for inscriptions inside or some clue as to James's loves and life, although he did not open the letters. He found several of James's sheep-dog trial certificates; he'd won several local competitions with Ben, his border collie, and there was a small silver-coloured cup bearing his name. The cup bore Ben's name alongside. It was called the Wolversdale Trophy. His mum would have been proud of that.

One by one, the contents of James's trunk were removed until George could see the base. There remained one large wooden box, just over a foot in length by some ten inches in width and two or three inches deep. It had a hinged lid, about an inch in depth. He wondered what it contained. He tried to lift it out, but it was very heavy, and two hands were required. Gingerly, therefore, he hoisted the weighty box from the trunk and placed it on the floor. Kneeling beside it, he slipped aside the two hooks which held the lid shut. It opened easily; he was shocked by the contents.

It contained a revolver.

CHAPTER SIXTEEN

When she returned to Thirklewood Hall, Lorraine went straight to her room to get washed and changed into something more casual for the evening meal. Mark said he wanted to know if anything of interest had cropped up during his absence, so he turned towards the Potting Shed, nerve centre of Operation Roots. Once he was inside, Detective Inspector Paul Larkin hailed him.

'Sir, there was a telephone call for you, from George Hartley of Pike Hill Farm.'

'I went to see him this morning. What does he want?'

'He wants to see you. It's important, but not desperately urgent, he says. He wouldn't tell me what it was about!'

'Right, I'll ring him before I eat,' promised Mark. 'Now, has anything else of importance happened here?'

'No, it's all quiet, we're ticking over nicely. The latest is that the Americans have drawn up a detailed list of Hartleys that the Vice-President intends to visit. It includes the cousins at Hull — I know you've been there — and of course he wants to talk to George Hartley and his offspring at Pike Hill Farm and see the graves at Wolversdale. The dates are the 12th at Wolversdale, the

13th at Hull, and he's talking of visiting the Borthwick Institute in York on the 14th, to see if they have any of his family records.'

'You've checked the known family members through the PNC to see if any have terrorist links or other associations that would cause problems, and you've checked with CRO for criminal records?'

'Yes, sir, we've done all the routine checks; nothing's emerged that would give cause for concern. One or two have convictions — there's a Caleb James born in 1929 who's got a conviction for GBH but that was way back in 1949. He'll be a half-cousin of the George you know. He lives in Durham.'

'The DPG and US agents will keep an eye on him, I'm sure, although I can't see him being a problem. So we have no youngsters with violent anti-American attitudes?'

'There is one younger member of the family called Andrew Caleb Sutton, born 1963, who is a known hunt saboteur. He gets carried away by his enthusiasm for stopping fox-hunters and has landed himself in court once or twice for causing a breach of the peace. He was bound over for two years last time — that was in February this year.'

'So long as he's against fox-hunters and not American Vice-Presidents, I don't think he'll cause problems. Again, the DPG will keep an eye on him and his activities over the next few days.'

'Good, and when he's out visiting, they don't want any of our men to accompany the party. Scotland Yard and the White House agents will see to all that.'

'Does the Vice-President intend bringing any of the Hartley clan here? Or taking them to one of the local hotels for a meal or anything like that?'

'I asked if any of them were expected here but it seems no. If the Vice-President has anything to show them, such as his own family records, he'll take the papers with him during his visits.'

'Good, that's one problem less to think about. It seems we'll be having a quiet time.'

'I got this latest gen from one of the Scotland Yard team, sir, a Detective Superintendent Birchall. He reckons the Home Office is not very chuffed about the Vice-President's private visit — they see him as a trouble-maker.'

'Trouble-maker?'

'Apparently, according to Yard intelligence, he has shown a lot of anti-British sentiment when he's been overseas, and he takes every opportunity to criticise this country and our government. We're not quite sure what he's up to.'

'Doesn't anyone have any idea?'

'He's got strong sympathies with Ireland, it seems; that dictates his overall attitude.'

'So why's he coming here to discover his English roots?'

'They suspect he's hoping to make some political capital out of it in due course, something along the lines that if he can show he really has British ancestry, his critical views will be taken more seriously, perhaps by foreign powers.'

'Politicians are wily animals,' said Pemberton. 'I'm glad I'm not in that profession. I wonder how he'll react if we can prove his grandad was a murderer?'

'It might shut him up, sir.'

'That's if he ever finds out — we might be told to keep it quiet!'

'We're good at doing as we're told, sir.'

'It's our job, Paul. So, apart from that, it's otherwise very quiet, eh?'

'Yes, sir, very quiet. Too bloody quiet, to be honest.'

'How about the programming of the Hartley file into HOLMES? Has anything of further interest come to notice?'

'Nothing, sir. I've reread the file but can't see anything that's going to help us come to a firm conclusion. Luke's still highest in the frame, but that's all; there's still no hard evidence of his guilt, certainly no proof.'

At this point, Mark explained about the movements of Thomas Hartley and asked Larkin if he could find out anything about train times on the North-Eastern Railway on 11th September 1916, suggesting the National Railway Museum in York as the best starting point. He explained why this was of interest and Paul said he would reread the relevant statements.

'See if there's any hint anywhere that Thomas was at Pike Hill Farm, or anywhere in the vicinity, on the day of James's death.'

'Now, sir?'

'No, it's gone five o'clock, Paul, it's knocking-off time.'

'I don't mind, sir, I've nothing else to do.'

'As you wish, but I'm not compelling you to work extra time — the Chief's given me a bollocking for always being at work and says I mustn't encourage my staff to do likewise. Anyway, thanks for your assistance. I'll give old Mr George Hartley a buzz now, then I'll get washed and changed and have a meal. See you in the bar later? I'll buy you a pint!'

'In half an hour?'

'You're on!'

In the privacy of his own office, Mark rang George Hartley at Pike Hill Farm.

'It's Detective Superintendent Pemberton,' he announced. 'I've just got in. You left a message for me to ring?'

'Aye, that's right, Mr Pemberton. You remember that trunk I told you about, Great Uncle James's stuff?'

'That's right.'

'Well, it's still here just as I thought, in the loft of the farm-house. It's untouched since James's mother packed it but I had a look inside this afternoon.'

'Is there anything that might interest me?' asked Mark.

'I reckon there is, there's a lot of personal things, but there's a revolver, Mr Pemberton. It looks like an army issue to me. I haven't touched it.'

'A revolver? Good God, what's it doing there?'

'Nay, Mr Pemberton, I've no idea. I thought you'd better look at it and mebbe take it away. Confiscate it or summat. It's not a very good idea having a thing like that lying around with kids in the house and I'll be happy for it to be removed.'

'I'll come and get it,' said Mark, feeling the flutter of excitement in his chest. 'What else does the trunk contain?'

'Bits of all sorts. His army stuff, things he had as a child, church things, books, certificates from school and so on, letters.'

'What sort of letters?'

'I didn't open them, Mr Pemberton, they're all wrapped up in ribbon.'

'What addresses were on the envelopes?'

'Oh, well, they were to his mum, here at the farm. At least the top one was.'

'I'll have something to eat, then I'll come straight over to Wolversdale. Would seven o'clock this evening be all right?'

'Aye, whatever you say, Mr Pemberton.' Mark had to tell Paul Larkin that the promised pint had evaporated, at least for the time being, and he explained the new development.

'Are you suggesting that revolver's the murder weapon, sir?' Paul asked.

'What else?' said Pemberton. 'The murder weapon was never found, the bullet had come from a .45 calibre weapon, and we still have the bullet. If we have a firearm to work on, we can at least get a ballistic comparison, Paul — after all these years!'

'It's a long shot, but if this was the murder weapon, how did it come to be hidden at the farm? I thought the police had searched the premises?'

'They did, but how long does it take to thoroughly search a farm for something as small as a revolver? You could conceal revolvers and even rifles all over a farm like that and they'd never be found, even by modern methods. I once knew a thief who hid an airgun between the corrugated iron sheets which formed the wall of a pigsty. He simply unbolted the interior lining, popped the gun on to a spar inside, and replaced the sheet. There was no way you'd have found that airgun without knowing where to look. I believe Luke did something like that. I think he kept it hidden until well after the police search. So, if this is the murder weapon, it puts Luke even higher in the frame. I reckon he used it to kill his brother, then returned to the farm with the revolver hidden among the tools he carried in the trap. He admitted carrying tools in a bag — that would be to explain any package that might be noticed. Once home, he hid the revolver.'

'But not in the trunk, surely?'

'Not at the outset. I'll bet he hid it in one of the outbuildings, then before he left the country, he smuggled it into this trunk, knowing his mother had gathered her mementoes of James and put them here. He'd know the trunk would never be opened, not while his mother was alive anyway, and so where better to hide the revolver than in the trunk among James's other things? If anybody found it here, they'd assume it had belonged to James, they'd think it was his service issue revolver. Luke would have access to the key, remember, being the eldest son. And, years later, if it was found, who would know its history? All would assume it had belonged to James, being among his other military equip-ment. Years later, if the gun was discovered, everyone would think James's mother had kept it as a souvenir, never thinking it was the cause of his death. But *we* know it wasn't James's service issue — we know that privates in the Green Howards weren't issued with revolvers or pistols. They did bring their rifles back home, however, minus ammunition. Soldiers who returned *after* the war would sometimes bring trophies — guns they'd captured from the enemy. In those days, to find a gun among a soldier's belongings was quite normal. So there are all sorts of sound reasons for hiding the revolver among James's own things — especially if it was the murder weapon.'

'So where would Luke get a revolver?' asked Larkin.

'The Boer War perhaps? He was a veteran — he could have brought his own revolver home, or he could have seized one as a souvenir. Lots of soldiers did, especially during the Boer War. He probably had a round or two to match it, but they've gone. And I wonder how many of his family knew he'd brought a revolver home? Maybe some, maybe none.'

'But James's rifle isn't with the stuff in the trunk. It wasn't retained.'

'No, the police would have seized that as evidence from the beginning, and it would have been returned to the Green Howards in due course. There should be a receipt for that in the file. But the army wouldn't want his personal clothes back, or the items of equipment which were expendable; they'd be written off just as if he'd been lost in the war. So Mum kept them — it's entirely understandable.'

'If this was the murder weapon, sir, and if Luke used it, I'm not totally convinced he would bring it out of hiding and place it among his brother's belongings.'

'If Luke had left it hidden, Paul you can guarantee that eventually it would be found. He would know that. You can't hide a thing like that without somebody finding it sooner or later and reporting it. If it was found in its hiding place, even months or years later, whether on the farm or elsewhere, it would clearly be considered as the weapon which had killed James. I'm sure you would agree. The mere fact that it had been hidden would suggest that.'

'Yes, I can understand that.'

'So Luke left home for a new life in Canada, totally unsuspected of being the murderer. Suppose the gun had been found after he'd gone, months or even years afterwards?'

'Yes, I can see what the reaction would be. They'd all suspect him — no one else would be able to account for the gun's presence and so the finger of suspicion would be directed towards Luke, who'd apparently run away to avoid capture. It might even have had his fingerprints on it — fingerprints were regarded as important even at that time.'

'Exactly, so Luke prevented all that by placing the gun among

James's belongings at some stage just before he left for Canada. Once his mother had filled the trunk with James's things, she'd not want anyone else to touch it, and that respect has passed right down through the family. Just think — if we hadn't alerted George, we'd never have found what might be the gun that killed his Great Uncle James. It was the perfect hiding place.'

'I can see that now, sir.'

'Which means, Paul, that if I'm right about Luke, he was a most cunning, clever and devious sort of character!'

'You'll seize it as evidence, then?'

'You bet I will, and I'll submit it to a ballistics examination along with the bullet we've still got. Fancy, after all this time, we might have found the murder weapon!'

'What about the rest of the stuff?'

'George mentioned some letters. I'd like to read them, Paul. The police of the time did read them but returned them to the family without making copies. We might find a clue in them.'

'What sort of a clue, sir?'

'Something to explain why James was murdered. We still haven't the remotest idea of a motive, have we?'

'And we'll be able to subject the actual letters to the scrutiny of dear old HOLMES?'

'Of course. We'll photocopy them before returning them to the family. I'd like Lorraine to read the letters; a woman's interpretation might be advantageous. I'll be interested to see what she thinks about James's mother.'

'OK, fine.'

'Look, Paul, I'm sorry to dash off again and leave you in charge, but tomorrow, you take time out and visit the Railway Museum. I'll stay in and do my stuff as the officer in charge!'

'Thanks, sir, yes — I'd welcome an outing.' Pemberton left Thirklewood Hall and realised he had ample time to reach Pike Hill Farm in Wolversdale. This time he was alone because Lorraine had said she wanted to wash her hair and he decided to occupy his spare time by calling on Millicent Roe. Rosenthorpe was but a short drive from Wolversdale. She'd been most abrupt with Lorraine and Mark was determined to interview her, the only known surviving witness from 1916.

When he arrived at the untidy cottage, the door was open, and a light was burning. He rapped on the woodwork, noting it could do with a coat of paint. Inside, he could see a fire smouldering in the grate and then an elderly woman appeared. She was carrying a teapot.

'Yes, what do you want?' she demanded.

'Miss Roe?' he asked politely.

'Aye, that's me. Who are you?'

'Pemberton is the name. Detective Superintendent Mark Pemberton.'

'If it's to do with that Hartley business, I'm saying nowt. I had one of your detective women snooping about yesterday, asking questions. What's going on, mister? Why are they suddenly asking about Jimmy Hartley all over again?'

'We've reopened enquiries into his murder,' Mark said. 'I'm in charge of the enquiries and you are the only surviving witness, you see. That means you're important.'

'I said my bit to Inspector Dawson. I told him what I'd seen.'

'You were just a child then, Millicent.' Pemberton was gentle with her although it was evident he was not going to be invited inside. 'I wondered whether, as you grew older, your memory of the horse and cart, or pony and trap, had grown any clearer.'

She sighed. 'I told Dawson and I'm telling you that what I saw I saw. I saw a man sitting in a horse and cart, that's all. I don't know who he was. I still don't.'

'Did you know Luke Hartley, when you were a girl?'

'There were lots of Mr Hartleys in them days.' She spoke quietly. 'They were a big family, allus knocking about our village, Rosenthorpe as well as Wolversdale.'

'You saw them a lot?'

'Yes, always coming and going, one or other of them, having their horses shod or cart wheels fixed. Decent folk, mister. I never knew which was which. I was only a kid — they were all grown-ups, all just Mr Hartleys to me.'

'So was the man in the cart one of those Mr Hartleys?' he pressed her.

'I don't know, God knows I don't! How many more times do I have to say I don't know who that man was!'

'I wondered if, as you grew older, you realised who it might have been.'

She merely shook her head, almost in exasperation.

He went on, 'I'm sorry to press you like this, but it is so important. Did you know any of the younger Hartleys?'

'Only that lad-fond lass of theirs.'

'Lad-fond?'

'Allus chasing the lads, she was. Her mother would send her down here to t'shops and she'd spend her time chatting to the lads instead of going about her business.'

'Why can you remember her?'

'Aye, I can. She was a right flirt, allus chatting to the lads, teasing 'em, leading 'em on. The local lasses didn't stand a chance when she was around. Bonny lass she was, older than me, of course. Same age as my elder sister, Dora. She's gone now, God bless her, my sister that is, but she never stood a chance against that Hartley lass. All our local lasses were jealous, I used to hear my cousin go on about her…'

'So that's how you remember her? She charmed the boys, eh? That would be Sarah, was it?'

'Aye, Sarah, that's the one. She went to Canada, I remember. And good riddance, that's what the local lasses said. allus trying to steal other lasses' boyfriends she was. My mother knew her, you see; my mother had been at school with her mum — Edith, she was. Edith Hartley.'

'Luke was Sarah's dad, Millicent. Did you ever see them together? As a family?'

'No, never. We never got up to the farm and they allus came down here themselves, Sarah would come on her pony. Allus well kitted out, she was, they seemed to have plenty of money. We had nowt, you see. I was right jealous of her then, but not now. Money's not everything, they've had their troubles.'

'What sort of troubles?'

'Well, Jimmy mainly. A murder in the family. That's awful, especially when they never caught the killer. I mean, there was bound to be suspicions, talk about family troubles, rumours, that sort of thing.'

'What sort of rumours, Millicent?'

'I might have repeated 'em as a bairn, Mr Pemberton, but I've grown up now and it's not for me to keep spreading tales that might not be true. There was talk of wartime spies being responsible, some said Jimmy had stumbled on a German doing summat and died because of it. Then some said it was nowt to do with the war, that Jimmy deserved to die, if you know what I mean.'

'No, I don't know...'

'Then if you can't find out, it's mebbe not true so I'd best shut up. Least said, soonest mended.'

'I'm sorry to keep pestering you like this, but as I said, it is very important. Even now, we have no idea why James was killed, and I just wondered if the man in the cart might have been Luke Hartley, Sarah's father?'

'It might, and it might not, I just don't know.' She sighed. 'Dawson kept asking me that and I couldn't say one way or the other, and I still can't. If I could say it was him, I would. But I don't know and that's God's honest truth. I might be a bit of a gossip, but I don't tell lies. If I said I was certain it was Luke in that cart, I'd be telling a lie and if I'd said that at the time, I could have got him hanged, couldn't I? Now think of that — suppose I had said it was him when it wasn't? Me, getting a man hanged... It could have happened, Mr Pemberton, me a lass of six getting a respected local man hanged for summat he might not have done... You see why I stick to my guns, why I can't say who I saw that day? God knows I've tried to think who it was but no, I just do not know. I have my principles...'

'You are right, of course, Millicent; you must tell the truth at all times.'

'I'd been brought up to be truthful, you see.'

'I congratulate you on that. So, even as a little girl, you knew not to say it was Luke — can I assume it wasn't anybody else you knew?'

'No, it wasn't anybody I knew. It was a man, like I said. I couldn't even describe what he looked like or what he was wearing. I just got a quick glimpse through the hedge as I went past. I mean, I never popped behind the hedge to see him, I just kept going, to get home for my tea.'

'Thanks, Millicent. I'm sorry to have taken up your time.'

'I can't think why you want to know all this,' and she closed the door, not slamming it as she had done with Lorraine. He left the dirty house and she stood at the window to observe his departure, framed in the light of the dim bulb which glowed inside. In spite of his brief interview, he felt sure she did have some idea of the identity of the man behind the hedge. She would take the knowledge to her grave, he believed; nonetheless, he did feel she had saved Luke from the hangman's noose. Positive evidence from Millicent and Lapsley would have convicted him.

Pemberton climbed into his car and turned towards Wolversdale. George Hartley was waiting when he arrived and wasted no time introducing him to his son, Alan, before escorting him through the corridors of the old farmhouse and up to the attic. Alan came with them; he was a younger version of his father with the distinctive sturdiness and colouring of the Hartleys. Even in him, Mark could see the resemblance to the photograph of the Vice-President.

'I've explained to our Alan that you're doing a bit of background checking before t'Vice-President arrives,' George said, not once mentioning the real reason for Mark's visit. 'But, well, when I turned this gun up, I thought you'd better take it. We don't want unlicensed guns around the house, do we, Alan? These things are dangerous, and I can't see we need to keep it as an heirloom of Great Uncle James.'

'I had no idea it was there,' said the younger Hartley. 'We've never once looked in that old trunk. We knew it held Great Uncle James's stuff and saw no need to go poking around.'

'I'll get rid of it for you,' said Mark. 'I'll treat it as a surrendered weapon.'

In the attic, Mark saw the neatly laid out contents of the old trunk and was immediately handed the revolver in its wooden box. He opened it to find a Smith and Wesson .45 revolver in good condition, well-greased and displaying the tiniest hint of rust on the top of the barrel. There was no ammunition with it, nor any other accoutrements such as cleaning rods.

'Nice gun,' he said, closing the box and tucking it under his arm. It was very heavy. 'I'll give you a receipt, Mr Hartley. Now, this is the other stuff, eh? All belonging to your Great Uncle James?'

'Aye, stuff his mother had kept for years, Mr Pemberton. You'll not be interested in this, will you?'

Mark inspected the other items, picking up the occasional piece of military kit, but decided there was nothing of any value to him, with the possible exception of the letters.

'I wouldn't mind a look at the letters,' he said, somehow feeling he was prying into their private lives. 'It'll mean taking them away, I'm afraid. I can't read them here, it would take a long time.'

'Well, I can't see any problem with that, can you, Alan? I mean, all parties are dead and gone, and you'd let us have 'em back?'

'Oh yes, of course. I'd have them back here before the Vice-President pays his visit, just in case you wanted him to see them.'

And so father and son allowed Pemberton to carry off the bundle of precious letters. He had a cup of tea and a piece of cake with Alan and his wife, Jennifer, and then thanked them, wishing them luck for the forthcoming Vice-Presidential visit.

After leaving Alan's house, however, Mark decided to ask George what he knew about the Hull section of his family.

CHAPTER SEVENTEEN

In his comfortable bungalow, George Hartley told Pemberton that he knew a little about his Hull cousins. He added that when his own father had died in 1975, several of the Hull cousins had attended the funeral.

'Was there a man called Patrick among them?' asked Mark. 'He'd have been about sixty then. Patrick Harland.'

'Cousin Patrick, yes. He worked for Hartleys of Hull, summat to do with the accounts side. A bachelor. No wife or family. I remember me and him having a chat about my accounts, saying how farmers were clobbered by the tax man. He said he might be able to help, but I never took him up on that.'

'Who was he, George?' asked Mark. 'Who was he? He was Cousin Patrick.'

'Yes, but whose son was he? What precisely was his relationship with the family? Do you know?'

'He was Aunt Sophie's lad, at least I always thought he was. Like I said before, I was never one for delving into family backgrounds. Why ask about him, Mr Pemberton? Is there summat else I should be knowing about?'

'He's not listed in your family bible, is he?'

175

'You've a good memory! But now you mention it, no, his name's not there.'

'I know the old bible was destroyed, but the new one, the one your father began to compile, did mention Sophie; she was married in 1912 to a man called Aiden Harland.'

'Aye, that's right.'

'But there was no mention of a family for Sophie and her husband,' said Mark. 'And our files, the ones covering the murder, hinted that Sophie couldn't bear children. She had none then, in 1916, and yet, according to the Hull Hartleys, via a man called Hurworth, Patrick was born in 1916.'

'Was he, by gum? Then she might have adopted him, eh?'

'That thought had occurred to me, Mr Hartley, which is why I'm asking you now. We couldn't find any reference to his baptism in St Ignatius' church in Hull where he made his first communion, but I didn't check any of the others.'

'But if he was adopted, Mr Pemberton, he could have been baptised anywhere. In those days, Catholics allus baptised their bairns on the very first Sunday after they were born. So you'd have to find out where he was born, then you'd find out if he was baptised in a Catholic church.'

'Thanks — I thought of checking on that, but it's hard knowing where to start, George. Formal adoption wasn't introduced until 1926, so I doubt if there are any detailed records about Patrick. I just wondered if you knew anything more about him. It was a long shot.'

'Nay, lad, I'm sorry, but Patrick's dead now, isn't he?'

'Last year, unfortunately. I'm told he would have loved to have met the Vice-President.'

'You could allus try the Catholic Adoption Society, they might know where to start looking. I know some folks hereabouts who have got good service from them.'

'Thanks, I might do that. Well, I must be off. Goodnight, George, and thanks for your help.'

'I hope you get it all sorted out before that American chap comes,' said George.

'So do I!' There was feeling in every word.

* * *

FIRST THING NEXT MORNING, Saturday 9th July, Mark Pemberton assembled his officers for a conference and gave them details of everything he had discovered to date. It gave them a welcome insight into the fact that this old murder investigation was far from defunct; the enquiry was very much alive and now that the murder weapon might have been found, it would add to the motivation of the teams.

'So...' Mark produced the Smith and Wesson from its box and showed it to them. 'Sarge?'

He passed it to Detective Sergeant Tony Ashton.

'Sarge, we have the bullet which was found in James's body and now we have that firearm. Have words with the ballistics lab in Nottingham as soon as you can to see if they can match the gun with the bullet. Drive down there if it's necessary. Tell them it's an old case, but stress that it's urgent in view of the impending visit of the American Vice-President. What I need to know is whether that bullet was fired from that weapon. I know it's Saturday, but they do function at weekends if it's urgent. And this is.'

'Very good, sir,' said Ashton.

'Lorraine, I want you to read through all these letters. I had a look at them last night when I got back. Some are from James to his mother, the others from mother to James, all written while he was undergoing training. Your feminine intuition might find something that our merely male minds have missed.'

'Such as what, sir? What am I looking for?'

'Some hint as to the reason for James's death. Some clue as to why it happened...something not shown in the files, something overlooked by the old detectives, something known only to the family, perhaps. Take your time, and when you've finished, get every one of them photocopied and we'll have them entered in HOLMES. Then we can return them to George Hartley.'

'Yes, sir.'

'Paul?'

Detective Inspector Larkin smiled. 'Sir?'

'I believe you're off to the National Railway Museum in York to check train times for 11th September 1916, if they've got any old timetables. We want the North-Eastern Railway, Thornborough to Rainesbury route and the Drakenedge to Rainesbury route.'

'Right, I'll enjoy that.'

'We want to know if it was possible for Thomas Hartley to leave Thornborough on one train, get off at Rosenthorpe, spend time with his family at Wolversdale, and then catch another train to complete his journey to Rainesbury, either the same day or the day following. I think he might have done that, but we need to know whether it was feasible.'

'Yes, sir.'

'Duncan?'

DC Young, the HOLMES programmer, put up his hand.

'You'll need photocopies of all this new stuff to enter into your magic box. I'll leave that with you. As always, we're looking for gaps in the evidence. Lorraine?'

'Sir?'

'When you've finished with those letters, I've another job for you. Concerning our mystery man, Patrick Harland. George Hartley has met him, at a family funeral, and regarded him as a cousin. He thought he was Sophie's son. What I need to know is whether Patrick was the natural son of Sophie, perhaps born late in life, or whether he was adopted. Try the Catholic Adoption Society for starters — George says they're very helpful.'

'Sir,' interrupted Larkin, 'I'm a Catholic and if Patrick was confirmed at St Ignatius' church, they would have needed to obtain his baptismal certificate before the confirmation could go ahead. If you can trace his confirmation record, it should give the date of the baptism and might possibly show the place; confirmation certificates weren't issued but if you can find the baptismal certificate, his confirmation details will be endorsed upon it. Baptismal certificates are produced later for weddings and they are considered important.'

'So I can ignore the church where he was confirmed; all I need is to find out where he was baptised!' Lorraine said.

'That's it, Lorraine. A nice job for you in Hull — perhaps with a bit of time to do some shopping!'

'Thanks, sir, I'll enjoy the break from routine!'

And so Mark was able to provide his officers with some positive detection work, while simultaneously retaining staff to man the reception desk and maintain security in the Hall.

Having despatched them to their duties, he did a tour of Thirklewood Hall to make sure there were no problems, had a brief chat with both Mr Dunnock of the White House staff and Superintendent Birchall from Scotland Yard. It seemed they were happy with the security arrangements and had no criticisms. He therefore settled down in his own office to study the old file once more in view of the very recent developments. Then the telephone rang.

'This is Mrs Preston from the Green Howards Museum at Richmond. We talked the other day, about Private James Reuben Hartley.'

'Ah, yes.' He remembered the very helpful Mrs Preston.

'Well, the regimental HQ does not have any training records left from World War One, I'm sorry to tell you, so we couldn't obtain details of Hartley's service with us. However, there is a history of the Green Howards, it's part of the Famous Regiments series. I've looked at that, Superintendent, just on the off-chance, and your Private James Reuben Hartley is mentioned. I said there was a reference in the *Gazette,* but he's also mentioned in the history book because he was murdered just before going to France. The book gives quite a detailed account of his life. It was an unusual thing to happen, you see. I wondered if you were still interested in it.'

'We most certainly are!' His voice echoed his delight at this news. 'Does it provide much information?'

'I can tell you a little over the phone if you want, and then I could send a photocopy along to you.'

'Marvellous. So what's it tell us?'

'When he completed his training, his CO recorded his conduct as exemplary. He got good marks for all aspects of his training — close combat, bayonet work, drill, trench warfare, and he qualified as a marksman with the rifle.'

'So he was no softie?'

'Not according to this. One report says he was always polite to his NCOs, far more so than many of his colleagues, and they recommended he consider something other than the infantry. Having no profession, you see, he wasn't placed in one of the so-called expert brigades — engineers or whatever. Farm work wasn't regarded as a profession or skill. James had expressed an interest in horses, so it says, and it was suggested he transfer to the Hussars and become a Horsemaster. The 15th/19th (The Kings) Hussars were looking out for men with experience in horse management.'

'He never got that far?'

'No, he was due to sail to France from Folkestone via Boulogne, en route to the Somme, on 13th September — oddly enough, the Hussars were sailing at the same time on the same ship and he'd expressed delight that he would be among horses for the crossing.'

'But he came home on leave? Wasn't that rather odd?'

'It was compassionate leave, for just one night at home. There was a telegram from Wolversdale, it's mentioned in the account, and it asked if Private Hartley could be granted one day's compassionate leave due to his mother's sickness. His unit received this on 10th September and the only available date for leave was the 11th. He had to travel down to Folkestone by train on the 12th to join his ship. There's a note here to say he would be allowed to leave training, one day early, which was a rest day anyway, travel to York and then go home.'

'This is good stuff. Any more?'

'Yes, he was due to return to York station the following day to catch his train to Folkestone. The rest of his companions would be aboard that train. But he never made it.'

'He got killed in the meantime,' said Mark. 'Yes, I really would like to have a copy of that account. Before I ring off, though, who signed the telegram? Is it mentioned?'

'Somebody called Luke. It says, "Urgent, come home, mother very ill. Luke." The wording is reproduced.'

'And did he reply by telegram? Do we know that?'

'It doesn't say so here, but I guess he would have done, to answer and to say what time he would be arriving. Our history included this account because it was so unusual to have a soldier murdered like that; there was talk of a spy being responsible, but army intelligence rejected that. They said it was a civil murder, but no killer was ever brought to justice.'

'Mrs Preston, that is a most useful piece of information. I'm most grateful to you.'

'I'll put a photocopy in the first-class post today; if I miss today's collection, there is one on Sunday. You should have it by Monday morning.'

Mark told her where to send it, using the Thirklewood Hall address, and thanked her again, then recalled Lorraine and acquainted her with the details. He asked her to check the letters for any reference to James's sick mother, then went in to speak to Duncan Young.

'Duncan,' he said, 'while you've been programming this stuff into HOLMES, have you come across any reference to either a telegram, or to James's mother being ill?'

'There was a statement by a telegraph boy, sir, it's tucked away somewhere in the file, but I can't remember anything about Mrs Hartley being ill. Hang on, I'll access HOLMES about the telegram.'

Mark saw that the relevant file had been cross-referenced with both telegram and telegraph, the practice then being to deliver urgent messages by telegram. These came to the village post office and were put into a yellow envelope for delivery by a telegraph boy. Sometimes these 'boys' were disabled pensioners — very old boys indeed!

But HOLMES produced a statement by a young lad called John Bennison. He said he had been delivering a telegram in Rosenthorpe at about eleven thirty on the morning of Monday 11th September 1916 when he'd noticed Mr Hartley walking from the station, along the road towards Wolversdale. He was not carrying anything. Later, a pony and trap came and picked him up.

'We haven't paid much credence to this statement, sir, and neither did the original investigating officers.'

'And why not?'

'Well, this child, sir, the telegraph boy, he's only twelve and he's obviously made a mistake. Hartley didn't get off the train until the middle of the afternoon, 3.35pm, before he started to walk towards Wolversdale.'

'Duncan, never underestimate children. They will tell the truth as they see it. Now, I've just sent DI Larkin off to York to find the rail timetables for that day. You know why?'

'Something to do with a Mr Thomas Hartley...' And his voice trailed away.

'Yes. We want to know if a Mr Thomas Hartley arrived at Rosenthorpe that day and here we have the answer! A telegraph boy saw a Mr Hartley but didn't say which one! And the police probably assumed the kid was making a mistake about the time...'

'No, sir, perhaps not. They did ask Hull police to enquire about Thomas's movements at the material time, and it was their report that cleared Thomas. Not Dawson's.'

'Full marks to Dawson. I wonder why he did not take this statement further? Surely, if a Hartley had been seen in the village earlier...'

'It was long before the time of death, sir, long before James got off the train.'

'But long enough for a killer to hire a pony and trap and hide in waiting for his victim, Duncan. So we need to check this one pretty carefully — I think it says that Thomas Hartley was in the village, or at the farm, at the time of James's murder.'

'I'm sorry, sir, I assumed the boy was mistaken...'

'It could happen to anyone. Now, this throws a whole new light on things. I want to find out just who was at that farm on that day — but in the meantime, what about the telegraph boy? Did he deliver a dreaded yellow envelope to Pike Hill Farm?'

'No, sir, it was to a Mrs Hayes in Rosenthorpe, to say her sister was coming to stay on Thursday.'

'So there was no telegram for Pike Hill Farm?'

DC Young actioned HOLMES again to search for other references to telegrams, but there was none. Dawson had clearly concentrated upon events on the actual day of the murder and not before, probably thinking that a telegram sent on the 10th was of no consequence to his enquiries.

'Sir,' said Duncan Young, 'if James had sent a telegram home, it might not have come via Rosenthorpe. After all, the postal address of the farm is Wolversdale. If the Hartleys wanted to send telegrams or receive telegrams, they'd surely use their local post office at Wolversdale? There is no railway station at Wolversdale, which is why they used Rosenthorpe station.'

'You're right, of course. So Dawson never checked to see who had sent the sickness telegram from, say, Wolversdale post office?'

'I've found no record of that in the file, none.'

'In which case, he would never have known that someone had sent a telegram saying that Mrs Hartley was ill, which in turn meant he would never have checked the truth of that. And if my memory serves me correctly, she was far from ill! She was working on the farm that day, preparing tons of food for the harvest workers...'

'So the telegram was fake, sir? The one that persuaded James to come home?'

'The message was false, but I'm sure Luke sent it; after all, he would have been well known hereabouts and wouldn't have been able to give a false name to the telegraph office. But because the murder enquiries were concentrated on the scene of the death at Rosenthorpe, that gem slipped through the net. Clever Luke, I think, a very clever Luke...'

'Are you saying he lured his brother home especially to kill him, sir?'

'That's how it seems to me, Duncan — and I'm beginning to wonder how many other members of the family were involved.'

'But he must have made his plans very carefully, mustn't he? In a small community like these villages, every move he made must have been noticed. Yet he got away with it — or they got away with it.'

'I'm not sure that he did, Duncan. I think he knew the police were getting close, which is why he went to Canada. But I don't know yet whether he made his preparations to go to Canada before he planned the crime or after he'd done it.'

'Can we find that out, sir?'

'Possibly. We need to discover the precise date he booked his passage and the precise date he left England.'

'Where can you find that, sir?'

'From the Maritime Museum at Liverpool, I should think, or

from ships' manifests of the time — or from that information that Lorraine obtained from Mr Dunnock. We'll try Mr Dunnock's sources first; we don't have the time to go over to Liverpool to search records.'

'Right, sir.'

'And I want to see if those American papers contain Luke's signature — so we can compare it against the one upon his statement in our murder file.'

Then the intercom buzzed.

'Sir,' said DC Napier, who was manning the reception desk, 'the Chief Constable is here. He wants to see you. Shall I send him through?'

CHAPTER EIGHTEEN

Even before Mark Pemberton could make his desk tidy, the Chief Constable strode into his office. He moved with a briskness that Mark had come to recognise and was smartly dressed in a dark lounge suit, looking as immaculate as ever with not a black hair out of place. Mark leapt to attention.

'Good morning, sir.'

'Good morning, Mark. All correct?'

'Yes, sir. Er, can I get you a coffee?'

'Yes, why not?'

Mark buzzed Barbara on the intercom. 'Two coffees, please, Barbara. Black, without sugar. Mr Moore has arrived.' Mark found a chair for his Chief who settled down and placed his brief-case on the floor.

'I've got a meeting at Rainesbury police station later this morning,' Moore said, 'It's a bit of a chore on a Saturday but I thought I'd drop in to see if things were progressing well with Operation Roots.'

'Very smoothly, sir. Would you like to look around? I can show you what we've arranged.'

'Yes, after my coffee. You get on well with the Americans? Scotland Yard? Special Branch? No conflicts?'

As they drank their coffee, Mark outlined the security arrangements for Thirklewood Hall, highlighting some of the more important aspects and providing the names of key personnel in the American and Scotland Yard teams. He also referred to the on-going redecoration of the suite to be used by the Vice-President, and the additional security arrangements which had been necessary. Moore listened with his usual intensity, asking the occasional pointed question, and then, having drained his coffee, asked for a quiet unannounced guided tour. Mark accompanied him; he saw the ground-floor security arrangements, the upper floor, the loft, the outbuildings and the private suites which would be occupied by the Vice-President and his key personnel. They now looked much more welcoming than they had only a few days ago. Moore asked about checks for bombs, snipers, bugging devices and long-range telescopic sights on cameras and night-sight binoculars. He talked to John T Dunnock and Superintendent Birchall and finally, after some fifty minutes, expressed satisfaction with what he saw. Mark took him back to his office.

'Thanks, Mark. I had to come and see for myself, but everything seems to be well under control. I hope you are taking the opportunity to relax a little!'

'It's a welcome change from routine, sir,' said Pemberton.

'And the Muriel Brown murder? Have your teams produced anything worthwhile?'

It was only then that Mark realised he had not informed Moore of his enquiries into Hartley's death. There was a sinking feeling in the pit of his stomach and he knew he must confess to this breach of protocol. He got up from his seat and went over to the office door, closing it firmly.

'Sir,' he said upon regaining his seat, 'I've just realised I've made a ghastly mistake!'

Moore looked at him with his dark, intense eyes. Mark could have withered under such a gaze, but he knew that Moore had no time for weaklings and no time for those who did not get to the point.

'We started to reinvestigate the Muriel Brown death, sir, but something else cropped up.'

'Go on, Superintendent,' was the cool response.

'I felt it would be advisable to know something of Vice-President Hartley's background myself, for security purposes — the background of his alleged family in this country, for example. So, as a prelude, I went to the family graveyard in Wolversdale to look at the tombstones.'

'And?'

'I found what I thought was a hero, sir, a James Reuben Hartley who had been killed in the First World War. I went to the local newspaper office to get details. I thought it would please the Vice-President to learn there was a hero in the family…'

'You're not going to tell me that James was one of those First World War soldiers who were shot for cowardice, are you?'

'No, sir. He was murdered. He was coming home on compassionate leave in 1916 when he was shot.'

'Shot? How?'

'By a murderer, sir. The killer was never caught.'

'Oh, bloody hell! You mean you've come here to undertake a simple security task and you've uncovered an unsolved crime, a murder? And the victim's a possible ancestor of the Vice-President?'

'Yes, sir. I'm sorry… But if the Vice-President had pursued the death of James, he'd have uncovered that murder himself, without any trouble — the local papers contain the story. I felt if we could get to the bottom of that murder, we could be well prepared for any questions or problems that might arise.'

'Who knows about this?'

'No one outside our team, sir — except George Hartley, the

senior member of the family. Not even the Scotland Yard officers or the Vice-President's minders have been told. We have more enquiries to make, you see...'

'More enquiries? What kind of enquiries, for God's sake?'

'I think the killer was Luke Hartley, sir. He fled to Canada.'

'And who's Luke Hartley?'

'The Vice-President's grandfather, sir.'

'Oh my God, Mark, this gets worse! You have been stirring the mud. Bloody hell... I don't know what to say. How far has this enquiry got?'

'I should have some final answers today, sir. I've found a revolver which may have been the murder weapon, and we still have the fatal bullet; I'm having ballistic comparisons made. Then there's a mystery child, sir. I have an officer looking into his background right now...'

'I don't think I want to hear any more of this!'

Mark then provided a more detailed account of what he had learned and offered the Chief Constable his own theories about the death of James. He expressed one theory that Thomas and even some other family members had conspired in James's death, referring to the telegram about their mother's supposed illness.

'It's a very complicated story, sir, and I think we should pursue the enquiries; if I was able to find out so much in so little time, then surely the Vice-President would be able to do so. If he made the discovery, through his agents, he'd think we, the British that is, were covering up his past. If we present him with the information, very discreetly, it might not get known to the wider world — we'd be doing him a service, sir, a spot of diplomacy, some good public relations or Anglo-American relations.'

'Just one thing, Mark. How sure are we that the Hartleys of Wolversdale are in fact related to the Vice-President?'

'As positive as anyone can be, sir. I'm ninety-nine per cent certain that the Luke who left here is the Vice-President's grandfather.'

'I'm not sure whether that's good news or not, after what you've just told me.'

'Well, sir, if you saw George Hartley and stood him beside a photo of the Vice-President, you'd think they were brothers. The likeness is astonishing. But we can provide better proof...something I was going to do this morning,' and Pemberton pressed his intercom.

'Barbara, find DC Cashmore, will you, and ask her to bring our copy of the American's Hartley file to me? Straight away please.'

'What's all this, Mark?' asked Moore.

'DC Cashmore has got photocopies of the research done by the Vice-President himself — she charmed one of his aides, sir! It contains the ship's manifest with Luke's embarkation details, as well as other material. I'm hoping there is something containing Luke's signature.'

'How will that help?'

'I have the actual murder file, sir, from 1916. It contains a signed statement by Luke. If the two signatures match, I reckon it confirms the link beyond all doubt. It's something I haven't tested yet — so you'll be the first to know the answer!'

As they awaited the arrival of Lorraine, Mark produced the thick murder file from his locked drawer and showed it to Moore.

This was the original; his team were working from photocopies. He checked the index before turning to a statement made by Luke Caleb Hartley.

'This is our Luke, sir, who used to live at Pike Hill Farm, the supposed ancestral home of the Vice-President. He went to Canada with his family in 1916, before moving down to America. There's his signature.'

Lorraine arrived looking flustered; word had circulated that the Chief Constable was with Pemberton and she wondered if she had done something wrong. She carried the precious American file.

'DC Cashmore is going through some letters, sir, that passed between the murder victim and his mother. We're trying to establish a motive for his death.'

'Morning, Miss Cashmore. Any luck?'

'Not yet, sir.' She blushed. 'But I've found no references to James's mother being ill.' She addressed that remark to Pemberton. 'And he seems to have enjoyed his training, contrary to what his mother said in her statement.'

'We thought James was a bit of a mother's boy, sir,' Pemberton told his Chief. 'That's what first came through to us upon reading the murder file, but he got a good training report from his CO and seems to have been a very capable chap.'

'No enemies, other than the Germans?' smiled Moore.

'No, sir. We can't think why he was killed. Anyway, Lorraine, let's have a look. Is there anything in that American file which bears Luke's signature?'

'Yes, there is,' she said. 'He signed a receipt for some items of luggage when he disembarked. Somebody's found a copy of that, it's in the file,' and she began to seek it. She found it without any trouble and opened the file wide so that it was in full view without removing it. Although it was a photocopy, the signature was perfectly legible. It was signed 'Luke C Hartley'.

'Now, let's see how it compares with ours in the murder file.'

Mark revealed the signature at the foot of Luke's statement. It was identical: 'Luke C Hartley' in the same smooth handwriting with two curls on the stem of the final y.

Moore smiled. 'I think that any handwriting expert would agree those had been written by the same person. You'll be having them expertly assessed, though?'

'Yes, sir.'

'So,' said Moore, 'we know that the Luke Hartley who left Wolversdale in 1916 is, without doubt, the ancestor of the Vice-President of America?'

'Thanks to this, yes, we do, sir.'

'And when did he leave for Canada?'

'He sailed from Liverpool on 6th October and arrived in November 1916.'

'I'd say that clinched it, Mark.'

'Really? Why, sir?'

'That's when the Germans were having one of their submarine campaigns in the Atlantic. They were torpedoing everything — even passenger liners. During October 1916 alone some 148,000 tons of British shipping and 164,000 tons of foreign shipping were lost to the German U-boats.'

'You ought to be on *Mastermind*, sir!'

'And you ought to know a little more about your history, Mark. Luke must have been fairly desperate to have left the country and sailed on the high seas with his wife and family when all ships were at such risk from torpedoes.'

'It's a fair point, sir, but it still doesn't prove he was a murderer. I like to think I've still got an open mind. A lot depends upon what we discover today. My teams are busy right now on several lines of enquiry.'

'So how long will it take to get these results in, to get a positive answer to all this?'

'By this evening, sir, I should have most of the background information that I'm waiting for.'

'You know, Mark Pemberton, there are times I wish you would just sit back and take things easy. If you'd been any other officer sent here to do this job, you'd have put up your feet and let the world go. You'd have let your officers do just the necessary amount of work. But no, you've got to go delving into Hartley's roots — and look what you've unearthed! A mighty can of worms if ever there was one. You've caused a huge problem, Mark — what the hell do we do with this information?'

'I'm sorry, sir, it just happened like that…'

'Look, you should have told me earlier, you know that, and I accept your apology. But I need to think this through — I'll contact you later. Tomorrow be all right? And not a word to anyone, especially not to the Americans or the press. God, I don't know what to do about this. It's unthinkable, Mark, our VIP guest having a killer as a grandfather!'

'It might not be so, sir. I've still got an open mind.'

'If you have a gut feeling that he killed his brother, for whatever reason, I tend to trust your judgement. But if we're going to present these facts to the great man, we need more than your judgement, Mark, we need proof. I wonder what the politicians will make of all this, when we tell them?'

'Should we tell them, sir?'

'Let's wait and see what today's enquiries bring, shall we? But I feel obliged to inform the Foreign Office — when you've produced more evidence.'

Lorraine dismissed herself to continue reading the letters and, after chatting to Mark for another five minutes, the Chief Constable departed. As he was leaving, though, he halted in the office doorway and said, 'You really should have told me about this earlier, Detective Superintendent.' He had a wry smile on his handsome face. 'And you should have taken things much easier.'

Mark called in Barbara and asked her to make yet more photocopies of the two Luke signatures; then he dictated a letter to the forensic laboratory at Birmingham where there was a specialist in handwriting comparison. He asked whether it was possible, working from the enclosed photocopies, to say whether the two signatures had been made by the same person. He asked that the matter be treated as urgent — Barbara could fax the letter to the laboratory and a reply by telephone would be acceptable at this stage. Confirmation by certificate could follow in due course; if necessary, after an examination of the original signatures.

Then Mark went to find Lorraine.

'I've been thinking,' he said. 'I cannot leave the Hall today because I've sent Inspector Larkin out, but you can. I know I asked you to read those letters, but can I suggest you get straight down to Hull, to check on Patrick? I'll go through the letters while I'm hanging around here — I'd like to get this Patrick business sorted out before tonight.'

'Yes, of course I'll go.'

'I have a theory which I'm not going to divulge just yet, Lorraine. A nasty theory, to be honest, in which I might be doing an injustice to the Hartleys. So I want to be sure of some facts before I give my views an airing — and Patrick is part of that theory.'

'You think there was a conspiracy, don't you? Between the family members? And James died as a consequence?'

'I'm going to read those letters from Mum to James and from James to Mum, and I'm going to reread the statements taken by Inspector Dawson and his crew. I do get the impression that there was some kind of family gathering at Pike Hill Farm on the day James died, but I'm not sure what it was about. Whatever it was, it was kept secret from the police at the time. The question is, why?'

Lorraine smiled. 'You know more about this than you are admitting, sir.'

'I've been giving it a lot of thought, Lorraine, but to be honest, I don't know anything yet. I might know more when you get back from Hull with Patrick's baptismal certificate!'

'I'll go now!' she said. 'The churches will be open on Saturdays.'

CHAPTER NINETEEN

By the time Charles Moore had left Thirklewood Hall, albeit a little later than he'd intended, Detective Sergeant Ashton had arrived at the ballistics department of the Forensic Science Laboratory in Nottingham. Because Ashton had telephoned in advance to outline his urgent request, the Police Liaison Officer, Detective Inspector Horton, was expecting him. Upon arrival, Ashton logged details of the weapon and ammunition which required analysis and was told by Horton that the Principal Scientific Officer specialising in firearms would immediately examine the revolver. He had been called in from his weekend off. Whilst he could not guarantee a firm result, he would be able to give a preliminary opinion having regard to the age of the gun and the bullet. Horton suggested that Ashton have lunch somewhere in town, and return in, say, an hour and a half.

Ashton returned to the lab shortly after 2.15pm and was ushered into the office of the PSO in question, a Mr Delaney.

'This is an old wartime revolver, Sergeant,' said Delaney. 'It's pre-First World War issue; this model was issued to several armies around the world. I can't say where this particular weapon has come from, but I'd venture an opinion that it was probably in use before the turn of the century. Actually, it's hardly been used and is in very good condition, although it has deteriorated slightly simply through lack of maintenance and lack of use: the barrel was full of dust, as one might expect, but I have carried out preliminary tests and have examined the bullet you supplied. I am reasonably confident that this is the firearm from which that bullet was discharged. That is what you want to hear, I'm sure.'

'That'll please my boss!' smiled Ashton.

'There are some distinctive striations on the surface of the bullet and they do appear to correspond to those which were reproduced during a test firing. Because the weapon has not been used a great deal, the striations are quite distinct — in an older revolver, pistol or rifle, the interior of the barrel becomes much more smooth, resulting in less prominent striations or marks. In this case, I was able to form my opinion very quickly, using a simple microscope. Now, the shell of the bullet is not with the exhibits, I note?'

'I don't think it was ever recovered,' said Ashton.

'It would have been interesting to examine the firing pin marks, but that is not critical. There's enough to work on. I have some further tests to make and will let your Mr Pemberton have a formal report in due course. I ask that you leave the exhibits with me for a week or so, just so that I can carry out the necessary further details which will confirm my findings. But yes, you have a match, Sergeant. I would swear that in any court of law.'

'Thank you, Mr Delaney,' and Detective Sergeant Ashton left for the long drive back to Thirklewood Hall.

* * *

DETECTIVE INSPECTOR PAUL LARKIN didn't conclude his enquiries with quite so much ease. The staff of the Railway Museum in York were most helpful, explaining that he should really have telephoned before arriving and asked to be issued with a reader's ticket. Having received the ticket, he should have telephoned for an appointment to view the timetables, and he would then have been allocated a time and date, because space for research in the library was somewhat limited. However, because he was a police officer and because his enquiries were connected with a murder investigation, he was immediately given a reader's ticket and shown to a place. The librarian, a youthful man with a mop of ginger hair, showed him the growing library of railway literature and memorabilia. He indicated the shelves containing old timetables and advised him how and where to begin his search.

Within a matter of minutes, he was shown a selection of old timetables from the North-Eastern Railway. Printed on flimsy, poor-quality paper, they were bound in very fragile covers, and were designed to survive no longer than a few months. Fresh timetables were issued every summer and winter and so the old ones were discarded. The small paperbacks were not intended to be permanent reference books, although these particular copies had somehow remained intact for almost eighty years.

There were some dating from 1916, and they did cover the routes from Thornborough to Rainesbury and from Drakenedge to Rainesbury. Before settling down to study them, Larkin asked whether the relevant sections could be photocopied, but this request was politely declined on the grounds that it might harm the very fragile paper. Accordingly, he would have to laboriously copy out the details by hand.

Having been briefed by Pemberton, he knew he was seeking the times of trains from Drakenedge to Rainesbury on 11th September 1916, and also from Thornborough to Rainesbury on the same day. The junction at Rosenthorpe was important; did all the services connect there, or were there long periods of waiting between trains?

He knew that Thomas Hartley had slept overnight in Thornborough on 10th September. He found that trains to Rainesbury departed from Thornborough at 7.30am, 9.30am, 11.30am,

1.30pm, 3.30pm, 5.30pm, and 6.30pm. These trains arrived at Rosenthorpe one hour after departure, so Larkin could see that Thomas could have arrived at Rosenthorpe at, say 10.30am; if a trap was awaiting him, he could have been at Pike Hill Farm around 11.00am and remained there until, say, six o'clock, in time to catch the 7.30pm into Rainesbury. He could even have stayed overnight and caught the early train, at 8.30am, and still been in time for a business meeting in Rainesbury.

The other section of line began at Drakenedge; trains left at 8.00am, 9.00am, 10.00am, 12 noon, 2.00pm, 3.00pm, 4.00pm, and 6.00pm. They arrived at Rosenthorpe thirty-five minutes later. There was provision for trains travelling in both directions to wait at Rosenthorpe for connecting services.

In copying down the simple times of these rural services, Paul Larkin realised that Thomas Hartley, although officially touring the North Riding of Yorkshire on business, had every opportunity to visit Pike Hill Farm for several hours, or even to stay overnight, without any disruption to his business routine. Paul also noted the times of trains running in the opposite directions, although these appeared not to be of any use. But at least the record would be complete.

His mission took him less than an hour and, because there was no great degree of urgency, he decided to tour the museum with its splendid array of engines and coaches.

MARK PEMBERTON, having dealt with the Chief Constable, enjoyed an early lunch, sharing a table with an American agent called Cissie. She was a member of Vice-President Hartley's staff and said how much she was looking forward to exploring the North York moors with him as he sought his ancestral roots. Mark smiled; he advised her to visit Whitby, Danby, Egton Bridge, Goathland, the coastal villages of Robin Hood's Bay and

Staithes, as well as Rosedale, Hutton-le-Hole and Lastingham, if she had the time.

Afterwards, Mark returned to his office to wade through James's letters. They had been ordered quite meticulously, undoubtedly by Sarah Hartley, James's mother. They were in sequence, each of her letters to him being placed next to one from him so that there was an almost continuous narrative, albeit with a day's gap in between.

It was quite clear from Sarah's letters that she had never wanted James to leave home; the letters were couched in loving terms, more like those of a mother writing to a child than to a young, but mature man. Clearly, she worshipped James; she missed him, she missed his laughter around the house and farm, she missed his companionship, the poetry she read to him, his skill with the sheep-dogs... She told of life without him at Pike Hill Farm, saying how she welcomed his letters and that he should be careful with his bayonet during practice, and to make sure his socks were always clean when marching and that his boots were always well fitting and kept in a good state of repair. She worried about him having to fire guns and march long distances... But not once during these letters did Mark find any indication that she was ill.

James, on the other hand, wrote of his training. He had met some rough men and some decent ones, he had met some with the table manners of pigs or worse, others whose sole aim in life was to chase women and others who stole anything and everything they could lay their hands on. He had been advised to keep his socks around his neck, for example! Whenever he washed them, he had to put them around his neck to dry, otherwise they could be stolen. When around his neck, they would also catch any lice that he might pick up in the trenches. He repeated stories of life in the trenches, stories based on tales that had filtered back to the Green Howards in training.

He told stories about parts of England he'd never before

known about; tales of Zeppelins dropping bombs over England and of flimsy aircraft trying to shoot them down. He had heard of the crash of an airship called the L21 at 3.00am on Sunday, 3rd September 1916 — it had caught fire and crashed at Cuffley near Enfield, the very first to crash on English soil. The man who'd shot it down was an English pilot, only twenty-one years old, a fighter with the Royal Flying Corps. Thousands had trekked to Cuffley to see the burnt-out airship.

There were stories from the trenches; on the first day of the battle of the Somme, 1st July 1916, 150,000 infantrymen faced the German army and by dusk, 20,000 were dead with 40,000 wounded. 600 of the dead came from Sheffield. Skeletons lay everywhere in the mud and there were awful rumours about the Germans using the dead bodies for making soap. It was said the Germans had found a way of abstracting glycerine from the bodies of dead soldiers and that the factory was near St Vith, near the Belgian frontier. He even described the factory — it was over 700 feet long and screened from the railway line by thick trees and an electric wire fence...

There were tales of other conscripts like James — those who had not wished to volunteer had gone to tribunals. One man, a farmer like James, had pleaded that he was a skilled man because he had once skinned 1,200 rabbits in one night, and so he was exempted. Another was exempted because he worked as a weaver by day, ran a fish-and-chip shop in the evenings, went to bed at midnight and played the church organ on Sundays. He also worked as a knocker-up, rousing other workers at 4.30am. The tribunal exempted him. Eric Hall, who'd joined with James, was enjoying the life; he'd excelled at trench warfare and the obstacle course and was always to the forefront in physical events such as cross-country running and other physical training.

James wrote that he and Eric had become quite good friends. Although he'd known Eric for many years, Eric being an apprentice farrier who'd often visited Pike Hill Farm with his father, the two soldiers hadn't struck up a friendship at the beginning. Eric was much younger than James for one thing, and James did say he'd noticed a coolness in Eric, something he had not understood. But as the intensity of their training had continued and as they'd found themselves sharing their lives, they had become friendly. Eric was a happy-go-lucky man with a lovely sense of humour and a way of charming the girls of Richmond. James had enjoyed his training alongside Eric.

Another hint of James's humour came in his stories about the epidemic of sock-knitting which had broken out in England. As part of the war effort, the authorities had pleaded with the women to knit socks for soldiers who were bound for the trenches and, as a result, they'd been inundated with tons of them. There were socks everywhere, far too many, and so the newspapers had pleaded with the women to knit fewer socks — which only made them knit more!

As Mark read the letters, he felt they were from a young man enjoying a new way of life. While James had not volunteered, he was facing his conscription with cheerfulness and determination; he'd beaten his colleagues in rifle-shooting competitions, he'd had no trouble adjusting to the discipline and had enjoyed most of his training.

There was another side to it all, of course — some of the meeker recruits were bullied, one lad could not march because he moved his right hand with his right leg, another was colour blind and couldn't distinguish green from red, another spent all his nights lying on his bed in tears, another had smuggled his cat into the barracks and gave it most of his own food...

Through the letters, he gained the impression that although James Reuben Hartley was a reluctant soldier, he was determined to do his best for God and his country. He always expressed his love for his mother and for the rest of the family, sometimes asking after Luke's children or Matthew who had become a priest. He'd heard that one trade union leader, Ben Tillet of the dockers, had suggested that all clergymen should be conscripted. Tillet had calculated that there were 20,000 of them and called them miserable cowards, asking why it was that men who so often said they wanted to go to heaven were afraid to put themselves in the position of going sooner than they intended. In fact, the truth was that lots of them had volunteered. Tillet was merely making mischief and political capital.

It was the mention of heaven that reminded Mark Pemberton of the verse which said James had gone to hell. Was it a reference to the trenches? Had the verse begun to circulate while James was in training? Or did it follow his death? As he ploughed through the letters, Mark found nothing which provided any indication that things were not all right at home.

Mrs Hartley wanted James back, clearly regarding him as her special son; that she doted upon him was evident from her letters. Mark guessed there had been more than a few tears at Pike Hill upon his departure to the Green Howards. But there were no problems, it seemed, no messages from girlfriends, no disgruntled men who might have wanted to contact James about anything, no unpaid bills, no old scores to settle. And no sign that Mrs Hartley was ailing or sick.

With regard to the final letters, Mark found that James had been told of his impending posting. He and Eric had been earmarked to serve in the area of the Somme in France, to add valuable support to the British troops already there. They were to sail from Folkestone on Wednesday, 13th September 1916.

James's CO had told him about the Horsemasters who were also sailing with their animals. James liked animals; he said in his final letter that he would not mind working with horses in France, doing spots of farrier work, grooming and so forth. That was his last letter. It was dated Friday, 8th September 1916 and had probably arrived at the farm on the Saturday following. There was nothing in it about coming home for a short embarkation leave — indeed the tone of the letter suggested he was going straight from Richmond to Folkestone and then to France.

The telegram from home had changed all that. And James must have responded by telegram — how else would the family have known what time to collect him from Rosenthorpe station?

As Mark rested from his studies, he felt that James had never considered he would be coming home before embarking, he had never expressed any fear about going to war and, most certainly, there was never a hint of his being suicidal.

So who had spread that kind of rumour, and why?

Pemberton knew he must digest the contents of those old statements yet again. There must be something he'd overlooked, some tiny item of evidence he'd missed. He tugged the huge file towards him and turned once again to the very first report. He would start at the beginning. He was sure that James Reuben Hartley had been lured to his death.

CHAPTER TWENTY

Pemberton began by reappraising the victim profile that DI Larkin had compiled from Dawson's earlier work. Now that his knowledge of the personalities was more detailed, he quickly found some contradictions — on the one hand, James was portrayed as a softy, a mother's boy, a man who was afraid of becoming a soldier, and yet during military training, he'd proved to be a good soldier, eager to learn and very capable at everything he attempted. There was not the slightest suggestion that he was a cissy or a mother's boy.

It was Luke who had hinted that James was not a strong man by saying his mother was worried about him walking from the railway station while carrying all his kit, something he would have had to do while serving in France. Soldiers were trained to march mile after mile carrying their kit, so a walk from the railway station to the farm, although five miles or so, would not have been a hardship for a countryman. Even old ladies and children would often walk that sort of distance, either to go to school or to visit the town by train.

But it dawned on Mark that it was James's mother who'd said he needed careful treatment.

Luke's statement contained phrases like, 'Mother asked if I would collect James because it was a long walk home...' Later, when he'd returned without James, 'Mother was in tears, worrying herself sick.' Mark therefore turned to Mrs Hartley's own statement; it was upon this that Larkin had relied for his victim profile.

He found phrases like 'James was the weakest one of the family, he was never very robust as a child, often off school with sickness of one kind or other.' 'He was a kind-hearted lad, he'd always be thinking of his parents, and would always give me a helping hand, carrying heavy buckets or even laying out the washing on the hedges.' 'He was very sensitive, he hated us having to drown kittens and wouldn't help with pig killing.' 'When conscription was announced, I thought he would never make a soldier, he was too sensitive and shy. I told him to go to the tribunal to get exemption, but he didn't want to. I think he was frightened that people would think he was a coward or avoiding his duty to the country, so he never went to the tribunal. I don't think he was a pacifist, but he was never one for a rough-and-tumble at home.' 'He couldn't make friends with girls too easily, he was very shy.' 'He had no enemies, he wasn't seeing somebody else's girlfriend or wife, he wouldn't do that sort of thing. He would sometimes talk to girls after church, he always drove me to church in the pony and trap, but he never brought a girl back home. I think some of the less savoury sort of girls would have liked to get their hands on him. They used to talk to him when he took me shopping and try to get him to take them for walks. He was a good-looking man, you see, and very kind and gentle. I know some of them couldn't wait until he got into a soldier's uniform, I had to warn him about the sort of things they'd do to force him into marriage.'

In Mark's opinion, this revealed an over-protective mother rather than a wimpish youth. The idea that James had not wished to fight appeared to have come not from James himself but from his mother; there was no doubt she had dominated the lad. He was not her youngest son, but he was the youngest still at home. The youngest of all, James's brother Robert, had married and gone to live in Newcastle on Tyne. Matthew, also younger, had gone away to become a priest and so James had remained to work on the farm with his elder brothers, perhaps knowing that he would never inherit the business, that he would never become owner — that he'd always be merely a farm worker at the beck and call of his father and his older brothers.

Mark's opinion of James was changing.

He now regarded James as a very considerate young man. He was the sort who would not want to hurt his mother's feelings by leaving home while she was alive; he'd sacrifice his own future for her and the family. If he went to meet a girl he would keep it a secret from his mother, Mark reckoned.

He also guessed that James had welcomed an opportunity to get away from the farm even if it meant joining the Green Howards to fight in the notoriously evil battles in the Somme. And typical of the lad, he'd written to his mother every day, but instead of pandering to her desires, he told her and the family all about his new and exciting world, the new friends he was making and the new experiences he was enjoying.

Mark realised that if this woman was neurotic and over-protective, the thought of her beloved son being despatched overseas, possibly to his death in France, could indeed have made her ill, but none of the statements referred to any illness. In fact, they all said she'd been very busy that Monday, preparing food for the twenty men and other family members who were helping with the threshing.

Mark plodded through the file. There were statements from a handful of those workers, men from the village who went from farm to farm assisting with threshing. The police had clearly thought it unnecessary to interview them all when all were at the same place at the same time. Threshing days in 1916 were always like this — umpteen workers all knowing their job and all working from dawn till dusk to get the task completed. The huge hissing traction engine was used to power the thresher, but the work of loading it, stacking the straw and storing the grain was all done by hand. It was a long slow job, but it was vital to get the threshing finished before winter and so the moorland farmers all helped one another.

The machinery would be hired, and it would travel from farm to farm in an endeavour to meet the demand, the hired workers followed it to earn some hard cash from their labours. As a consequence, Pike Hill Farm on the Monday of James's death would have been a hive of activity. Every available assistant, whether child or adult, would have been welcomed.

Mark checked the statements taken from a sample of the workers; they all agreed that Luke had taken the pony and trap at the time he'd stated, and with the intention of collecting James from the railway station. Those who knew James did not have a bad word to say about him. They respected his decision to join up without appealing to a tribunal and they said he had no enemies in the locality.

A third fact which clearly emerged from the statements was that those who knew James said he was a fine and intelligent young man who could have made a career in a town because he had a good brain and he liked reading and writing. They all said he was quiet and somewhat shy, but he was never a cissy, as they put it.

Mark also found a statement from Father Clifford, the parish priest at Wolversdale. He expressed an opinion that James Reuben Hartley was a fine upstanding young man with a deep social conscience and a high intellect. He had no enemies, he was well mannered and considerate to everyone. Father Clifford knew of no reason why anyone would wish to harm him, nor did he think James would ever contemplate suicide.

Most certainly, he would not shrink from something as

important as fighting for his country. Before leaving home to join the Green Howards, James had talked about it to the priest, not to seek advice but merely as one man talks to another, and he had said he was quite looking forward to the experience — he'd even said he had no fear of dying for his country because he had every faith that God would look after him.

Mark returned to the statements which dealt with that fateful day, a hectic time for Pike Hill Farm in which even the children had a part to play. One statement was made by a Mrs Gloria Bowen; she said she'd been at the farm all day assisting with the feeding arrangements and also looking after the Hartley children. Luke's son, Caleb, aged eleven, had been considered mature enough to work on the stack while Paul, only nine, had been given the job of sweeping up the stray bits of straw. George's eldest, also called Caleb and also eleven, worked beside his cousin on the stack, while Joseph, almost ten, had the chore of sweeping up the fallen grains of corn and taking them to a large bin in one of the outhouses. Young Maria, aged only seven, stayed with Mrs Bowen and helped carry the food out to the men or the empty mugs and dishes back into the kitchen for washing. Everyone had had a job.

Mark's scrutiny of a mass of other minor statements, made by those who had known James, all confirmed James's status among the villagers and tradespeople — he was a charming young man who was universally liked and respected.

Girls wanted him to pay attention to them, but his mother always seemed to be in the background. She seemed to be jealous of any girl who threatened to take him from her. Mrs Hartley was always steering him away from those she regarded as not suitable — it seemed that no young woman was good enough for her favourite son. There was no sign, in any of the statements, that James had any close male friends either — he was not a sportsman or a team player, although he had partaken in sheep-dog trials and shown a high degree of skill with a rifle. He was something of a loner, it seemed, preferring to enjoy those activities which did not require a team. All the indications that James was a softy were now regarded by Pemberton as untrue. Both Dawson and Paul Larkin had relied too heavily upon the mother's statement. He must have words with Larkin.

Mark began to see James as something of a lonely man, perhaps not necessarily through his own choice. Sixth in a large family, living on an isolated farm and having to obey his neurotic mother's whims, he might not have been able to make many friends, certainly not of the opposite sex. There were the poetry books among his belongings too — Mark saw him spending a lot of time alone with the books, perhaps reading them in his room or walking in the beautiful countryside which surrounded the farm.

There had always been the family's feelings and reputation for James to consider; if he had wanted to leave home to follow a more Bohemian lifestyle, his family might not have approved. Mark wondered whether James had come to regard the army as a means of escape from his restricted existence. He had not volunteered for military service, perhaps because of pressure from his mother, but the moment conscription had been imposed on all unmarried men of military age (ie between eighteen and forty-one), James had applied to join the army. Mark felt sure this had provided him with the necessary impetus to leave home and make his own way in the world.

After reading all the letters James had sent home, Pemberton was satisfied that none referred to embarkation leave or a short visit home before leaving for France. Likewise none of his mother's letters ever said she was ill or in need of his presence. Yet James had responded to a telegram suggesting his mother was ill. He'd been granted compassionate leave of one night — just enough time to draw him back to his death. So why was the telegram sent? Was it a summons to meet his death? It bore Luke's name but not his signature — the words would have been written by a postal clerk at Richmond before delivery to the Regiment.

Was it from Luke acting alone? Or was it the brothers together, all working in some form of conspiracy? Or was it even from James's mother, making use of Luke's name? But if there had been a conspiracy among the brothers, why plot against the likeable, quiet and shy James?

Mark then asked himself how many brothers were on the farm that day. He sought the answer by turning to more of the collected statements. He needed to know where every member of the family was on Monday, 11th September 1916, so he drew a pad of notepaper towards him and listed each member against a sequence of columns bearing headings denoting the time of day.

He jotted down the times beginning at 7.00am with hourly intervals until 9.00pm. Then it meant plodding through yet more statements to determine the whereabouts of every member of the family at any particular hour.

He began with Caleb Hartley, aged sixty-four. Caleb had been on the farm all that day, his task being to organise and supervise the threshing operation. When interviewing Caleb, Inspector Dawson had obviously asked the specific question, 'Did you leave the farm at all on Monday, 11th September 1916?' because there was a sentence in his statement which said, 'I did not leave Pike Hill Farm at all during that day.'

Mrs Hartley had been at the farm all day too. Her statement said she had been feeding the team of about twenty threshers, aided by other women. Six of the other women had been interviewed and corroborated Mrs Hartley's statement. No one had noticed any woman departing from the farm at the material time.

Luke had left the farm, as Mark knew only too well. He'd departed alone in the pony and trap at 2.30pm specifically to collect James. He had intended arriving at the station at 3.35pm. Several witnesses had seen him leave and verified the time. Luke had not found James at the station and had waited in the village in case he turned up later; Luke had returned home just before

6.00pm. Luke's wife, Edith, and their children had been helping too. They had been on the farm all day.

Mark turned to a 1916 map of Pike Hill Farm and its environs which showed the farm's position in relation to Wolversdale and also the roads to Rosenthorpe, both the public road and the toll road. There was a long track leading across fields from the high road to the farm; it hadn't changed since 1916, except that it was now surfaced with tarmac. Pemberton remembered it from his own visit to George Hartley — if anyone had driven along that road, they would have been noticed quite easily by the people working around the premises. No one could have sneaked away without being observed.

George Stanley Hartley was the second eldest son and, according to his statement, he'd been threshing with the rest of the family all day. He had disappeared once or twice to attend to matters about the premises but had not left the farm. His wife, Mary, and children had been helping with food during the threshing. This was the present George's grandfather.

Samuel was a butcher and was living away from the farm at the time of the murder; Thomas and Sophie the twins had moved to Hull, Matthew was a priest in Manchester, Jessica was living in Lincoln and Robert had married and was living in Newcastle on Tyne. But the police had never interviewed any of those brothers about their whereabouts. So had they all come home on Monday, 11th September 1916? After all, Dawson had not been too concerned with the people who had actually been on the farm that day; he needed to know who'd left it or who had been at or near the scene of the crime at the material times.

Mark knew that it was customary for all the brothers to assist with the harvest and with the threshing; even though they had their own work and their own families to care for, it would not have been unusual for them to arrive that day to give their assistance. The other helpers would not have considered it worthy of comment. Indeed, it was their absence which would have prompted comment. Mark then asked himself whether, if Thomas had in fact come home, there would have been any necessity to do so in secret. Surely, the family threshing day was the perfect reason.

But had the presence of the brothers been concealed for some unsavoury purpose? If the brothers had all come home on the very day that James had been falsely summoned to visit his sick mother, what was the real reason? Had they all been told she was ill? Why had James's homecoming required such deception and why did it result in his murder?

CHAPTER TWENTY-ONE

Mark Pemberton was convinced that the thick file of ancient statements contained a clue to the reason for James's death. But as he pored over them until his head ached with the effort of concentration, that clue stubbornly refused to reveal itself. There was no proof, for example, that Thomas Hartley had visited the farm that day and yet Mark felt sure he must have done. He was known to have been in the district and the train times did allow him time to call. The sighting of a Mr Hartley by the telegram boy added strength to that belief, and it was the kind of action that Thomas would surely have undertaken. If he had gone to the farm, perhaps in secret, then would the other brothers and sisters have also been there? Had Father Matthew come all the way from Manchester, and had Samuel left his butcher's business for the day?

There was nothing to indicate that they had. The implication was that, of the family, only Luke and George, and their father, had been working at Pike Hill Farm on Monday 11th September 1916; the other threshers had been contract men, hired for the day. And yet, Mark told himself, there was nothing to say that the brothers, or other members of the family, had not been there.

Inspector Dawson had not seen fit to list every person at the farm because their presence was not material to his case. Dawson might well have checked in a way that was not immediately apparent; he might not have recorded every one of his actions, particularly those with a negative outcome. Mark knew that Dawson was interested only in anyone who might have been at or near the scene of the crime — and that was some five miles away, a considerable journey in 1916.

Of the family members, only Luke filled that particular role and yet the other Mr Hartley, whoever he was, must have walked past the murder scene if he'd gone to the farm from the railway station. But he'd have passed the scene during the morning; Dawson was interested only in the afternoon hours. And that's when Luke was known to have passed by.

Luke, Luke, Luke… Whichever way Mark turned, he was faced with the fact that Luke was the central figure in the puzzle. Luke who had apparently fled to Canada, Luke who had gone to meet his brother, Luke who had returned without his brother, Luke who had spawned a family which had produced the Vice-President of the United States of America. Where were they now, Luke's other offspring? His daughter, Sarah, who was thirteen when her uncle James was murdered, his eldest son Caleb James who was eleven and had helped with the threshing that day, and little Paul, only nine, who'd also helped…

Pemberton remembered that it was James's niece, Sarah, who had set up the James Hartley Foundation in America; she'd be Luke's daughter, Sarah. She'd named her Foundation after her deceased Uncle James, a touching memorial to him. Suddenly Mark realised that Sarah had not been helping at the farm on the day of James's death. She was not mentioned in the statements. That was the thing he'd been seeking, that one little clue — Sarah's name had not cropped up in the context of working on the farm that threshing day. Quickly, he turned to the statement made by Mrs Bowen, the lady who'd been looking after the children.

He scanned it again just to make sure she had not mentioned Sarah. Was Sarah too old to be regarded as a child, he wondered? At thirteen, she'd be almost a woman, working as a woman maybe, baking, doing kitchen work, perhaps even holding a job as a domestic in another farm or country house?

But the lack of any reference to Sarah set him along another train of thought and he became determined to discover where she was that day. Did it matter? Was she as important as the mysterious Patrick, for example? He began to peruse the statements all over again, seeking references to Sarah. Trace her, interrogate her and eliminate her.

Then the telephone rang.

'Pemberton,' he said.

'Sir,' said the distant voice, 'it's Detective Sergeant Ashton. I'm ringing from ballistics at Nottingham.'

'Oh, hello, Tony. Any luck?'

'Yes, sir. I thought I'd ring with the good news before I set off back. There's a match, the bullet was fired from that revolver. The lab will confirm it in writing as soon as possible, but I thought you'd want to know. It means we've found the murder weapon after all this time!'

'That's great news, Tony. Well done. I'll see you when you get back. There's no rush, things are quiet here.'

'It's nearly five o'clock now, sir, and it takes well over two hours to drive back.'

'Get yourself a meal on the way, put it on expenses. It's Saturday, so treat yourself to a glass of wine — but remember you're driving!'

Flushed with triumph, Pemberton went through to Duncan Young, who was finishing his stint for the day. He told him the news, at which the HOLMES operator beamed.

'It's taken us nearly eighty years to find the weapon, sir, so I reckon that's a good piece of police work!'

'So all we have to do now is find the killer.' Pemberton smiled wryly. 'Now, I've got a task for tomorrow. I'm not sure whether you've got all the data entered yet?'

'Not yet, sir. There's a huge amount of stuff in that murder file.'

'Right, well, if you've a minute, I'd like you to check for references to Sarah Hartley, daughter of Luke.'

'Any specific enquiry, sir?'

'She was his eldest child, a girl of thirteen at the time of James's death. I've just done a check of the names of everyone on the farm on the day of his death, and she's not mentioned. I realise that's not conclusive, but I am curious to know where she was if that's possible — it was customary, you see, for the whole family to turn up for a threshing day. So, where was she? Working away, perhaps? Poorly? Visiting friends or relations? I just wondered whether she was referred to in any other statements.'

'I'll check now, if you like, sir.'

'Will it take long?'

'A few seconds, sir. Hang on.'

Mark watched as Duncan activated the various menus on HOLMES and the computer told him that Sarah's grandmother was also called Sarah Hartley. There were two Sarah Hartleys.

'I know that Sarah senior was at the farm all day,' Mark said.

'Due to the way it's been programmed, sir, HOLMES won't distinguish between the two Sarahs, but it will identify all the files in which either one or the other is mentioned.'

'That'll do,' agreed Pemberton. 'We can soon eliminate the elder Sarah.'

The computer speedily drew up a list of statement numbers in which the name of Sarah Hartley was mentioned. Mark thanked Duncan and returned to his office to study the file anew. This time, he had a list of all the references and he began to examine them.

Then Detective Inspector Larkin walked in.

'Hello, sir,' he said. 'Still wading through that file?'

'My head's aching, my eyeballs are aching and my back's aching, but my brain tells me the answer is in here, Paul. The answer to who killed James Hartley and why... Anyway, how did you get on at the Railway Museum?'

'Wonderful, sir. It's a fabulous place, all those gleaming railway engines from my childhood dreams. It was like playing with a giant train set, a lad's dream to be sure.'

'And timetables from the North-Eastern Railway dated 1916?'

'They're all there, sir, in the Library and Archive Department. I've copied down all the times for September 1916, the summer timetable.'

'So would Thomas have broken his journey at Rosenthorpe?'

'Yes, he could, quite easily. He could have left Thornborough on either the first or second train to Rainesbury, got off at Rosenthorpe and spent the day at Pike Hill Farm. He could have caught the last train to Rainesbury, or even the first the next morning; he could have spent the night at the farm and still have got to his Rainesbury appointment on time.'

'Thanks — write it all up, Paul. And so the question remains: did Thomas visit home that day, and if so, why?'

'I didn't find that answer in the Railway Museum, sir!'

'You've let me down again, Paul,' joked Pemberton, who added seriously, 'But you did let me down on James's profile!'

He explained to Paul Larkin how he felt the victim profile of James Hartley was not quite accurate and asked him to have another look at it.

'Now, sir?'

'Later, Paul, it's knocking-off time now. I fancy a shave, a shower, a change of clothing, and a nice long cool pint of beer before I eat.'

'Me too. See you in the bar then?'

'Sure.'

'Is DC Cashmore back from Hull yet?' asked Larkin.

'No, she's not, and there's no word from her. I wonder how she's getting along?'

* * *

LORRAINE HAD NOT FOUND the beginning of her enquiry as simple as she'd anticipated. Before leaving the office, she had telephoned the Catholic Adoption Society to ask for advice about tracing the origins of Patrick Harland. The society was very cautious, especially about giving information over the telephone, but when she explained that a confirmation memento had been issued to Patrick by St Ignatius' church in Hull, the advice was that that church must be the starting place.

'But I want to find out where Patrick was baptised,' she stressed. 'I'm not concerned with his confirmation.'

'That's the biggest hurdle of all,' Lorraine was told. 'Unless someone can tell you which church it was, it means a long, long check through piles of baptismal certificates — or, of course, a search through the country's national registers, either in London or locally. It's all very time-consuming.'

'I haven't a lot of time,' she sighed.

'You could try the Nicholas Postgate Convent in Hull,' advised the girl. 'They used to run a home for orphans. I think it closed after the Second World War. A lot of children from there were adopted by Catholic families, but I doubt if records from 1916 will still be available.'

Lorraine thanked her for her advice, jotted down the address of the Nicholas Postgate Convent, rang to make an appointment for later that afternoon, had a quick coffee and set off for Hull.

Within an hour she was sitting in the secretary's office with another coffee. The secretary, a lay worker called Miss Philomena

Lynch, made her feel welcome and listened as Lorraine unfolded her story. She omitted references to the murder investigation but concentrated on her desire to discover the whereabouts of the supposed relations of Vice-President Caleb Hodgson Hartley.

'Patrick is very important to our enquiries,' she concluded. 'He died very recently, aged seventy-seven; he remained a bachelor and we believe he was adopted by a Mr and Mrs Harland, Sophie and Aiden that is, around 1916. They lived here in Hull and Sophie was a founder of Hartleys of Hull. I was given to understand he might have been an orphan, perhaps one who went from here to the Harland family.'

'We did work with waifs and strays in the latter years of the last century, but we also took in children who were, shall we say, born in secret.'

'Secret?'

Miss Lynch smiled. 'Young people the world over were having illicit relationships, Miss Cashmore, and the outcome was often a poor child that no one wanted or even owned.'

'So nothing changes!' commented Lorraine.

'Well, in those days it was important to conceal any hint of scandal in a family and so, if a girl got pregnant before marriage, she would often come, here. She would come, or be sent, in conditions of some secrecy, to the convent to give birth to her child. The convent cared for mother and child until the mother could go home.'

'And suppose the girl could not take the child home?'

'Then the child was kept here, and adoptive parents were found.'

'This would be long before the formal rules of adoption were drawn up in 1926?' asked Lorraine.

'Indeed it was, which is why I fear we might not have any very detailed records of 1916. Secrecy was regarded as important — the Catholics of that time were very cautious about a girl being seen to be a sinner and so their pregnancies were concealed...

hypocritical behaviour it certainly was, and I say so as a Catholic myself. The fact is that lots of children who passed through the orphanage weren't orphans in the true sense of the word. They were unwanted babies, born out of wedlock. It's so sad, so unchristian.'

'So if Patrick Harland was born here in 1916, under whatever name he then carried, would there be a record?'

'Yes, there may well be, but it will be extremely brief. We would not have his baptismal certificate, for example — that would be at the church. This convent has a chapel, but the chapel does not qualify as a parish church where such records are retained. However, we do have some old ledgers here, we keep them for families doing research. I can let you look through the 1916 books.'

'I'd appreciate that,' said Lorraine.

The register was a huge leather-bound volume with gold lettering down the spine. It said, 'Child Register 1916'.

'It's heavy,' said Miss Lynch. 'You can read it over there if you wish,' and she pointed to a small table and chair in the corner of the office.

Lorraine bore it across and began her search.

The register was a sad record of human behaviour. Babies born out of wedlock were processed by the nuns of this convent; unwanted by their parents and causing embarrassment to their families, they were hidden behind these walls and given away to those who wanted them. She checked the long lists, all written in beautiful copperplate handwriting. The lists were in chronological order, month by month, and gave the date the child entered the orphanage, the name of the child, the date he or she was born, the name of the mother if known and father if known and the fate of the child — adoption, retained in orphanage, death and so forth. She saw that quite a lot had died in infancy.

And then, in September, she found a Patrick. His surname was Hartley. The entry said, 'Date: 3rd September 1916. Name:

Patrick Hartley. Date of Birth: 3rd September 1916. Mother: Sarah Hartley; Father not known. Adopted November 1916.'

And that was all.

Sarah Hartley? Without the file for quick reference, Lorraine puzzled over the name. Who was this Sarah? In spite of that doubt, Lorraine felt sure that this child later became the man known as Patrick Harland. She checked the rest of the register, moving right through to the end of 1917 without finding another Patrick, or anyone with the surname of either Hartley or Harland.

'Excuse me.' Lorraine turned in her chair to address Miss Lynch. 'You mentioned earlier that children born here were not baptised in the chapel. Do you know which church they used?'

'Yes, St Chad's. It's just around the corner from here, a hundred yards or so to the left outside the main door.'

'I believe the child was baptised very soon after birth, so who would attend the ceremony?'

'The mother was always encouraged to attend the baptism, to be with her child at that very important moment. She would sign the baptismal record.'

'And after the child had been born and baptised, where did the mother go?'

'If she was from a good home, we would encourage her to return to her parents or family home as soon as she was able; they often said she'd been away on holiday or working.'

'And if the mother had no home or had been thrown out?'

'In those circumstances, she could remain here until such time as she could find work or other accommodation. There were problems if the babies were not adopted — the longer the mothers stayed, the more attached to their children they became. So we did encourage them to leave very soon after the birth if adoption was being planned.'

'And in the case of this entry here,' she held up the register bearing Patrick Hartley's name, 'you would not know what happened to the mother?'

'No. Most of our files of that period were destroyed by an incendiary bomb in the Second World War but some of the stuff was saved. That old register was one of the survivors!'

'Thanks, you've been most helpful. Now, I wonder if I'll be able to see the baptismal register at St Chad's?'

'I'm sure there will be no problem. I'll ring Father O'Neil for you, shall I?'

'Thank you.'

And within twenty minutes, Lorraine was sipping a cup of tea with the genial Irish priest. With eyes full of happiness and a smile perpetually upon his lips, he said, 'Sure I don't mind, Miss Cashmore. 'Tis a genuine pleasure.'

As she sipped, he rummaged around in a huge green safe which seemed to serve as a filing cabinet and pulled out masses of cardboard-backed registers and books.

Muttering '1916' and '1917' under his breath, he eventually found the right volume.

'I'm anxious to find out if Patrick Hartley was baptised here. Would that be in your records?'

'If he was born at Nicholas Postgate's and received into the church here, at the tender age of a day or two, then it'll be here, to be sure,' and he flicked through the entries. Then he found it.

'10th September 1916,' he read aloud. 'Here we are. Patrick Hartley was baptised in this church.'

'Does it give the name of his parents?' she asked, heart beating with anticipation.

'It does. Sarah and James Hartley.'

'James?' she cried.

'So it says here.' He stabbed the entry with a finger.

'Can I have a copy of that?' she asked. 'It's for the Vice-President of the United States of America to see.'

'Then how can I refuse?' He grinned. 'I'll do it right away.'

'So James was Patrick's father!' she said to herself as the priest went off to find the necessary documents. 'So who is this Sarah?'

CHAPTER TWENTY-TWO

After an enjoyable meal in Hull, Lorraine returned to Thirklewood Hall and did not visit the bar area. It was almost nine o'clock and all she wanted was a hot bath and an early night. She did peep into Pemberton's office, wanting to impart her news to him, but on finding it deserted, decided she would tell him tomorrow morning.

Next morning, Sunday, she found him at breakfast, sitting alone at one of the corner tables with his muesli and orange juice.

'May I?' she asked, pointing to an empty chair and producing one of her beautiful smiles.

'I looked for you last night.' He indicated she should join him at the table. 'I checked at reception — they said you'd returned late and had gone to your room. I didn't want to disturb you.'

'I appreciate that.' She did not use the word 'sir'. 'I was pretty shattered when I got in and didn't feel like socialising. It's a mighty long drive across those Wolds to Hull, but aren't the roads quiet!'

'Driving's a genuine delight over there — it's like motoring in the past. But I guessed you'd be tired. There are times I need space. It's nice to be alone sometimes.'

'But not now?'

'No, this morning I welcome your company. But enough of all this small talk! How did it go yesterday? Did you track down the elusive Patrick?'

'I did, and guess what?'

'What?'

'James Hartley was his father. He's named on the Baptismal certificate. I've got a copy.'

'James? Good God!' Mark could guess what was coming next. All along, he'd had his own suspicions about the parentage of Patrick. 'And his mother? Who's she?'

'I think you know,' she said. 'I think you had a bloody good idea, otherwise you wouldn't have been so determined to track down Patrick's ancestry, would you?'

'Sarah?' he asked, his knowing smile revealing his own early conclusion.

She nodded. 'That's the name on the certificate. I wasn't quite sure which Sarah until I had a look at the file.'

'It wouldn't be James's own mother, if that's what you were thinking at the start! Now that really would be tainted behaviour! It's got to be the younger one, Luke's daughter,' he said softly. 'The family would regard it as incest, even though uncle and niece are not forbidden categories in English law. But what a shocking discovery for a father to make. That his own brother had fathered a child by his daughter...'

'Enough to make the father kill the seducer, sir?'

'I very much suspect so.' Mark tried to envisage the anger that the rigid Luke Hartley must have felt when the discovery was made. First, there would be the realisation that his daughter was pregnant, then the awful knowledge that James was the father...

'When do you think Luke learnt the truth?' she asked.

'I can only guess. I think it would have followed the baptism. I think family members would have been there, young Sarah most certainly was, as well as Sophie and Thomas, and their respective spouses.'

'With Sophie awaiting the adoption of the child?'

'I don't think the adoption would have been finalised by then — I reckon Sophie might have put forward the idea of adoption because, as we know, she was unable to have children of her own. So she and probably her husband and even her brother Thomas would have gone along to support the girl. But imagine their horror when they saw that Sarah had named her uncle as the father — she actually recorded his name on the baptismal certificate. That was a secret they could not contain.'

'But the way it was done, sir, it looks normal. Anyone outside the family who read the entry would have no idea of the near-incestuous relationship. The names of the parents look like those of any normal mother and father.'

'But the family knew all right. I think either Thomas or Sophie must have written to tell Luke and I think that's when Luke sent the telegram to James to bring James home. I think the original idea might have been a confrontation with James; he'd have to face the family before going to France. They might have been threatening him with banishment from the family home, but over the intervening period, Luke worked himself up into a rage and shot his brother. I think he planned the cover-up very carefully. I think he told the police that James was suicidal when in fact he was not, and I think he hoped it would look like suicide, the reason being given as a reluctance to go to the Somme. But James wasn't like that, he was quite prepared to go to France. I reckon Inspector Dawson soon realised that Luke was the killer but was never able to secure the necessary proof. Certainly, there wasn't enough to have him brought back from Canada — Luke had made a good escape. I doubt if the police knew of Sarah's pregnancy; that would have been a very well-kept family secret.'

'What about the conspiracy theory you had?'

'I don't think the family was plotting murder. I think they

might have gathered on that threshing day, a day when it was normal for them to assemble without anyone wondering why, and I think their purpose was to discuss the future of the child and to arrange a long-term family cover-up. I think that's why Thomas came — it might even have been the real motive behind the telegram.'

'Maybe the others did not come to the farm that day?'

'Perhaps you're right. It might be that when Luke sent the telegram, he had no intention of killing James; his purpose was to get James home by one way or another, at least for that one night, to confront him with Sarah's condition. Perhaps James never knew she was pregnant. She'd have gone away to the convent while he was doing his training, but his mother never mentioned that in her letters. And James never showed any particular interest in Sarah when he was away. Do you think Thomas revealed the secret of Patrick's father that day, the day of James's death? Over lunch perhaps? And if so, it's not surprising that Luke responded in that violent way. Once he'd done the evil deed, I think the family realised it was Luke who had killed James — the adult members, that is. I don't think Sarah ever knew her father had killed James, not even when she was an adult woman.'

Lorraine sat in silence, listening to Pemberton's theories, and found herself in agreement.

He went on, 'Whatever the outcome of that meeting, I reckon the family would have agreed to Patrick being adopted by Sophie, which is what happened — and which is why Sophie kept in touch with Luke's family when they went to Canada. Remember they wrote to say Patrick had made his first Holy Communion.'

'Can we prove any of this, sir?'

'I doubt it. The evidence is a bit thin. Most certainly it is too slight for modern requirements — I couldn't see the Crown Prosecution Service authorising prosecution on such meagre evidence if this was a modern case.'

'But there could have been a prosecution if all this had been known at the time?'

'Very possibly. The courts took a different attitude in those times. In a modern investigation, though, we'd have better scientific evidence. In this old case, circumstantial evidence is all we have; the murder weapon has been found, by the way, and we've linked it with the bullet that was in the old file. The revolver was among James's belongings which his mother had kept. I think Luke hid it there, so it would never be found until long after his death and long after the murder was forgotten. I reckon old Caleb decided to destroy the family bible and all references to Luke. Caleb might have banished Luke to Canada — certainly, it was a risky thing to do, to cross the Atlantic during the German submarine campaign, and that alone smacks of a forced voyage. The outcome, of course, was that Luke effectively became a nonperson. Caleb probably thought that out of sight is out of mind. But the old man could have had no idea that records would be retained in old newspapers and elsewhere. I'll bet he never gave that a thought. He would have gone about his exclusion of Luke in the belief that future generations would never know of his existence.'

'He must have been a fairly simple chap.'

'Simple, but not stupid. Unsophisticated, perhaps. But it was a forlorn hope, even though it has taken three-quarters of a century for the truth to emerge. But the clues were there even for a modern generation — George, the next brother, did not have the Caleb name, so purists would realise he was not the eldest. They should have realised that there was another brother somewhere.'

'Like Patrick, sir,' she said. 'Is that why he was not given a Caleb name?'

'I never thought of that! Of course, he was the eldest son of James, wasn't he, so he should have been called Caleb too. But without that name, he might never be associated with the family...'

to all intents and purposes, he'd be an adopted child of unknown parentage!'

'Until a nosy detective with time on his hands begins to start delving! So what do you make of that curious verse, Mark?'

'Tainted. An odd word to use. I don't think it was lightly used, Lorraine. I reckon someone knew of the goings-on at the farm. Sarah was a teaser, you know. She had a reputation for chasing the men — Millicent Roe told me that. I see a Sarah who was rather advanced for her years and I suppose it's not surprising, in a remote place like that, that she was made pregnant by her uncle. The gossips must have had a field day — they'd know the girl had been put out of circulation for a while. Village women were not stupid or blind.'

'You mean the village women would have sensed there was an illicit pregnancy?'

'I'll bet they did. Somebody outside the farm must have known what was going on, hence that peculiar verse.'

'Women do sense these things, I suppose,' Lorraine acknowledged. 'Perhaps they saw signs of pregnancy in Sarah, although girls did wear loose-fitting dresses, didn't they? They — or Sarah herself — would be able to conceal the pregnancy for quite a long time.'

'Perhaps, at first, they believed she'd been caught by one of the local Romeos. Remember, such a union between an uncle and a child niece would be tantamount to incest in their view, and that does taint any family.'

'I suppose he would be regarded as tainted after that kind of behaviour,' she said. 'It was a strong Catholic district. So they might be right in singing about James going to hell.'

'Indeed, and the brother mentioned in the verse? Well, I'm sure that was Luke. Remember the verse didn't say he'd gone to hell, it said he'd gone 'as well' — and so he had. He'd gone to Canada. It's typical of the kind of verse sung in rural areas at that time, especially when there was a murder in the vicinity. I think the people of the area would have known Luke was the killer, even though it was never openly proved.'

'The younger Hartleys were probably teased unmercifully with the song.'

'I doubt if they knew its full meaning,' he said. 'George knew of it but had no idea of its underlying message. You know, Lorraine, I never knew anything about my grandfather's brothers or sisters, and he had lots. And they weren't trying to hide anything.'

'Me too,' smiled Lorraine. 'I know my aunts and uncles, but not my great aunts and great uncles, and their offspring. If those offspring turned up now, they'd be like strangers.'

'So we know how Vice-President Hartley will feel when he learns what we have discovered. Poor man.'

'So, what do we do now?' she asked.

'I must tell the Chief Constable of our finding and of what I think was the course of events in September 1916. I know he wants me to write it all up for the Foreign Office.'

'There can never be a prosecution, though?'

'No, of course not, but I think we can close the file now. I reckon we can name the killer without fear of reprisal, so we can record this old crime as "detected" — it'll all help the crime figures! I'm told our leaders would like to use it to persuade Vice-President Hartley not to be so critical of the United Kingdom's overseas and Northern Ireland policies.'

'He's in for a shock, isn't he?' smiled Lorraine.

'Well, he wanted to find his roots and we've done it for him. Operation Roots has been a huge success. He should be pleased.'

'Pleased? To learn that an aunt was a victim of a near-incestuous relationship and that his grandfather murdered his own brother who'd fathered a child by his niece? There's no way I'd be pleased to discover all that about my precious family!'

'I'm glad I don't have to tell him,' said Mark. 'Well, after breakfast, I must go and inform the others.'

'Make a full and detailed report, Mark,' said the Chief

Constable over the telephone. 'Just as if you were presenting the case for consideration by the DPP and the CPS. With recommendations. I will hand a copy to the Foreign Office for them to pass, with our compliments, to Mr Vice-President Hartley. I know they want to do this; they are absolutely delighted at the way you have produced this background and feel sure it will help Anglo-American relations.'

'That's one way of putting it!' laughed Mark Pemberton. 'I would like to tell George Hartley of the final outcome, sir, I owe it to him, and then we can resume enquiries into the Muriel Brown murder. It's still unresolved.'

'Fair enough. Take it easy, though, don't wear yourself out. I wanted this to be a holiday for you.'

'Yes, sir.'

'And let me have your report tomorrow, by noon. I'm meeting our Foreign Office contact at two. I want to give him the file. It's needed for the Vice-President's arrival later in the day. You'll have to drive it over to me, it's urgent.'

'Yes, sir,' said Mark Pemberton.

Next day, Monday, 11th July, the Chief Constable rang Pemberton.

'Mark, the file has been handed over and the Vice-President has read it. He thanks us for our work in producing the document. You have saved him a lot of time-consuming research, but he still intends to visit his ancestors' graves, his cousins at Pike Hill Farm and those in Hull.'

'So I can expect him to arrive at Thirklewood Hall later today?'

'You can,' said Moore. 'And he has some information for you, he says.'

'Really, sir?'

'He has told the Foreign Office that Luke died in 1958 without admitting any murder, but he did enter a monastery in 1953, a year after his wife's death. He gave all his money, which was a considerable amount, to Sarah's Foundation. Apparently, they specialise in coping with sexually abused children.'

'Conscience money, perhaps?'

'Well, I'll let you make your own judgement. He's also got a letter which came to light — that's what set him searching into his own roots. It was left by his Aunt Sarah when she died; she was, by then, Mrs WJ Swinburne. She died in 1991, aged eighty-eight.'

'In the USA?'

'Yes, in Connecticut. After her death, her family found a sealed note among her belongings. It was addressed to the head of the family — and in her family, that was Caleb Hodgson Hartley. He opened the letter and it contained a confession, Mark. From Sarah. She said that when she was a little girl, she had falsely accused her Uncle James of violating her. She'd even named him as the father of her child on her child's baptismal certificate. She did it out of spite, to get her own back on him. But the letter said James had never touched her. As a maturing girl, she was not a virgin, she'd attracted lots of admirers, but she'd often tried to seduce her uncle. He was the one man who always rejected her advances. She was determined to make him suffer for that...'

'The little minx!' cried Pemberton. Moore continued. 'The Vice-President said that when she was a young girl, she had never realised the serious consequences of her behaviour. She married but was never able to have any more children and had spent years trying to make atonement for her actions; she established and ran a home for abused girls and boys and became a pillar of her neighbourhood. The letter, which could be opened only after her death, said the father of her son was an apprentice farrier who used to call and see her at Pike Hill Farm. He was called Eric Hall.'

'The farrier's son!' sighed Pemberton. 'He joined up with her uncle James but was killed at the River Aisne on 28th May 1918, when the entire 4th and 5th Battalions of the Green Howards perished. His body was never found. She had learned this from her Aunt Sophie. Vice-President Hartley said that one of his reasons for coming to Yorkshire was to find out what happened to the Uncle James to whom she referred. His aides learned from Hull that James had been shot in the war and that he was buried at Wolversdale...'

'The scheming little bitch!' cried Mark Pemberton. 'So James died unnecessarily... God help us! Hell certainly hath no fury...'

'Forget it, Mark, it's not your problem,' said Charles Moore. 'It's the Vice-President's now. What's done is done, the past must be forgotten. He'll be with you soon and I'm sure he'll want to discuss your findings in person. But in the meantime, there's some proper work to do. We have learned, through international intelligence, that the Iranians have discovered the whereabouts of Hartley while he's in the UK. They've organised a hit team to get him. It could spell trouble. The SPG will explain it all, and it means there may be a genuine threat to your Vice-President Hartley. So it's time to do some real work, Detective Superintendent Pemberton!'

'Yes, sir,' said Mark.

SUSPECT

NICHOLAS RHEA

CHAPTER ONE

'You're happier these days, Mark, and it shows.' The Chief Constable's smile was warm and friendly. 'You're more at ease, more relaxed.'

Detective Superintendent Mark Pemberton, seated on a chair before his boss's desk, sipped a black coffee. 'Yes, I am, sir, thank you.'

'You've got over your wife's death?'

'Not entirely, but I've come to terms with it. And I'm taking more time off, making friends outside the job too. It's not easy, mixing a social life with police work, but I'm managing.'

'So what are you doing in your spare time?' Charles Moore was showing a genuine interest in Mark's welfare.

'I've joined a rambling club, we explore the dales and moors. I'm discovering parts of Yorkshire I never knew existed.'

'I'm glad you're making the effort. I must admit I prefer the new, relaxed, and not-so-gloomy Mark Pemberton. There was anger in you. You'd become very introverted, you know, and you were working far too hard.'

'I had to keep busy, sir, there was nothing to keep me at home. I used work to get rid of my anger, get me over my loss, I suppose.'

'I understand.' Moore's tone was sympathetic. 'But it's down to business now. I'm faced with the ever-present need to spend less money while making better use of existing manpower and resources, and, at the same time, I have to detect more and more crime.'

'Hoary old regulars!' grinned Mark Pemberton. 'So long as I've been in the job, we've been told to spend less, get more officers on the streets, and detect more crime, but I'd say we're detecting a greater number of crimes than we did say, fifty years ago ...' He realised Moore was regarding him calmly and began to appreciate why the Chief had called him in. 'If it's cuts we're talking about, I suppose it'll affect the Muriel Brown enquiry?'

Mark could envisage that investigation being wound up. It wouldn't be a great surprise. Being allowed three detective constables to work full-time on that old enquiry was something of a luxury — Pemberton's long-term worry was that a lack of funds and a shortage of staff could result in that murder remaining forever unsolved. That thought was highly frustrating — that a lack of money could enable a killer to evade justice seemed very wrong indeed. The Chief now addressed Pemberton's concerns.

'Don't forget that Muriel Brown was murdered a long time ago, Mark, before I became Chief Constable of this force. The chances of discovering her killer are remote by any standards.'

'But not impossible.' Mark wasn't going to let this crime be forgotten.

'To be honest,' Moore spoke softly and smoothly, 'I can't see that we need to fret unduly about an undetected murder which is some fifteen years old. Besides, even if we do crack it, it'll be just one more crime detected. A single clear-up. That won't make a very large contribution to our "Detected Crime" figures — give me a batch of a hundred detected burglaries any day. They're much more impressive on paper!'

'You can't compare burglary with murder, sir!' Pemberton had to defend his desire to keep this old enquiry active. 'Some yobbo admitting a string of break-ins is no comparison with a murderer caught by good police work. Paper-pushing policemen and Home Office clerks will be our downfall! Statistics of that kind make nonsense of our work! I regard it as my duty to do all in my power to identify the murderer. The fact that the crime's an old one doesn't matter — in fact, this one ensures that my officers remain up to date with HOLMES and current investigative techniques. It allows them an opportunity to work with computers, and it's taught them how to abstract important data from statement forms, even very old ones. It's highlighted mistakes made by their predecessors, mistakes that will benefit future enquiries. All that is most important — we all learn from mistakes. Muriel Brown has been a first-class means of providing extra training for young detectives, far better than any exercise we could devise. It's real too, which means there's the job satisfaction aspect. We might get a result — we might identify the killer. That's important even if it is only one detected crime.'

'I appreciate what you say, Mark, and I admire your spirited defence. You'll be pleased that Muriel Brown is not going to be totally abandoned. I'm replacing your three plain-clothes officers which means the murder enquiry can continue. Inspector Hadley will join your staff; he will replace those detectives.'

'Vic Hadley? George Washington incarnate?'

'George Washington?' grinned the Chief. 'Who calls him that?'

'Most of the force, sir,' smiled Mark Pemberton. 'It's because he says he cannot tell a lie.'

'That's a lie in itself.' The Chief was bemused by this. 'I don't believe anyone goes through life without telling some sort of a lie. I must admit I've never come across that nickname for Hadley. Anyway, Inspector Hadley, George Washington or whatever you call him, is going to join your department.'

'I thought he was on sick leave, sir, something to do with stress?'

'He is, Mark, but he's on the mend, he needs to be usefully employed.'

'But he's a uniform inspector, sir, they're detective constables.'

Pemberton's instinctive response was adverse. Why choose Hadley? Of all the officers in the force, Hadley was the last person Pemberton would have selected for any task in the CID.

'I know what you're thinking, Mark. But his advisers — doctor, psychologist, therapist and counsellor — are all agreed that some undemanding work, free from operational pressures and stress, will help towards his rehabilitation and restore his confidence. That's why I want him to work in your department.'

'Undemanding work, sir? In a CID office?'

'If you gave him the Muriel Brown case, more as occupational therapy than anything else, he'd feel useful. He needs to believe he's still a skilled operational policeman who can be trusted with important work. I don't have to remind you, Mark, that it's best he keeps out of the public eye, at least for the time being; you'll need to keep him away from the attentions of ex-Councillor Newton and his family too. That man's never off our backs — I still get letters from him, demanding justice or wanting to reopen the enquiry. He's still as bitter as hell about his brother's death. That aside, I'm sure you can usefully employ Inspector Hadley.'

And as he issued dial challenge, the Chief flashed one of his handsome smiles.

'There's always work in a CID office, I'll grant you that,' Mark Pemberton responded without enthusiasm and placed his empty cup and saucer on the Chief's desk. This morning's meeting was almost over and his gut feeling was that Hadley would be a burden rather than an asset. The Chief had made it impossible to refuse — but to take away three good, keen young detectives and replace them with a sick senior officer who would work shorter hours and require very careful handling didn't seem a good bargain for Pemberton and the Criminal Investigation Department — or for the Muriel Brown enquiry.

Pemberton's ambition was to solve that case before he retired; it was the only undetected murder on the force books. Some fifteen years ago, Muriel Brown, then a twenty-seven-year-old secretary, had been raped and murdered in her own car, her death resulting from a bout of frenzied stabbing. The car, with her body inside, had been abandoned on the moors, but her killer had never been traced. That crime had occurred prior to DNA testing, HOLMES and the other modern support services and computers which had become such an integral part of murder investigations. Old techniques had been used and Pemberton felt that if all the relevant data could be fed into a computerised data-processing system, the enquiry could be revitalised. The case of Muriel Brown might yet benefit from modern technology. In any case, undetected murder files were never officially closed. Nonetheless, Pemberton felt that the chore of logging all that old data into a computer was not really demanding enough for a high-ranking officer, even one who was recuperating after a long illness.

But orders were orders and you couldn't deflect the Chief Constable once he had made up his mind — and it was clear that his decision had been made. Whatever Pemberton might think or say, Inspector Victor Hadley, the former officer in charge of the force firearms unit, would join Pemberton's team.

'He will start on Monday morning.' Charles Moore flashed one of his dazzling smiles. 'And I shall require weekly reports on his progress.'

Printed in Great Britain
by Amazon